"But you're not in love with me," she objected softly.

"Well, neither are you in love with me," he replied. "Still, over the past few weeks I've noticed your relationship with these children. I think you would make a splendid mother...and wife."

Cassie marveled that his voice sounded so strong and steady. She felt like a quivering mass of jelly herself.

"I do have some scruples, you know," she told him. "If you think that I could treat such a commitment so lightly, then you really don't know me at all."

"Think about it, Cassie," he urged her. "You'd be able to do so much more for the kids here."

It was all so confusing. And she had no one to confide in.

You always said you'd only marry for love. Her conscience pricked her once more. *Yes, but if you marry him, you get to keep the house for the kids. You could continue the work God called you to.*

"Help me," she prayed silently. "You gave me the job. Now show m̲e̲ h̲o̲w̲ t̲o̲ make the right decision."

LOIS RICHER

credits her love of writing to a childhood spent in a Sunday school where the King James Version of the Bible was taught. The majesty and clarity of the language in the Old Testament stories allowed her to create her own mind pictures while growing up in a tiny Canadian prairie village where everyone strove to make ends meet. During her school years, she continued to find great solace in those words and in the church family that supported her in local speech festivals, Christmas concerts and little theater productions. Later, in college, her ability with language stood her in good stead as she majored in linguistics, studied the work of William Shakespeare and participated in a small drama group.

Today Lois lives in another tiny Canadian town with her husband, Barry, and two very vocal sons. And still, her belief in a strong, vibrant God who cares more than we know predominates her life.

"My writing," she says, "allows me to express just a few of the words God sends bubbling around in my brain. If I can convey some of the wonder and amazement I feel when I think of God and His love, I've used my words to good effect."

A Will and a Wedding

Lois Richer

Love Inspired™

Published by Steeple Hill Books™

This book is dedicated with much love to my parents, Dorothea and Wilfred Schill, who taught me the value of faith and tenacity when striving for my goals. Thanks, Mom and Dad.

STEEPLE HILL BOOKS

Steeple Hill™

ISBN 0-373-87009-4

A WILL AND A WEDDING

Printed in U.S.A.

"Wherefore lift up the hands which hang down, and the feeble knees;
And make straight paths for your feet, lest that which is lame be turned out of the way: but let it rather be healed."

—*Hebrews* 12:12-13

Chapter One

Jefferson William Haddon III wanted a son.

Badly.

The problem, as Jefferson defined it, was that at age thirty-five, he had yet to find the type of woman with whom he would consider raising a child. And the very last thing he had expected was that someone would find such a woman for him.

"Would you say that again, please?"

Jefferson turned to stare at the woman across from him once more, unable to believe that his Aunt Judith had considered her suitable for marriage.

Not to him.

She wasn't the type to be his wife.

If he had wanted one.

Which he did not! Not like this.

"Miss McNaughton will continue her sponsorship of you in your endeavor, Miss Newton, provided that you and her nephew, Jefferson Haddon, marry within the next two months. Until that time, you may both reside in her home, Oak Bluff, all expenses paid." Judith's old family lawyer cleared his throat.

"Mr. Haddon, when you marry you will receive Miss

McNaughton's fortune less Miss Newton's yearly allowance of one hundred thousand dollars. You will both receive the deeds to the house and its entailments, free and clear. Miss Newton will, as your wife, continue to live in the house as long as she wishes." The snowy haired gentleman paused to glance up at the couple seated before him. His light blue eyes darkened as he continued.

"If you should choose to ignore her wishes, Miss McNaughton has directed that neither of you shall benefit. Miss Newton will be forced to make other arrangements for her work and Mr. Haddon will have no further claim on her estate. The property will be sold and the money will go to an animal shelter she has so named."

Even as he wondered what the woman's 'work' was, Jefferson's mouth fell open.

"But surely we can contest the terms of this will, Mr. Jones. You were her friend for years, surely you realize what a terrible position this places us in." He stopped, conscious of the glowering countenance of the old lawyer.

"Your aunt was of perfectly sound mind when she made out this document." The wrinkled old hand shook Judith's will in front of them both. "Should the opportunity arise, and you decide to contest, young man, I will be happy to testify to her sanity. In court. Under oath." The old man's tone was frosty with contempt.

Jefferson was furious. He raked a hand through his perfectly groomed dark head in agitation. Yes, he wanted a child, but he had no desire to get married for money. And he certainly would not be forced into it by a busybody old aunt with nothing better to do than play matchmaker.

Blast, what a mess.

That woman, what was her name? Cassie, he remembered suddenly, Cassie…something. Anyway, she sat staring at him in horror. As if she could do worse than marry into one of the oldest families in Toronto!

"I'll move out immediately." He heard her words through a fog and turned to stare.

"What?"

"Are you hard of hearing, Mr. Haddon? I said, I will move out of the house immediately." Her voice was sharp with scorn. "I have no intention of marrying you or anyone else to provide a roof over my head."

She surged to her feet with all the pomp and ceremony of a miniature warship, sailing off to battle. She stood in front of him, hands on her shapely hips. Grim determination turned down the edges of her mouth. Jefferson laughed at the absurdity of it, and then watched fascinated as her body went rigid with fury.

"Your aunt was a gracious woman who treated everyone with dignity and respect. It's too bad you didn't turn out the same."

He studied the wide green eyes, huge and full of turmoil in a face white with strain. Her black hair curved around her oval face in a riot of curls that bounced merrily with each move she made.

She was not like any woman he had seen before, Jefferson decided. This Cassie person's appearance fell somewhere between comfortable unconcern and brilliant chic. She wore a bulky red sweater that hung well below her hips. A flaring skirt in a wild pattern of reds and oranges dropped to her ankles. She had on some type of granny boot that should have looked ridiculous and instead suited her crazy outfit. The gypsy look was further embellished by gold hoops that hung from her small earlobes.

Jefferson found those turbulent eyes fixed on himself. Coldly.

"Look, Mr. Haddon. I'm not a charity case. I lived with your aunt because she asked me to. She was lonely, I think, and gradually she developed a fondness for some of my charges. I think they provided some amusement for her when she couldn't get out anymore." Her glittering eyes reminded him of a cat's when it was hissing with fury, ready to strike. "But I am not, I repeat not, going to live with you in that house, let alone marry you, just so I can get my hands on a hundred grand."

She stared down her pert little nose at him, which would

have been effective if she hadn't had to tip her head back
so far to meet his eyes. He wondered where she had learned
the slang terms for money even as he appreciated the fact
that she also had no intention of going along with Judith's
machinations.

Grinning, he held up one hand.

"No offense, Miss, er, uh—" Jefferson looked toward
the lawyer to fill in the gap.

"Newton, Cassandra Newton," she repeated, her voice
seething with unspoken emotions.

Jefferson watched as she rolled her eyes upward and then
closed them. She was whispering. Some kind of a prayer.
He recognized the same habit his aunt had employed during
his own rebellious youth. He listened unashamedly to her
softly spoken words, a half smile on his mouth.

"God, I need some help here. I know you're leading me
and I'm trying to remember that this is Judith's nephew, so
for her sake I'll try to be polite." She sighed deeply, her
shoulders rising. "But, Lord. You know I don't tolerate
egotistical, arrogant, spoiled brats very well."

That said, she wheeled away toward the door, ignoring
Jefferson as she spoke directly to Mr. Jones.

"Thank you for inviting me to hear the will, Mr. Jones.
I appreciated Miss McNaughton's help when she was alive,
but I just can't marry someone because she wanted me to."
She cast a disparaging look over Jefferson.

Especially not him, her turbulent sea green gaze seemed
to say.

Mr. Jones thoughtfully stroked the snowy white beard
that made him look like a jovial Santa Claus. He held on
to the tiny hand she had offered, while silently contemplating her determined stance. Finally he spoke.

"You have two more months to live in the house before
the will dictates that you must move out, Miss Newton.
May I suggest that you stay there and use that time to sort
out your plans for the future? In the meantime, Miss Mc-
Naughton has provided some funds for your living expenses."

Jefferson watched as the woman accepted an envelope, which he assumed contained a cheque, from Jones. They spoke quietly together for a few moments before she left. Jefferson smiled as she deliberately ignored his presence.

Good! He had no desire to deal with some moneygrubbing female just now.

The next few hours were fraught with tension as he and the older man went over the legal documents several times. Finally Jefferson was forced to give up in defeat. There was little hope of breaking this will. And he wasn't sure he wanted to, not really.

Aunt Judith had been the one person to whom he'd been able to run when life got rough during those difficult childhood years. She had always been ready to offer a shoulder, a handkerchief and a cookie when he desperately needed all three. She had been the calm mothering influence he had never found at home. She had also been tough and uncompromising when her mind settled on something. If Judith McNaughton wanted it, she invariably got it. Apparently she wanted to see him married.

"Mr. Jones, I have to tell you that this doesn't fit in with my plans at all. Not at all."

He fingered his mustache and considered the older man. There was nothing but courtesy and consideration in that lined face and Jefferson decided to explain his blueprint for the future.

"I have invested a substantial amount of money and a large of amount of time researching the possibilities of obtaining a surrogate mother and defining exactly what her rights in such an arrangement would be."

"You want a child badly, Mr. Haddon."

Jefferson nodded.

"I want a son. I've interviewed couples who have gone through the process and inspected the children produced from such a union. I'm satisfied that they seem normal healthy children with a parent who truly wants them."

Mr. Jones coughed discreetly behind his hand, hiding his thoughts behind a large white handkerchief.

"And after this research you feel you have an idea of what you want?"

"I know exactly what I want in the mother of my son, Mr. Jones." He enumerated the qualities for the lawyer. "Calm, rational, levelheaded, to name a few traits. Unemotional. A woman who won't expect to be involved in my life other than in matters to do with my child in the first few months of his life."

There was a gleam in the older man's eyes that was extremely disconcerting.

"This hypothetical woman, then. You believe she will just calmly hand over her child and disappear? That the two of you would live happily ever after?"

Jefferson nodded.

"Yes, that's exactly what I want from the contract. A calm, rational agreement between two adults." He barely heard the mumbled aside.

"Seems to me a woman would have to be very calm to agree to such a thing. Dead, in fact." Mr. Jones shook his head slowly.

"I would make it worth her while," Jefferson rushed in and then stopped, appalled at how the words sounded when you said them out loud.

His face flushed a deep red at the intensity of Jones's scrutiny. Jefferson had always known he came from a family of wealth and prestige; tact and diplomacy were the rule. Never once had he been tempted to misuse his assets. But suddenly he wished he could spend a portion of his father's overblown bank account to buy back those words, unsay them.

Lawyer Jones evidently felt the same way for he frowned, his wise blue eyes accusing in their scrutiny.

"But what about this woman? How long will you need her? What happens to her once the first few months of the baby's life have passed and you no longer need her? Do you expect she will have no feelings for the child...that she'll just disappear with cash in hand?"

When stated in those terms, Jefferson's plan sounded arrogant; even slightly odious.

The older man snorted in disbelief.

"And what if the child is a girl?"

Jefferson hadn't thought about that.

"And what do you tell the child about his mother in ten or fifteen years?" the old man asked in a no-nonsense voice.

It was too much information overload, especially on a day when everything seemed out of sync.

"I don't know. But I'm confident that I can handle whatever needs to be done." Even now, Jefferson's mind whirled with plans.

He had chosen a name for the boy. Breaking with eons of family tradition, Jefferson had decided his son would be named Robert, Bobby for short. It was all planned out, everything was in place. His lawyers had the financial details organized into a formal agreement.

"Mr. Jones, I merely require the right woman for my purpose. It will mean that my business plans for expansion will have to be shelved for the moment, but I feel it's worth it." Jefferson hoped the man understood that he would not be swayed by these trivial problems.

Willard T. Jones sat polishing his round spectacles, staring at them for a long solemn moment. When he finally glanced up, Jefferson caught a sparkle of amusement in the old man's eyes.

"Well, Mr. Haddon. I'm sure you've thought about this long and hard. If I may, I'd like to offer a suggestion."

Jefferson nodded.

"My advice is this. Put everything on hold. The issue of Miss McNaughton's estate has yet to be settled and if you recall—" he smiled dryly "—your marital status may well change."

"Oh, I don't..."

"In six months' time, the entire picture will look very different. I suggest you take the time necessary to think everything through. You might start with the estate." Jones

tipped back in his chair and gazed at the ceiling while
speaking. "Judith Evelyn McNaughton was a cagey, stubborn old woman who went to the grave with a last-ditch
effort to manipulate you into marriage. She specially chose
Cassie Newton."

Privately, Jefferson thought Judith's latest bid for control
of his future made all her other matchmaking attempts pic-
ayune by comparison.

"She knew how hard you've worked to make a success
of your company. Just last month she was telling me of
your need to expand your business. And of your need for
more cash."

Jefferson was startled by the words.

"I didn't realize she had kept such close track of me
while I've been out of the country," he murmured, staring
at his hands.

"She wanted you to have the means to expand."

Jefferson grinned. "But only if I got it on her terms.
Good old Judith."

"The way I see it," the older man continued, "she gave
you two months' grace. Think long and hard before you
decide, my boy. Make very sure you won't regret giving
up the very things Judith wanted you to have."

As he walked down the street, Jefferson Haddon shook
his head at the ridiculous situation he found himself in.
Memories, sharp and clear, tumbled around in his mind. He
could still visualize Judith's thin, severe face with that prim
mouth pressed into a firm line as she bawled him out.

"One must always consider the other person, Jefferson.
For in one way or another, whatever you do will affect
him."

That had been the time Freddie Hancock has socked Jefferson in the nose for saying Freddie's mother was fat.
Well, Jefferson grinned fondly, it was true. All the Han-
cocks had been fat. But Mrs. Hancock was enormous and
when her arms wrapped around him in a hug, his eight-
year-old body had been suffocated against her overflowing
abundance.

He'd also been embarrassed. Aunt Judith had remonstrated with him on the social niceties before patting his hand gently.

"That's the way many people show their affection for you, dear," she had said. Her golden eyes had been sad. "I wish you would open up more. Most people just want to be friends. If you give them a chance, you will enjoy them."

Needless to say, that had not been Jefferson's experience. There were few opportunities for boyhood friends in the austere home his father maintained and very little free time to pursue such interests. There were even fewer people in Jefferson's young life who had ever hugged him.

Aunt Judith had understood that. She had also been one of the few to whom he had granted that particular privilege. And as she gathered his gangly body against her thin, frail frame, he'd felt warm and cared for inside.

His mouth curved in remembrance.

Of course, Melisande Gustendorf had tried to hug him a number of times in those days. Usually when he was with the guys. Mel would sneak up behind them and wrap her arms around him. She was weird that way. And at twelve, what boy wants to be hugged in public by a girl?

Jefferson smiled fondly as he remembered the lesson about birds and bees that Aunt Judith had related when she heard about Melisande. Aunt Judith had never married; never had children. Explaining the details must have been embarrassing, but she had persevered until Jefferson's every question had been answered. And then he had made darned good and sure Melisande never got within six feet of him!

His memories of Aunt Judith made him chuckle as he drove back to his penthouse apartment on the waterfront. Most of the time he was satisfied with the place. But today he felt hemmed in, constricted by his aloof tower.

"Dinky little rooms stuck way up in the sky," Judith had scolded him constantly about his chosen lifestyle. "You live out of reach of people. Why, you can't even touch God's wonderful creation, the earth, without driving for twenty minutes.''

In a way, Judith was right. From his panoramic living room windows, he could see the city clothed in her glorious fall colors. By late October the leaves had all turned to vibrant oranges, brilliant reds and sunny yellows. Many had fallen, but there were still enough to create a picturesque view.

But it would take a while to drive to one of the reserves, park his car, and walk among the beauty.

"You should be out in the fresh air, chop a few logs when the weather gets crisp. A fire feels good in that stone fireplace when winter sets in."

"But Aunt Judith, I have to be near my work."

She had glared at him then and his eyes had dropped first.

"You know blessed well that your work could be conducted from anywhere. Why, these days some folks use a computer for everything. Don't have to leave home to talk to people, shop or even go to the library."

She had tapped her walking stick against the bricks of the patio, almost knocking over one of the pots of rusty orange chrysanthemums she always set out in the fall.

"Don't hold with it myself. People need people. A body should have a time to work and a time to play. Too many folks taking their work wherever they go. And those danged cell phones."

Jefferson grinned in remembrance.

"The blamed things always ring at the wrong time." She had glared at him angrily as his own pealed out. "A body can't have a decent conversation nowadays."

At Judith's estate, Jefferson knew there would be crunchy crisp leaves underfoot when you first stepped out the door. They would float down on the fall breeze, covering the vast expanse of lawns. A few pumpkins and some of the hardier vegetables would sit outside in the garden, and he could almost taste the ripe red crab apples weighing down slender trees in the orchard.

The decision was made without thinking and moments later, Jefferson found himself ensconced in his luxury sedan, hurrying toward Judith's huge estate, aptly named Oak Bluff. Suddenly, he had a longing to see the old, sturdy brick house with its huge oak and maple trees standing guard around the circular driveway; to walk in the naturally wild terrain at the back of the grounds and feel the fresh air wash over him.

It was exactly as he remembered. Stately majestic and yet welcoming. The house stood firm against the elements, its pottery red brick and spotless white trim gleaming in the bright fall sunshine. Bennet had cleaned the debris off the walkway and the front lawns, but Jefferson knew there would be a thick carpet of crackling, wrinkled red and gold leaves just outside the back door.

He let himself into the house with the key Lawyer Jones had given him and dropped his overcoat on a hall table before glancing around. Richly polished oak paneling led the way into the library, his favorite room in the entire house.

Aunt Judith had a vast number of books, both old and new, crowded onto the shelves, carefully catalogued and indexed by subject, then author. Nestled into a nook on the far side, Jefferson knew there was a computer, printer and fax machine that Judith had frequently used. In one corner, under a window, stood the old desk her father had given as a birthday gift many years before. Its rolltop cover was closed now that the owner was gone. He brushed his hand over it fondly.

"Hello? Anyone home? Bennet?"

There was no answer. He wandered through to the patio.

The deck was littered here and there with golden yellow poplar leaves that whirled and wafted down on the delicate breeze. The redwood patio furniture was still out and since the afternoon was warm, Jefferson decided to sit outside until Mrs. Bennet returned. In his mind he could hear Judith's voice as she fondly reminisced.

"No one can ever deny the power a home has on a

family. It's like an old friend. It wraps its arms around you and shields you from life's problems while it draws people closer together.''

This was exactly like coming home, he thought, staring at the beauty around him. And it was nothing like the house he'd grown up in. This house was made for laughing children, a family, love. Suddenly, Jefferson wished he might raise his son here. When he had one, he reminded himself.

Obviously, Aunt Judith had wanted him to have that experience. But at what a price—married to someone he didn't even know!

Voices from the garden area penetrated his musings and he got up to investigate. Down past the patio, a shortcut through the maze and Jefferson was almost across the lawns when he identified the happy laughing shouts of children.

"Chicken! I let you roll me."

"No, you didn't. I made you."

"Ow! David! He pulled my braid."

What were they doing here, he wondered? The estate was fenced but there were no nearby neighbours with children. At least none that he could recall. From the sounds quite a few people were present now. And they were having a riot on his aunt's property.

"Can't catch me."

When he finally rounded what Judith had called the summerhouse, Jefferson Haddon III stopped dead in his tracks. There were at least ten of them, he decided. The oldest was no more than fifteen or sixteen. They were carrying the cornstalks from the side of the garden to the center, forming a huge cornstalk teepee while one person stood at the edge, arms outstretched to the sky.

"Autumn leeeves begin to faaall…"

At least the shrill voice had good volume, he decided, wincing at the wobbling pitch.

They all had jeans on, from the toddler holding another child's hand, to the eldest who seemed intent on adding a few more stalks to the already monstrous heap. All except for one boy, the tallest of the group. He wore tight black pants that looked painted on, and a red checked shirt that hung way down his lean body.

Startled, Jefferson watched as the skinny one lit the tee-pee. In seconds there was a huge crackling bonfire in the center of his great aunt's garden, and a pack of kids were dancing round and round, laughing happily.

"Ring around the rosy!"

Disgust and anger coursed through his veins as Jefferson watched the scene unfold. They had no right to intrude, he fumed. No right at all. This was private property. For some reason the Bennets were not here, so these children were trespassing. They certainly didn't have permission to light a fire.

Breaking into a run, Jefferson jogged across the lawn and through the black tilled soil of the garden to grab what he thought was the ringleader by his jacket.

"Exactly what do you think you're doing?" he demanded through clenched teeth and then sucked in a lungful of air as shimmering green eyes glittered out from a tousled mop of black hair.

"Having a wiener roast, Mr. Haddon. Want to join us?"

Cassie Newton stood grinning up at him as the children ran circles around them happily. She looked like a child herself in the bulky old coat and decrepit jeans. Her face was smudged with dirt and her blunt fingernails were filthy.

"Who are all these children?" he asked, ignoring the grin. "And what are they doing here?"

"They're mine," Cassie told him proudly. "And I already told you. We are going to roast wieners." Her voice dropped to a whisper as she hissed a warning up at him, green eyes flashing. "For the short time they have left here, this is their home and their party. And you will not spoil it, do you hear me?"

Sensing the tension surrounding them, most of the children had stopped their wild play and stood staring at the two adults facing each other.

Jefferson watched as the tall, skinny boy sporting the tight pants moved forward to stand protectively next to Cassie. He topped her by a good ten inches and it was clear from his stance that he would take on anyone who challenged her.

Jefferson was flabbergasted.

"All of these children are yours?" His voice squeaked with surprise and he heard one of the kids snicker. He strove for control. His eyes moved over her assessingly. "How old are you, anyway?"

But she ignored him.

"David," she addressed the young soldier at her side. "Would you please tell Mrs. Bennet that we're ready. Then you could help her carry out the hot dogs and the hot chocolate."

A sweet smile accompanied her words and Jefferson was surprised to see the sour-faced lad grin back good-naturedly before loping off to do her bidding.

She directed the rest of the children to arranging a picnic table that stood off under the trees, and finding wiener sticks. Satisfied that everyone was occupied, Cassie turned back to face him.

"I'm a foster mother," she told him matter-of-factly. "The kids stay with me until the agency is able to find them families." Her green eyes glimmered with mirth as she spied his Gucci shoes filling rapidly with rich black garden soil.

"You're not really dressed for this," she observed, eyeing his pure wool slacks, black vest and once pristine white shirt. "Perhaps you should wait inside until I am finished if you wish to speak to me."

Jefferson seethed at the dismissing tone of this—this interloper. So she thought she could reject him so easily? He grabbed her arm as she turned away. His eyes opened wide as she turned on him like a fiery virago, ramrod stiff in the filthy garments.

"Mr. Haddon, you will let go of me. You will not create a scene to spoil our day. You will return to the house and wait there."

Her voice was as crisp as a fresh fall apple and he found

himself turning to obey her militarylike orders before he realized what he was doing and turned back.

"Just a minute here," he protested, angry that she had him dancing to her tune. He pointed to the fire.

"You cannot let that thing rage away. What if it got out of control? The city has bylaws, you know."

The urchin before him drew herself to her full height, which Jefferson figured was maybe a hair over five feet, before deigning to speak. When she did, her resentment was clear.

"I am in charge here, Mr. Haddon. If I need help I can call on Bennet. But I won't." Her hands clasped her hips and he couldn't help but notice the way her hair tossed itself into silky disarray around her face. "And for your information, I have a permit to burn."

Jefferson shook his head. He refused to be deterred. Someone had to protect Judith's wonderful old estate.

"Bennet's nowhere to be seen. Fat lot of help he'd be."

She refused to answer him, her full lips pursed tightly. Instead, one grubby fist pointed toward the shed in the corner of the garden. Jefferson saw a man leaning against the side, watching them.

"We'll manage, Mr. Haddon. You'd better go before you ruin those designer duds completely."

Jefferson almost choked. The stately old butler Aunt Judith had insisted wear a black pinstripe suit coat and spotless white shirt stood clad in a red flannel shirt and tattered overalls with a filthy felt hat on his silver hair.

Jefferson whirled around to speak to Cassie but she ignored him as she dealt with one of the children's requests. When the little girl had toddled away, he tried a more conciliatory approach.

"My name is Jefferson," he told her softly, intrigued by a woman who would don such unsightly clothes to stand in the center of a dirty garden with a pack of homeless kids for a wiener roast in late autumn.

She whirled to face him, having obviously forgotten his presence.

"What?" Her voice was far away, lost in some never land.

"My name is Jefferson." He told her again, more clearly this time.

That sent her big green eyes searching his for something. He didn't know exactly what, but evidently she was satisfied. Moments later she moved forward to help Mrs. Bennet set out the food. He thought he heard her clear tones whisper softly through the crisp air.

"Goodbye, Jeff."

As he watched her walk away with that energetic bounce to her step he was coming to recognize, Jefferson tossed the sound through his mind several times.

Jeff. Jeff, he said to himself. He'd never had a nickname before, not with his father's strict adherence to family traditions. At boarding school he'd always been Jefferson or Jefferson William.

Jeff.

He liked it. A smile flickered across his sober face. He had never been to a wiener roast, either. Perhaps it was time he broadened his horizons. So that he could teach Bobby, he told himself.

He strode back to Judith's house with anticipation as his companion. The boy, David, was just coming out and looked suspiciously at him before moving aside at the door. He avoided Jeff's eyes, striding quickly past, obviously eager to join the group in the garden.

"David," Jefferson called after him. The boy stopped, unsure. Finally he turned around, angling a questioning black eyebrow up at the older man.

"What?" His voice was sullen.

"I need to change clothes. Do you know where there are some old things I can borrow?" Jeff ignored his petulant expression.

They stood facing each other for long moments, searching brown eyes scrutinizing him steadily, before David nodded. Moving into the house, he stopped to let Jeff remove his dirty shoes.

"Mrs. Bennet will skin you 'live if you track that dirt through the house," he ordered, his tone smugly superior.

As they marched the length of the upstairs hallway, Jeff noticed that every room seemed to be occupied. It was odd. He'd been here hundreds of times before and no one had ever occupied the second floor.

Other than Judith.

They finally stopped at the linen closet at the far end of the hall. The boy tugged out a cardboard box and began pulling things out.

"Here, you can wear these," the kid offered, measuring Jefferson's body mentally before choosing his attire.

Jefferson winced at the ragged denim shirt and much patched jeans that were proffered from a box that had undoubtedly come from the Goodwill center. There was very little to commend the shabby articles except that they would save his own clothes from stains the black garden soil would inflict.

"You can change in my room if you want," David suggested hesitantly.

"Thank you very much." Jefferson kept his tone properly appreciative, considering this was half his house. David stood staring out the window while he slipped out of his pants and into the rags.

"Why do you have your own room?" Jefferson asked curiously, having already noticed two beds in each of the other bedrooms.

The boy's head swung round, his grin wide.

"Cassie says a guy who's sixteen should have some privacy. So I get to have my own room. I never had that before." His serious brown eyes stared at Jefferson. "In most of the foster places we don't have half the fun we have here." His solemn face brightened.

"Cassie says this is a fun stop on the highway of life. While we're here we get to do lots of neat things. Like the bonfire." His eager eyes inspected Jefferson from head to stockinged feet. "There's some old boots in the back porch," he said softly. His dark head tipped to one side, anxiously waiting.

"Are you just about ready? They're gonna be cooking the hot dogs soon an' I'm starved."

Jefferson nodded and they went down the stairs together. Well, sort of together. The boy bounded down happily in front, eager to rejoin the fray.

Jefferson slipped on the boots slowly, mulling over the child's explanation. If he understood correctly, this boy was in limbo. Waiting. And while he was here, that woman, Cassie Newton, made the time seem like a holiday. It was a curious occupation; one he didn't understand. What did she get out of it?

They walked toward the others, David half running until he stopped suddenly. Wheeling around, he asked, "Are you going to live here, too?"

Jefferson paused, head tilted, wondering how to answer.

"I'm not sure yet," he hedged finally. "Why?"

"Just wondering what we're s'posed to call you," David mumbled, turning away.

Jefferson reached out impulsively, pulling at the boy's sleeve.

"My name is Jeff..." The rest died away as the teenager bounded toward the others, yelling as he went.

"This is my friend Jeff," he bellowed to the assembled throng. That settled, he got to the matters at hand. "I'm having four hot dogs."

They crowded around Cassie eagerly as she handed out wieners and sticks to the younger ones first, then the older children. To his credit, David waited until the last for his portion, Jeff noticed. He took his own place behind the patient boy and only belatedly wondered if there would be enough of everything for the adults to share in the feast.

He would have backed away then, but Cassie thrust a stick and a wiener at him.

"Slumming, Jeff?" she asked, one eyebrow quirked upward expressively. There it was again, he mused, that shortened form of his name. To his amazement, he found that he enjoyed hearing it on her lips. He was even starting to think of himself as Jeff, he decided.

He ignored the hint of sarcasm and threaded the wiener on the stick crossways. It didn't look very secure and he wondered how long it would stay on.

Evidently, Cassie Newton was mentally posing the same question for she reluctantly took the items from his clumsy hands and patiently demonstrated the fine art of roasting hot dogs.

"You have to do it like this," she instructed, pushing the meat on lengthwise. "Otherwise it will fall off when it begins to cook."

Her eyes took in his curious outfit then, widening in surprise as she focused on the sizable tear above his left knee. She forwent the obvious comment and, with a grin, turned to skewer a hotdog for herself before moving toward the fire.

Jeff followed her, wishing he'd had this experience before. Feeling totally inept and out of place, he watched carefully, noticing the way she turned and twisted the stick to get each part of the meat cooked. He tried to follow suit but after several minutes, Cassie's wiener looked golden brown and plumply delicious while his was shriveled and covered with black spots. Even the youngest child in the group had done better than he.

"Good for you, Missy. That looks great!" She praised the littlest imp with a glowing smile.

Jeff decided he liked the way her face lit up when one of the children teased her. A softening washed over her clear skin as she spoke to each. She didn't talk down to them, he noted, and she didn't boss. Cassie Newton treated each child as an adult person, entitled to her full attention. And as she listened to their little stories and jokes, Jefferson sensed her pleasure in them.

"We're very happy to have you here, sir." It was Bennet, grinning like a Cheshire cat as he bit into his own food. "Miss Judith used to say that sweet dill relish was what made the difference between a really good hot dog and a great one.''

Jeff smiled while his brain screeched to a halt. Aunt Judith had done this? Joined in a wiener roast in the garden? Stiff and stern Aunt Judith who wouldn't tolerate a speck of dirt under seven-year-old fingernails?

He could hardly imagine such a thing. His curious eyes moved over the assembled throng.

It was like watching a huge family, he mused. Something like Norman Rockwell would have painted and totally unreal. He munched on the liberally ketchuped, but still charred, hot dog and thought about the curiously vibrant woman laughing down at seven wildly active children.

That Cassie managed all this with children who weren't her own was wonder enough. But when you considered that they were children who were here for a short duration only, the bond she managed to create was amazing.

He wondered how she had achieved such a rapport with them even as a tinge of jealousy wove through his mind. He wanted, no, he dreamed, of having such a relationship with his own children.

Just then the real-life Norman Rockwell portrait happened right before his eyes. A little boy, no more than five, tucked his hand into Cassie's and proceeded to tug her behind him to the lush green grass beyond the garden. On one end, it was covered with a pile of red and gold leaves in various stages of drying. As Jeff watched, they took turns tossing handfuls of the vibrantly colored foliage over each other, giggling merrily as the leaves stuck to their hair and their clothes. The picture stayed in his mind, clear and bright long after the game ended.

A whole new plan began to form in his mind.

One that involved the son he had longed for.

One that involved the petite dark-haired woman, industriously swiping at the mustard stain on the mouth of one of her charges.

One that involved Judith's extensive estate and the money she'd wanted him to have.

Jefferson William Haddon III sipped his hot chocolate and thought about that idea.

A lot.

Yes, he decided at last. It might just be workable. As long as he kept his mind focused on the long term plan: A business that stretched around the globe and a son to leave it to.

Chapter Two

"Oh, Lord," she prayed, "why me and why now?" Cassie wasn't nearly as nonchalant about the sudden appearance of Jeff Haddon as she would have liked him to believe. In fact, the sight of those broad muscular shoulders and lean, tapered legs had quickened her heart rate substantially in the lawyer's office. And again when he appeared in the garden. But he need not know that.

Neither did he need to know the way her heart sped up when she looked into those rich chocolate eyes. Maybe it was because he sometimes looked like a lost little boy himself.

She laughed at the thought. Boy, indeed.

Don't be a fool, she scolded herself. *Jefferson Haddon certainly doesn't require your mothering skills.*

So she continued her ministrations with the children, hoping they would enjoy the wonderful fall weather while it lasted. And if ever there was a place for them to run and yell, free of the constant strictures of their everyday life, it was on the grounds of Judith McNaughton's estate. The place was like a bit of heaven God had sent specially for their use. It seemed that now He was changing the rules.

When the afternoon sun lost its warmth, she scooted them all inside.

"Come on, guys, let's go in and watch that new video Mrs. Bennet rented." They trooped into the TV room with barely a complaint and settled down while she took the opportunity to relax for a moment in the sunroom.

Cassie glanced out the window longingly, thinking wistfully of what she would lose when she moved out in two months. Not that she wanted to; the place was made for hoards of children and Judith had been the best surrogate grandmother Cassie could have ever asked for.

She remembered the day she had filled out the first forms to become a foster mother. It seemed like yesterday and yet there had been a variety of children since then. And nothing had ever been as wonderful as Judith's invitation to stay at Oak Bluff. That will had come as a surprise. Fondly, Cassie recalled the old lady's words about the children.

"They need stability and order, my dear," she had said. "And I think you are the one to give it to them."

Cassie's lips tightened as she remembered Judith's comments on her nephew.

"He's a stubborn one, is Jefferson, but underneath he's a good lad. Honest and kind. Maybe a bit reserved."

Judith had been fond of rambling on about her family and Cassie hadn't paid as much attention as she should have.

Obviously.

She was still amazed that the 'boy' Judith had talked about was over thirty years old, tall, dark and handsome and from one of the city's oldest families.

That he was here now seemed unbelievable. After all, he had not made an effort to see the old woman during the last few months of her life.

"It's a wonderful old house, isn't it?"

Cassie whirled around to find the object of her thoughts standing languidly behind her. His deep voice sounded friendly, without the arrogant tones she had heard at the lawyer's. She decided to give him the benefit of her many doubts and listened as he continued speaking.

"I used to come here quite a lot as a child. Aunt Judith had a way of making me feel better at Oak Bluff when things at home weren't going very well."

She cocked her dark curly head to one side, appraising him with quizzical jade eyes.

"You haven't been around for quite a while," she accused. "I've been living here for six months and in all that time Judith never saw you once."

Jeff shook his dark head. "No, she didn't."

He refused to justify himself to her, Cassie noted. He might as well have told her to mind her own business. Still, she had needed to ask.

"Where will you live when they sell the house?" she asked curiously. The way he kept watching her made Cassie nervous.

"The same place I've been living for years," he commented sarcastically. Jeff's dark eyes stared down at her unperturbed.

Cassie bristled at the condescending note that filled his low voice. Her temper was one of the things she constantly tried to rein in, but inevitably she forgot all about control and let loose when she should have kept cool. This was one of those times.

"Look, *Mr. Haddon*," the emphasis was unmistakable. "Perhaps I don't have the obvious resources you have and your aunt had, but I am not some subhuman hussy trying to swindle you. I am interested in what happens to this house because it involves my family and my employment. When I move, I will lose these children because I don't have the housing resources to meet government standards. Pardon me if I seem concerned!"

She would have angrily spun out of the room, but Jefferson Haddon grasped her arm and forcibly tugged her back. When she looked up, his rugged face was stretched in a self-mocking grin. His long fingers plucked the ragged denim away from his lean form.

"I'm sorry," he proffered humbly. "I'm dressed like a bum and now I'm acting like one. Can we at least try to be friends?" When she didn't answer, he pressed her hand. "For Aunt Judith's sake? I'm sure she thought a lot of you to ask you to live here."

Cassie eyed him suspiciously through her narrowed eyes. Regardless of what attire Jefferson Haddon III donned, she doubted if anyone would ever question his status as the lord of the manor. And that mildly beseeching tone didn't suit him at all.

Expertly cut black hair lay close against his well-shaped head, the back just grazing the collar of his shirt. Broad forehead, long aristocratic nose and a wide mouth seemed chiseled into classically perfect proportions which screamed blueblood.

Jeff Haddon had the lanky, whipcord-strong type of body Cassie had always assumed belonged to cowboys, not playboys. His shoulders looked muscular and wide beneath the torn flannel, his hips narrow with long, long legs. He looked what he was, a rich business tycoon dressed in let's-pretend-we're-slumming clothes.

Right now his dark eyes beseeched her to understand. Grudgingly she accepted his apology even as she tugged her smaller hand from his. She hated having to tip her head so far back just to look at him and vowed to buy some four-inch heels to wear when he was around.

"I don't think friendship is exactly what your aunt had in mind when she made up that will," Cassie quipped, curious about the red stain that covered his pronounced cheekbones.

"Then I guess we'll just have to pretend," he retorted.

"Fine. Truce." Cassie turned to leave.

"Where are you going?" His voice was an exact replica of two-year-old Mark's and Cassie smiled at the sound of petulance.

"I thought perhaps you would prefer to be alone. This house is big enough to get lost in and failing that, I can go help in the kitchen," she replied, moving toward the door.

His rumbly voice stopped her.

"Why don't you have coffee with me instead?" he asked, holding out a slim hand toward the huge armchair that had always been Cassie's favorite. "Mrs. Bennet just brought a fresh pot in," he cajoled.

Cassie studied him for a few minutes, assessing his intent with all her senses on alert. Finally, she allowed herself to be guided to her seat. Her fingers closed around the mug of steaming coffee with pleasure. She sipped the rich dark brew slowly, closing her eyes in satisfaction.

"Don't you just love coffee?" she murmured, inhaling the aroma that steamed off her cup. "I can never get enough."

"I limit myself to three cups a day," Jeff told her. "Too much caffeine is unhealthy."

Cassie ignored him, rolling the hot liquid around on her tongue. "Nothing that tastes this good could be that unhealthy," she countered, curling herself comfortably into the chair.

She watched him sit stiffly erect in the straight-backed chair. His silent appraisal unnerved her.

She could feel the tension building as electric currents snapped in the air between them. She had felt it before, that nervous awareness whenever he watched her.

Suddenly, she felt extremely conscious of that same, powerful attraction she had felt earlier today. It made her jittery. Cassie had plenty of contact with men in the course of her work, but they were colleagues, older than her, often balding with paunches.

And none had sent her pulse soaring or her heart thudding the way this man did. It was disconcerting. She tried to bury feelings she didn't understand under a bluster of bravado.

"Coffee's not a risk. It's a necessity." Her gaze fixed on his. The silence in the room yawned between them. Cassie searched her mind for trivial conversation that would break the current of magnetism drawing her into the dark depths of his eyes.

"Are you married?" she blurted out and then chided herself for her stupidity. When would she learn to control her tongue?

Jeff stared at her through narrow-slitted eyes, his mouth tight. "Obviously not, if my aunt is trying to marry the two of us off." His answer was short and did not welcome further comments.

Cassie ignored that. "I just wondered what you would do with all this room if you did live here," she pondered, glancing around the beautiful space. "It's a home meant for a family."

"What would you do?" His tone was razor sharp but Cassie ignored that, preferring to lose herself in a world of dreams. "Cassie?" His voice had softened and she dragged open her eyes to find his dark gaze resting on her in an assessing manner.

"I'd fill it with children," she told him simply.

"Ah, you're planning on getting married, then?" he asked shortly, dark eyes glittering.

Cassie sat up straight at that, untangling her feet from under her.

"Good grief, no." She laughed. "I meant with foster kids."

She was pretty sure her face gave away her thoughts. She'd never been much good at pretence and there was no point in trying to hide her plans for this house.

Not that it mattered now.

"There are so many kids who could really benefit from a few months here. Away from the pain and confusion that have left them wondering about their future. This is a place where they could feel safe and carefree." She grinned up at him. "Sorry. When I get on my soapbox, I tend to start preaching."

Jeff's eyes raked over her curiously.

"But don't you want your own children? I can't imagine that you would waste all your efforts on someone else's offspring. Don't most women want to get married and have children?"

He was watching her again. His eyes were bright with what she privately termed his banker's look, as if he were assessing her net occupational worth.

"Oh, but these are my children," she exclaimed. "Every child that comes under my care has a special place in my heart."

"You can't possibly love them all," he snorted derisively. "There's no way anyone could have enough love for all the needy children of the world. Obviously even their parents can't provide them with what they need."

Cassie smiled sadly, her eyes glistening.

"I didn't say all of them, just the ones I come into contact with." Her small hands stretched out toward him in explanation. "And if I never have my own children, at least I will have the experience of loving these. But you know—" her green eyes twinkled across the room "—love isn't something that you run out of. The more you give, the more it grows."

It was a strange statement, he decided. And it proved that Cassandra Newton had no real grasp on reality. He sat quietly in the flickering firelight, lost in his own thoughts.

"It's been my experience that there is never enough to go around," he murmured finally, staring down at his toes. He let the silence stretch starkly between them uncomfortably before speaking again.

"What will you do now?" he asked, curious about her plans now that her access to the house would be denied. "How will you be able to look after all your children when you have to move?"

Jeff watched Cassie closely, noting the white lines of strain that etched themselves around her eyes and the thin line of her mouth as she considered his question.

"I don't know. The younger ones won't have as much difficulty finding a place. It's David and Marie I'm really worried about. And all the other kids like them."

"Why will it be so hard for them?" Jeff asked curiously. "Are they in trouble with the law or something?"

"That's usually what everyone thinks." Cassie smiled

sadly. "They'll take the younger ones because they're cute and cuddly. But the teenagers always have a more difficult time." She grinned at him, tongue in cheek.

"After all, how many adolescents do you know that are easy to get along with?" she queried. "Usually they're already struggling to find out who they are. Fitting in to a strange home is just another problem added to an already staggering load."

Jefferson thought about his own teenage years. They had been difficult, all right. And he'd had the advantage of knowing that there would be food and the same place for him to sleep every night.

As he sat watching her slender form, slim legs tucked beneath her, Jeff could see the enthusiasm and concern Cassie brought to her job. He considered his own idea once more. Somehow he doubted that the small spitfire in front of him would welcome his idea just yet. He decided to hold off for a while. Perhaps once they got to know each other, Cassie Newton would be more amenable to the plan that was floating half-formed in Jefferson's busy mind.

Jeff made it his business to go out to Aunt Judith's a number of times during the next weeks. He made more than two dozen trips over the next three weeks to the stately old home, and not all of them were to do with settling Judith's estate.

He was drawn to the family atmosphere that prevailed but his curiosity was piqued by the small, green-eyed sprite who played board games sprawled on the floor, drank coffee incessantly and squealed in delight when the children tickled her. Oak Bluff was as comfortable for him now as it had been when Judith was alive. More so. Now he felt an insatiable interest in the inhabitants that he had never experienced with his aunt.

With a little ingenuity and a few well-framed questions, Jeff managed to inveigle himself into the household routine without much fuss. Before long Bennet was relaying bits and pieces of information that were very enlightening when one was trying to understand Cassie Newton. He also learned more about her charges.

Friday afternoon he found Cassie alone in the library. He wandered over to the armchair and stood peering down at her, noticing the tearstains on her pale cheeks. She glared back at him impolitely.

"Do you ever work?" she demanded rudely.

"You forget," he teased. "I have my own company. I'm the boss." Jeff smiled. He had her rattled. That should help.

She raised her eyebrows as if to say, so what? Jeff grinned.

"It so happens that I just finished the graphics for a new computer system and I'm taking a break. How's it going with you?"

She sat cross-legged on the floor. Some tight black material clung to her shapely legs and stretched all the way to her hips where a big bulky sweater covered the rest of her obvious assets. Her hair was mussed and tousled in disarray around her tearstained face.

"It's not going, not at all," she muttered, staring at her hands.

"I thought some of the kids had moved." Jeff flopped into a big leather chair and propped his elbows on his knees.

"They have. Only David, Marie and Tara are left now. Tara has a place to go on the first of the month, but the other two..." Her voice died away as huge tears plopped onto her cheeks. "I just can't seem to find anywhere for them to live. If nothing comes up, they'll have to go into temporary care, or worse, the juvenile home. They'll hate that."

She slapped her hand against the newspapers spread out on the floor around her. Jeff felt the energy she projected buzzing in the air around him as she jumped to her feet.

"Why did Judith have to make those stupid rules?" she demanded, standing in front of him. "I could have tried to purchase the place outright if she had put it up for sale, but this way, even when I move out, there's no opportunity to get it." Her tone was disparaging. "A cat home, for Pete's sake!"

Jeff grinned. He'd seen this side of her quick temper before and he knew there was at least one way to calm her down. He grasped her slim arm and tugged.

"Come on," he urged. "Let's go for a walk."

Seconds later they were striding through the dense, musky woods. Cassie might be short, but she set a fast pace and Jeff was forced to move quickly to keep up.

She strode along the path muttering to herself, clad in a brilliant red wool anorak that left her long, slim legs exposed in their black tights. Cassie's raven curls glistened like a seal's coat in the autumn sunshine as they swirled around her taut face.

"Absolutely ridiculous," he heard her mutter as she stomped on a rotted tree, splintering it in the crisp air. "People shouldn't be allowed to waste valuable resources just because she wants her nephew married."

Jeff picked up the pace, anxious to hear this.

"Can't he find himself a wife?" she mumbled angrily.

"I haven't really looked," he told her and watched, satisfied, as her skin flushed a deep rose. "Are you volunteering?"

"I don't want to get married," she told him as she looked down her pointed little nose. "I just want the kids and the house."

Jeff pursed his lips to stop the chuckle from escaping. "Isn't that putting the horse before the carriage, so to speak?" he queried, teasing her. "You should probably marry me first before we start discussing children."

Cassie stopped in her tracks at his heckling tone, which sent him colliding into her from behind. Jeff struggled to regain his balance, but they both went crashing to the ground anyway with Cassie's firm little body landing squarely in his lap. He sat there winded while she scrambled off him, and wondered at the reaction her tiny presence always created.

Her giggles of sporadic laughter sent his head tipping back to scrutinize her laughing face.

"You look like you've landed in something particularly nasty," she told him, chortling at his discomfort.

"It sure felt like it," he muttered, dusting the pine needles from the seat of his pants. Her laughing green eyes stared down at him curiously.

"What did you mean?" Her soft voice was hesitant, as if afraid to hear the answer.

Jeff thought for a moment, rehashing their conversation.

"Aren't you at all interested in volunteering for the position of my wife?" he asked, his voice teasingly serious.

But Cassie didn't laugh as he had expected. Her haunting green eyes stared at him, assessing his meaning.

"Why would you need to hunt for a wife?" she inquired, walking slowly beside him, her earlier ill humor dissipated like a morning mist now that curiosity had taken over. "I'm sure there are droves of women who would eagerly offer themselves on the marriage block to the infamous Jefferson Haddon the fourth." Her tone was softly disparaging but her companion seemed not to hear it.

"It's the third. And there are hardly droves," he drawled. "Anyway, that's not the kind of woman I want for the mother of my son," he mused, his thoughts turned inward.

Cassie stopped dead in her tracks as she stared at him in shock.

"What did you say?" Cassie squeaked, sure she had misunderstood. "What son?" She wrinkled her brow in thought. Surely there must be something she had missed. When he didn't answer, Cassie shook the muscled arm hanging loosely at his side. "Do you have a child, Jeff?"

"Not yet," he told her, black eyes snapping fiercely. "But I plan to."

His pronouncement left her speechless, mouth gaping in wonder. Jefferson William Haddon the third was going to get himself a child? How, she asked herself dryly. By mail order and stork delivery? She stared unblinkingly at the grim determination turning up his wide mouth. When she heard his next question, Cassie's jaw dropped a little further.

"Want to help?" As a come-on it lacked finesse. As a proposal, it left something to be desired. It also left her gasping, as if someone had ploughed their fist into her midsection. She moved weakly down the dusky trail, totally ignoring the illustrious Mr. Haddon, flummoxed by his ridiculous statement.

In fact, the whole conversation was preposterous, she told herself. Totally ridiculous. The inane concept of marrying him and helping him provide an heir to the family fortune was...

The answer to her prayer, a small voice whispered. She tried to brush it away, but the flow of words refused to stop. For years, it reminded Cassie, she had dreamed of raising her own children. Now, at twenty-eight, she had almost lost hope that the right man would ever come along.

Maybe he had finally shown up.

What are you holding out for? Prince Charming? her subconscious chided her. *There are all kinds of love. Some of them are learned, like your love for the children. Forget the fairy tale—take reality.*

Cassie replayed the lawyer's voice as it read Judith's will. Marry him, it said, and she could live in this house, have her foster family, continue with her work and have a large amount of money as well.

Flickering images of her own family's needs slipped through her mind. Samantha desperately needed cash with the second baby on the way and her husband's death just last month. Ken was struggling, too, with two stepchildren who needed some professional help.

And Mom and Dad. Cassie pictured the couple's dilapidated old farmstead. Neither of her parents were in good health and the place had become worn and rundown. One hundred thousand dollars would make an immense difference all around.

But one thought kept surfacing. She would be a kept

woman, Cassie reminded herself. She would be marrying Jeff for the money.

And for a child.

Strangely, that thought didn't bother her as much as Cassie expected it would. Instead, darling little cherub babies floated across her mind, kicking their chubby legs and gurgling in happy voices. The agency never brought her the babies. Her arms ached with the need to hold and cuddle one of those baby-lotion scented bodies.

And there was David. If anyone needed a father, he did. Could Jefferson Haddon possibly be the man God had sent to ease David's path into adulthood? It seemed impossible; it didn't jibe with the dream she'd held for so long.

A godly man, proud to be a follower of God, happy to share her work in the church and take his place as the head of their family—Jeff Haddon? A man who would share the same pain she felt when broken, unhappy children were brought to their home; a loving husband who would stand next to her and help in the healing process? Would marriage and children with Jeff give her that Christian family she'd planned for so long?

God, is this really from you?

Cassie heard a voice and turned to find Jeff's long lean body directly behind her. He was speaking in a low tone that riveted her attention.

"We could both benefit, Cassie. Obviously that's what Aunt Judith intended."

She stared at him, transfixed by the dark conviction glinting from his stern face.

"But you're not in love with me," she objected, softly. "And I consider that a prerequisite to marriage."

His gleaming dark head came up at that, his eyes boring into hers.

"No, I'm not," he agreed dryly. "But then, neither, I think, are you in love with me." He peered at her as if assessing her ability to understand what he was about to say. Cassie felt an anxious quiver spring up inside. "I'm thirty-five years old. I am fully capable of deciding what it is I want out of life. I want a son.''

Cassie marveled that his voice was so strong and steady. She felt like a quivering mass of jelly herself.

''I've been noticing your relationship with these children over the past few weeks,'' he told her, his long stride adapting to match her shorter one. ''You have the kind of rapport a child needs during its formative years. I think you would make a splendid mother.'' His voice added reflectively, ''and wife.''

He was serious, Cassie realized. Prince Jefferson actually expected her to agree to marry him and provide the heir to his kingdom.

''Is it so important, this successor for the Haddon family,'' she demanded disparagingly, ''that you would marry someone you don't love, someone you barely know, just to continue the family line?''

''No,'' he smiled at her sadly, tiny lines radiating around his sardonic mouth. ''It's not important at all, for that reason. But it is important for me to have my own child.'' He straightened his shoulders then and grasped her elbow briskly as if getting down to business. ''Think about it, Cassie. You would be able to do those things you're always talking about for kids who need your help.'' His voice lowered provocatively. ''And you would be able to continue your writing without the kind of interruptions that any other place would afford.''

Cassie whirled to face him, amazed that he knew of her secret life as a children's author. Then she realized that a man like Jefferson Haddon would have had her thoroughly investigated before considering the possibility of proposing.

The air went out of her suddenly.

''So it would be a business proposition,'' she intoned softly, glaring up at him in the silence of the woods. ''I get money and the run of the house to continue my work and you get your child. I do have some scruples, you know,'' she told him, furious at his extended silence.

''I can't just coldly and callously go to bed with you

because you want a child. Lovemaking is a part of marriage and that's a serious step that two people take because they want to commit themselves to the future together. If you think that I could treat such a commitment so lightly, then you really don't know me at all.''

She wasn't prepared for his strong arms as they wrapped around her. Jeff tugged her against his muscular frame, a tiny smile turning up the edges of his lips. His head tipped down, his mouth meeting hers in a kiss that rocked her to her boot-clad feet.

Cassie felt a longing stretch deep inside. It surprised her with its strength. As she felt his lips touch hers, Cassie curled her arms round Jeff's strong neck and twined her fingers through his dark, immaculate hair.

She knew that time passed, that one kiss had become many. But each gentle touch of his lips created a need for more.

When he finally drew away from her, Cassie felt bereft. He pressed her head against his chest while they each drew deep calming breaths of crisp fall air.

His voice, when it rumbled against her cheek, was softly mocking as his hand stroked over her windblown hair.

''I don't think anything that happened between us could be cold or calculated,'' he told her, a smile of satisfaction curving his tight mouth.

Jeff tipped her chin up, forcing her turbulent gaze to meet his melting dark chocolate one.

''We both know there's something smoldering between us,'' he rasped. ''And I think it's only a matter of time until it bursts into flame.'' He held her gaze steadily. ''But I'll guarantee you this. I'm not going to force or coerce you into anything. Whatever we do, it will be after a mutual decision.''

Cassie felt as if the ground were falling away and she wrapped her fingers around his arm.

How could this be happening to plain, ordinary Cassie Newton? She seldom dated. Goodness, she didn't even know many men who weren't involved with the children's agency or her church.

"If you'd prefer, we can go the route of artificial insemination." His mouth tipped up wryly. "Although, personally, I don't think it would be nearly as, er, interesting."

Cassie felt her cheeks burn with the implication behind his words. How could he say these things? It wasn't, well, decent somehow.

"The direction of our relationship will depend on you, Cassie."

She knew her mouth was open; that she was gaping at him like some starstruck teenager. She couldn't help it. The world had tilted in a crazy angle and she couldn't get her bearings.

"Come on. If we don't walk, we'll freeze."

He tugged her along beside him then, continuing their walk as if nothing unusual had occurred. Except that he kept her hand enfolded in his.

Cassie let the whirl of emotions pirouette through her mind in fast forward. Marry him? She hardly knew him, although he had somehow become an intricate part of their lives over the past weeks.

And always, Jeff watched her with David. Dark head cocked to one side, he would listen intently as she spoke with the boy. Subject matter wasn't important. Jeff seemed to focus more on the child's acceptance of Cassie as the authority on the matter. At least marriage to Jefferson Haddon would ensure a home for David and Marie, she thought ruefully.

Nasty suspicions crowded into her confused brain and Cassie stopped dead in the pathway to cast a curious glance at the tall man beside her.

"What's really behind this proposal?" she demanded, hands on her hips. "Why do you suddenly need *me* for your plan?"

He looked sheepish. And not a little embarrassed.

"The truth this time," she ordered. "All of it."

"I do want a son," he said firmly.

"And?"

"Well, the fact is that most of my funds are tied up in the family trust. Oh, I make a good living," he offered quickly as she frowned. "My company is doing very well. But I want to expand and that takes a lot of capital. It's a private company and I'd like to keep it that way."

He studied her face as if deciding whether she understood what he was saying.

"You mean you don't want to offer stock or something to raise money?" Cassie asked him doubtfully.

"Yes, and I don't want to take on private investors unless I have to. Computers are a risky business right now. The markets are changing so rapidly and new advances occur daily. I'd rather not risk anyone else's hard-earned money."

Cassie sank onto the iron bench nearby, thinking about what he'd said.

"Judith once told me that your father has money. Maybe he could..."

"No!"

It was a vehement denial that brought two red circles to his cheeks. He flopped down beside her, hands shoved into his pockets. Cassie couldn't see his face, he was turned away from her. But she could hear the cold hard tones and the anger under them.

"My father would never agree," he told her. "He wants me in the family business and would be just as happy to see Bytes Incorporated go down the tubes." He watched her speculatively for a moment. "If he knew about the son idea, he would have a fit. He's had my wife picked out for twenty years now. He won't take it lightly when he finds out I've married someone else."

"Oh, but I don't want to create more problems. Family is very important." Cassie stared out in front of her, barely registering the beauty of the fall landscape.

"Mine isn't," she heard him mutter sotto voce.

"This marriage, if it happens, will already be starting out with a lot of obstacles," she protested. "If only Judith hadn't tied everything up.'' She swung her head around to stare at him. "Does your father know about the will?''

He shook his head, then bent to pull an oak leaf from her hair.

"He knows she died, of course. And that she left a will. But beyond that, nothing. I specifically asked Jones to keep things quiet until it was all settled.''

Cassie pulled herself to her feet and wandered farther into the woods. It was all so confusing. And she had no one to confide in. On the one hand, it would be ridiculous to turn down such a wonderful opportunity. On the other...well, it certainly wouldn't be a love match.

You always said you'd only marry for love. This is business. Her conscience pricked her once more.

Yes, but if you marry him, you get to keep the house for the kids. Lots of kids. You could continue the work God called you to. It could become a sort of sanctuary.

It was an internal argument that went on for the duration of their walk. Jeff spoke no more about the issue, leaving Cassie time to sort through in her own mind all the ifs and buts that flew like quicksilver through her muddled thoughts.

How could she deny David and Marie the opportunity that Oak Bluff with all its wonderful prospects presented to the two homeless teenagers? They could have a stable life without worrying about the future. They could blossom and develop into capable, responsible adults without worrying whether or not they would be able to continue their activities tomorrow or next week, or whenever they moved on.

And what about the other children who came into her hands? Cassie asked herself. Could she deny them all the things Judith's money would buy just because she was holding out for love? Was this windfall really from heaven, or did she just think so because she'd benefit?

It wasn't an easy question. And it was one Cassie decided to think on long and hard. But after all, she reminded herself, it wasn't as if she had ten other offers sitting on the table.

And there *were* definite sparks when Jeff had kissed her back there. More than sparks!

"Help me," she prayed silently. "You gave me the job. Now show me how to make the right decision. Direct me away from the biggest mistake of my life."

Chapter Three

"Chocolate cake! Thanks, Mrs. Bennet. It's my favorite." David's pubescent voice was squeaky but full of happiness.

Jeff and Cassie ate dinner with the children, feasting on a succulent stew and featherlight homemade biscuits that Mrs. Bennet had prepared.

The older woman stroked her hand over the boy's perpetually tousled head and winked at Cassie.

"I know it's your favorite, dearie. Yours and someone else's." Her gleaming eyes settled on Jeff's loaded plate. "That's why I baked it."

Cassie watched David inhale the generous slice and marveled at his appetite. Of course, teenage boys did grow by leaps and bounds, and devoured everything edible along the way. David was shooting up by inches and Cassie had taken him shopping several times to accommodate feet that expanded in direct proportion to the seemingly endless stretch of his legs.

"Are you finished your homework, Marie?" Cassie watched the girl shift restlessly in her seat.

"Almost. I'll be done before Nate phones later."

"Well, don't stay up all night talking to him. You will

see him at school tomorrow, you know.'' She smiled at the happy little grin that appeared on Marie's face.

"I'll try not to be too long, Cassie."

The flush of pink in the girl's cheeks gave her a glow of beauty. It was too bad people couldn't see how kind and loving these two were, Cassie fumed. David and Marie had been subdued during the meal, barely speaking unless they were addressed first. It bothered Cassie.

They were afraid of a future over which they had no control, she realized. Worried that they would be separated after having spent so much time depending on each other. A permanent home, one they could rely on, would make such a difference in their young lives. And with so few people interested in raising teenagers, Cassie doubted anyone would create much fuss if she asked to keep the two on a permanent basis.

She studied Jeff as she ate, watching him speak to the teens. He was especially good with David, drawing the quiet boy out with each comment. He had a knack of treating David as if he were an equal. He listened to what he had to say with interest most people would only offer an adult. It was a manner Cassie had found sadly lacking in many of the homes that housed foster children.

"How about a Monopoly tournament after dinner?" she asked brightly.

David grinned at her, eyes shiny with mischief.

"You must be feeling lucky," he teased. "Watch out, Jeff. She owned everybody last time. I'm lucky I'm not still paying back what I borrowed."

They played for an hour before Marie's soft voice broke into the silent concentration.

"You'd better get started on that science project," she reminded David in a sisterly tone. "The proposal is due in a week and you haven't done any research."

"And you'd better go phone Nate before he dies from not hearing your voice."

It was typical sibling banter and Cassie smiled as she

heard it. David and Marie were not related at all but from their teasing demeanor no one would have guessed.

Marie left the room quietly, her long blond hair flowing behind like a cape, but not before she tapped David on the shoulder.

"Jealous?" she asked pertly.

Groaning, David stretched to his full five-foot-ten-inch height.

"You wish!" He carefully replaced the game pieces in the box and snapped it shut. "I hate science," he muttered, before glancing shamefaced at Cassie. "Sorry, Cassie, but it's so boring."

"What kind of a project are you supposed to do?" It was Jeff's deep voice. Cassie stared at him in surprise.

"We can choose," David replied, kicking his toe in the carpet. "That's worse," he confessed, "because I haven't got a clue what he expects us to do."

"I know a little about science," Jeff murmured softly. "Could I look at your text? Maybe together we could come up with an idea that would get you started."

"Cool" was all David could manage to answer.

Cassie smiled as they left the room, talking and gesticulating. She hadn't expected Jeff to take such an interest in the boy. In fact, she recalled, he had spent several evenings doing things with both children this past week.

Well, since he had taken over the science problem, it left her free to start a project that had made her fingers itch for weeks. Cassie buried herself in the library for the next three hours, refusing to allow her mind to dwell on the marriage proposal she had just received. She'd always found her work the best panacea for solving personal problems.

Cassie was knee-deep in sketches of Bored Boris, the magical dragon, when she startled at the soft touch on her shoulder.

"Don't do that," she squeaked, holding a hand over her heart. "People my age have been known to keel over from a shock-induced heart attack."

"That's okay." Jeff grinned. "I know both CPR and mouth-to-mouth. Want a demonstration?"

Cassie frowned at him reprovingly. "No! Thanks, anyway."

She studied him closely. The immaculate shirt was unbuttoned allowing her glimpses of dark curling hairs that covered Jeff's broad chest. His tie hung haphazardly out of one of his jacket pockets and his made-to-order jacket was slung carelessly over one shoulder.

The perfectly creased black trousers he'd sported earlier in the day were dusty and wrinkled. And that impeccably trimmed hair was tousled and disorderly, one black lock hanging over his left eye.

He looked smug, Cassie thought. As if he had swallowed a whole bowl of canaries. She stood in an attempt to bolster her bravado which was a little shaky after this afternoon.

"Well, did you come up with something?" she demanded, her low voice sharper than she had intended.

But Jeff merely stared at her curiously before answering.

"Depends," he replied cryptically, head tipped to one side as he studied Boris. His dark eyes met hers. "Can we use that big empty room downstairs for a lab?"

"A lab," she repeated, wondering what on earth they had concocted between them. "Why do you need a lab? It's just a simple science project."

Jeff stepped backward and pushed the door closed with his foot before speaking.

"That kid is very bright," he told her seriously. "And mighty ambitious. But he hasn't had much encouragement and he doesn't know where or how to begin." The muscled shoulders shrugged.

"I would have thought the teacher could have done a bit more explaining, but at any rate, I want to get him interested in some preliminary physics so that later on he won't be overwhelmed by everything. He's got a natural curiosity about things that hasn't been stifled."

Jeff studied her quizzically through those melting chocolate eyes. Cassie rushed into speech before he could say anything more.

"But what about when the house is sold and he can't have his lab anymore?" She stood straight and tall in front of him, prepared to do battle for her child. "What about when you get tired of teaching him and want to go back to the playboy scene? What does David do then?"

Cassie could see the brown sheen change to black in Jeff's darkening gaze. His eyes were like a sheet of the notorious black ice that covered Toronto highways in winter. You could sail along with no problems until you needed to put on the brakes. Then you were in big trouble.

When his hands tightened around her upper arms, Cassie was pretty sure this qualified as big trouble.

"Will you please get it through your head that I am not, nor have I ever been, a playboy."

The words snarled out between lips so tightly pursed, Cassie wondered if they had ever been as softly caressing as she remembered.

"And this house only has to be vacated if you refuse to marry me." His mouth was a straight line of disapproval. "I like the kid and I want to help him with this." He stared down at her furiously.

"Or maybe you're jealous because you wanted to do it?" he demanded suddenly.

Cassie tipped her head back and laughed. She fixed him with her own gaze.

"I'll have you know that I hate anything to do with grade ten science projects." She laughed again. "It's a great relief not to have to help him with his homework." She pushed his hands away before stepping backward. "I am concerned only for David and his welfare. I have to be sure that this will be a positive experience for him and not one where he'll feel abandoned when it's no longer convenient for you to help him out."

The air crackled with tension as they stared each other down. Jeff was the first to move by thrusting out his hand toward her.

"Okay, truce," he mumbled. "I know your primary duty is always to protect the kids' interests. I promise I won't leave him in the lurch regardless of what happens between us." His black eyes sparkled down at her.

"Although, if you hate science that much and you're going to opt for the artificial route to children of your own, I suppose someone will have to do some remedial work with you, too." He grinned at her, obviously delighted with the flush of color that stained her cheeks.

"Close your mouth, Cassie," he teased. One finger brushed down her tip-tilted nose. "It's a part of life…grade eight health, in fact. Certainly nothing to be embarrassed about. And it's something we do have to think about. I still want that son."

Cassie was embarrassed. It was nice to know that he had given some thought to their future situation, she supposed. It was good that he was considering all the pros and cons. But how could he say such things out loud with absolutely no warning? And how could one touch of those long fingers make her all quivery and shaky inside. Could this be from God?

"You are a very lovely woman, Cassandra."

And then she forgot everything. His arms surrounded her and hugged her against his muscular form. She could feel the silky brush of his mustache against her cheek, the smell of wood smoke on his clothes.

But most of all, she could feel his heart thudding just as quickly as hers. And she knew that Jefferson Haddon was no more immune to her than she was to him. Which should have been reassuring.

Shouldn't it?

Moments later, when all Cassie wanted was more of his touch, Jeff pressed her gently away from himself, easing her arms down from his neck. She couldn't even remember how they'd gotten there.

"Think about what I said," he whispered in her ear.

Then, leaving her bemused and befuddled, he walked out of the room. Moments later Cassie heard the powerful roar of his car. But it was virtually impossible to think coherently as she carefully put Boris and his friends away. And if she listened, Cassie was sure she could hear Judith's hearty laughter resounding through the room.

"Go for it," she seemed to say and Cassie smiled as she fingered the portrait on the old desk of her benefactor.

"Perhaps I will, Judith," she murmured. "Perhaps I will. But not before I get a second opinion."

She picked up the phone and dialed, a faint smile tipping the corners of her lips.

"It said what?" Robyn's voice squeaked with surprise. "You mean to say that if you marry the guy, you get to keep the house and a pile of dough besides, and you can't decide what to do?" She snapped her fingers in Cassie's face. "Earth to Cassie. Hello?"

"I know it sounds simple," Cassie admitted. "Take the house and the money and go with it. It would solve a lot of problems." She thrust away the thought of her own family. "But this is serious. I have to *marry* Jeff, as in forever. And that's serious business. I can't just go into it with a way out already prepared. I don't believe in divorce any more than you do."

"Yeah, that's heavy stuff all right," Robyn agreed. "But I wonder if you're looking at this right." She frowned, her blond head tipped to one side as she considered her friend.

"What do you mean?" Cassie frowned. "I've thought about nothing else for ages. I just can't see a way through."

"Think, Cass. Think about the book of Genesis. In those days there were arranged marriages all the time. In fact, that's how they got started. Isaac needed a wife and Rebekah was the one that was chosen by God. They didn't even know each other until after she'd already promised to marry the guy!"

"That was thousands of years ago," Cassie protested. "We do things differently nowadays."

Robyn laughed sourly.

"Yeah, we do," she agreed. "And does the world seem

any better for it? There are kids all across this country growing up in homes where the adults have separated because they've lost that love that seemed so wonderful when it first grabbed hold of them.''

Cassie nodded.

"I know, Rob. I know. But this is my future I'm deciding here. It's not at all what I had planned...." Her voice died away as she let her mind roam.

"Cassie," Robyn said, drawing her attention back to the present. "Wasn't it you who told our entire grade nine class that you wanted to look after kids who needed help?"

"Yes, but..."

"And wasn't it you, just last week," Robyn continued unfazed, "who said that even though Judith had died, you still believed God would provide a way for you to do this work?" She waited for Cassie's dark head to nod agreement. "Well, then. Maybe this is God's way of providing for you."

Cassie studied her friend as she thought about her work. She had always felt a connection with children; but she was especially drawn to the needy ones. They lacked so much that mere human kindness and a stable home could provide.

"I know you said Jeff's not religious. I know he's got a problem with his family. And I know you said he loved Judith." Robyn's face screwed up in thought. "Maybe that's the key," she muttered.

"What key? What are you talking about?"

"Yes, it makes sense. Don't you see, Cass? Jeff likes what he sees in you."

"Which is?" Cassie frowned.

"You're resemblance to Judith, your faith in God and His power in your life. Maybe it's what he craves for himself. You can be His light, Cass. Maybe your job is to show him the way to the source of that light, to help him understand that God loves *him*."

"It sounds like an awfully convenient excuse for me." Cassie shook her head dubiously.

"I think this is the only way there is for you to keep the

kids. At least right now. And while you're doing that, you can help influence Jeff's life in the right way." Robyn studied her. "Have you got enough courage to take a leap of faith and trust God to work it all out for the good?"

Cassie stared at the ceiling, her mind whirling with problems. It was a lifelong commitment, she knew. Marriage was a solemn promise to another person. It was not to be entered into on whim, or discarded when things got tough.

"I'm praying for you, pal." Robyn patted her on the shoulder. "Whatever decision you make, I'll still be here."

"Thanks," Cassie muttered, picking up her handbag and moving to the door. "I think."

"Are you telling me that you *will* or that you *won't* marry me?" Jeff queried, his eyes darkening to a deep sherry brown.

Cassie focused her own gaze on his left shoulder and said the words that needed saying.

"I'm saying that if we can come to some agreement on the conditions of this marriage, I will agree to it. The first thing is the children. I want us to adopt David and Marie. Legally," she added when he continued staring at her.

"And?"

"And I want to continue to accept foster children whenever I'm asked, for whatever time. If the arrangements become too unwieldly, we can discuss it then." She said it in a puff of energy, as if she were afraid to stop.

He stood there, tall and silent, staring at her. Cassie could feel his eyes pressing into her, but she stood firm.

"Fine. I agree."

It was as if someone had punched her in the tummy. Just like that he was agreeing?

"So, what date shall we set?"

Cassie sucked in a lungful of air. "There is one other thing."

He frowned.

"I think we should wait out the two months' grace period that Judith gave us. We'll be engaged but free to break

off the arrangement if either one of us changes our minds."
Her heart lost its regular beat for a moment and then re-
sumed a breakneck speed as she met his dark eyes.

"Why?"

"We have to be sure, Jeff. Both of us. I don't believe in
divorce and I'm not going into this marriage with a way
out already prepared. If I'm going to be married, it will be
wholeheartedly. For life."

"But waiting means another five weeks," he complained. "That puts us right before Christmas."

"I know. It's enough time to really think things through,
don't you think?" Why did her voice sound so uncertain,
Cassie wondered. She'd gone over this a thousand times
and this was the way it had to be.

Those liquid chocolate eyes were fixed on her, staring
deep into the doubts and fears that filled her tortured mind.

"I don't need to think about it," he murmured, never
breaking the stare. "I feel quite sure we can both achieve
satisfaction from this arrangement, but if you need the extra
time, I'll go along with it." He tugged a small leather-
bound booklet out of his jacket pocket and consulted it for
several moments.

Cassie wanted to say something—anything. They
weren't having an *arrangement*, for heaven's sake. They
were getting *married!*

"Saturday, December 10th," he muttered. "That would
give us time to prepare for the Christmas celebrations afterward." One long lean finger tapped the book thoughtfully as Jeff glanced up, eyes gleaming. "How is December
10th for a wedding day, Miss Newton?"

Cassie blinked. That was it? He agreed to everything and
then checked his calendar? Somehow she had expected a
fuss or an argument. Anything but this calm acceptance.

"Cassie? The tenth?"

She stared up at him, bewildered and confused.

"Uh, yes, okay. I think so."

"Good." He brushed his lips across her cheek before
rechecking his book. "Now. About the ring. I think if we

were to go now it would be best. I know a jeweler who will meet with us privately and design exactly what you want. Maybe he can do everything right now, while we wait. Then we can announce it to the children and the staff. I assume you'll want the Bennets to stay on?''

He was holding her red wool coat out, ready for her to shrug into. Cassie didn't move. She couldn't. She could only stand there staring at him. He was moving way too fast.

"Ring? What ring?"

"Your engagement ring, of course." His tone was soft and gentle. Teasing even. "We are talking about a marriage, you know. A real marriage. And like you, I'm fully prepared to make it work."

"Yes, but…"

He had her bundled into the coat and moving out the door before Cassie could even think. She stopped on the step, stubbornly refusing to be moved.

"Wait a minute!"

Jeff stopped politely, tugging his collar up around his ears as the cold north wind whipped down from the roof and tugged at their clothes. His eyes were mildly inquiring and he didn't move his hand from under her elbow.

"Is there a problem?"

"Yes! I don't need a ring." She said it fast so she couldn't retract it. "And there won't be any big wedding. This is an agreement between us two. That's all."

"I don't think so." He grinned boyishly.

Cassie felt the strong warm arm around her shoulders as he hugged her against his side. If he had ordered or hollered she wouldn't have listened. But this soft cajoling was something entirely different.

"I asked you to marry me. You agreed. That means we're going to be man and wife. And I'm going to give you a pledge of my commitment."

"Yes, but…"

He cut her off, blithely ignoring her objections.

"We will now move to the next stage of this courtship

which entails finding an appropriate ring for this finger."
He rubbed her ring finger with his hand.

"Yes, but..." Cassie stopped as his lips brushed across
hers softly.

"I am not finished, Cassandra." His deep voice whispered in the still silent evening, effectively stifling her pro-
tests. "Maybe we're not the traditional love match, but we
can still go into this as friends. And totally committed to
making this marriage work. I don't want anyone thinking
anything else. The ring will solidify our position."

He sounded so loverlike one moment and businesslike
and coldly calculating the next that a shiver of apprehension
rippled down her spine to dissipate like the morning dew
at his next softly spoken words.

"Besides, I don't think any bride should miss out on the
old traditions. Especially not one as lovely as you."

Cassie swallowed her nostalgia. A diamond ring didn't
have to mean love, she told herself. It was just a stone. It
could signify friendship as well as love; or commitment to
making something work. Why not relax and enjoy it?

She curtsied.

"Thank you, kind sir. I would be pleased to accept your
ring."

It began as a fun evening which came as a surprise to
Cassie. She hadn't expected that someone like Jefferson
Haddon would be able to unbend so easily. They laughed
and joked about the strange customs of marriage as they
visited Jeff's favorite jeweler but neither could agree on
just what type of ring Cassie should wear.

"I work with kids, Jeff. I don't want some big, gaudy
showpiece. Something small and practical will be just
fine."

"This isn't overly large." He held up an opal close to
the size of a golf ball with glittering diamonds surrounding
it.

"It's both ostentatious and pretentious. Besides that, it's
ugly."

He frowned at her. "All right. You pick one."

"This is lovely." Cassie chose a small diamond perched on a thin band of gold.

"Hah! I can't even see where the diamond is—if there is one. How about this?" He held up a dinner ring that nearly blinded her.

"I don't like clusters," she told him, grimacing. The thing would take arm supports just to carry it around.

"And this?" It was a rock the size of a cherry.

She shook her head in dismay. "Jeff, that thing would cost a fortune to buy let alone insure." She glanced at the display cases once more. "I do like this." She fingered the tiny sparkling stones imbedded in the thin gold band.

He snorted with disapproval.

"So do I, for two kids in high school maybe."

She watched as Jeff buttoned up his coat. Then, thanking the jeweler for his assistance, he ushered her out the door without a word. Cassie found herself being led toward a dark and rather intimate-looking restaurant moments later.

"I thought we were supposed to go shopping," she protested, casting worried glances at his annoyed face. "Are you giving up on our marriage already?" It was supposed to be teasing, but Cassie held her breath until he answered.

"We'll discuss this over dinner" was all he replied in an exasperated tone.

She watched speechless as the maître d' greeted him by name.

"Mr. Haddon! Good evening, sir. I didn't realize we had a reservation for you tonight," he added nervously.

Jeff smiled that broad grin that made him look like a mischievous boy and laughed.

"Your memory's not slipping, George. You don't. Is there anything available?" Cassie watched him slip the man a twenty dollar bill.

"We're very busy, sir. I'll just check." It took George less than three minutes to return smiling. "We have a small table in the corner, Mr. Haddon. Right by the fireplace. Will that suit?"

Apparently it did as Cassie found herself being seated mere seconds later.

"Cassie," Jeff said, "George here is a good friend of mine." He slipped his hand on top of hers and squeezed gently. "George, this is Miss Newton, my fiancée."

The older man beamed down at them both.

"My congratulations, Mr. Haddon. That's wonderful news!" His voice dropped. "Miss McNaughton would have been so pleased."

Cassie watched the smile tug at Jefferson's wide mobile mouth.

"Yes," he drawled. "Aunt Judith would be very happy."

When they were alone, Cassie leaned forward.

"I'm really not dressed for such an expensive restaurant, Jeff. And I'm not very hungry, either." She heard the whine in her own voice and endeavored to get rid of it. "Why are we here?"

Brisk and to the point, that was better.

He leaned back in his chair, smiling benevolently at her across the candlelight. A waiter arrived with champagne in a silver bucket, forestalling any further conversation.

Jeff picked up the glass and held it aloft.

"A toast to us, Cassandra."

She frowned at him and he laughed.

"Don't worry," he told her. "It's nonalcoholic. I guess that's another detail you should know. I don't drink. Ever."

His voice was cool, almost hard and Cassie wondered if she should ask why. The dark look on his face was not encouraging, however, and she decided discretion was the better part of valor. Slowly she picked up the slim, fluted crystal and tinkled it against his.

"What are we toasting to?" she murmured.

"To us and the solutions we're going to find to our disagreements. All of them."

As she sipped the bubbly concoction, Cassie looked around curiously. The restaurant glowed warmly in the flickering light cast off smoothly polished oak walls. It was a gracefully elegant room with brass fixtures, potted flowers and tall willowy plants strategically placed here and there to provide privacy for its diners. The sound of softly soothing classical guitar played in the background as the tinkle of good china, silver and crystal rang out occasionally.

"I'm having a steak," Jeff declared, laying down the huge menu. "What would you like?"

"I've heard about this place," Cassie mused, staring at the preponderance of items listed. "A friend of mine said the veal is excellent. I'll try that."

Somehow, Cassie felt Jefferson Haddon wouldn't understand that her friend Moira had only been able to enjoy the veal on her twenty-fifth anniversary because her children had surprised their parents. He probably had no idea that not everyone frequented Vicenzo's on the spur of the moment.

The waiter bustled away to return seconds later with their soup, a delicious mushroom blend that teased and tantalized her tongue.

"I don't recognize all of these greens," Cassie admitted when her salad arrived. "But the dressing is fantastic." She licked her lips at the flavor of it only realizing how childish her action was when Jeff's laugh rang out.

"It's nice to see someone enjoy their food," he assured her. "And you don't have to worry about dieting, thank goodness."

Cassie grinned.

"Are you kidding? With kids around all the time, I'm lucky if I get to eat." She peered up at him through her lashes. "Why are we here, Jeff?"

She watched as a tiny flush of pink colored his cheeks.

"I, um, well, you see I was hoping that, well," he stopped, obviously at a loss.

Cassie smiled. For once it was nice to see the elegant, assured Jefferson Haddon stumble for the correct phrasing.

"Just say it," she advised. "Don't worry about how it sounds."

"Very well. I was hoping to show you, by coming here

tonight, that your choice of a ring is important in more ways than one.''

Cassie frowned. ''It is. Why?''

He placed his fingertips together, tent-style and studied them for several minutes.

''Perhaps I'm not being very clear. I don't want to offend you.''

''You won't,'' she assured him as she frowned again. ''Just let's get the truth out between us. Then we'll deal with it. What seems to be the problem?''

''Cassie, do realize how big a company Bytes Incorporated is?''

She frowned. He wanted to talk about his computer company?

Now?

''No, I've never really thought about it. Why?''

His brown-black eyes met hers almost apologetically.

''It's a worldwide enterprise. Which is why it will take so much money to expand. I travel quite frequently to Europe, Asia and Australia.''

She wasn't getting any of this, Cassie decided. It was nice that he was successful, but so what?

''Would you please just say whatever it is clearly,'' she demanded.

''Cassandra, your ring is important because more people than you and I will see it. And misinterpret it.'' The last part was muttered under his breath.

''I want something that represents me, my status, if that doesn't sound too arrogant.'' Jeff frowned at her, but kept speaking. ''I'm not exactly a pauper, you know. I have a certain status, an image, I guess you'd say. I want people to recognize you as my wife and the ring should symbolize how highly I esteem you as my wife.''

A light dawned. Cassie glared angrily across the table.

''Oh, I get it. You mean that people will think you're cheap if I have just a small ring.''

''Well, no, not exactly. I mean that people will think it's

only a temporary liaison, without duration. A sort of affair. That's not the impression I want to give.''

He looked angry, Cassie decided, noting the tightening around his mouth. She should have realized sooner that she was marrying into an elitist group. Judith had never been flashy about her wealth but she certainly had not denied herself anything, either.

Cassie called herself a fool. She couldn't care less about his money and hadn't given it a thought. Which was obviously a mistake. Clearly the money and the image it could create were very important to Jefferson Haddon.

"I'm sorry." Jeff's dark eyes were frowning down at her. "I didn't express that very well."

"No, it's all right," she murmured softly. "If you want a larger stone, then, of course, that's what we'll get. After all, as you've just pointed out, you are the one who's paying for it."

It was a mean and nasty remark and Cassie wished she had never said it, but it was too late now. So she bent her head over her meal and tasted the famous dish.

"You are determined to misunderstand me. I merely meant that if I could afford it and you liked it, why shouldn't you have the nicest ring we can find."

They ate in silence after that with Jeff glancing up at her from time to time. He tried to initiate some small talk, but Cassie couldn't carry the conversational ball. Her mind was on other things. Like how a farm girl from the sticks was going to carry off this charade.

She ordered coffee and sipped the dark fragrant brew.

"This is excellent." She smiled up at the waiter. "Colombian Supremo with just a hint of mocha, isn't it?"

The solemn face creased into a smile.

"Madam knows her blends," he affirmed. He held out the pot toward Jefferson. "And you, sir?"

Cassie watched the dark head shake.

"Never at this time of night," he replied. "I'll have herbal tea. Mint."

She shuddered and sipped another mouthful of coffee for courage.

"Mint tea? Now? I always have a good strong cup of coffee before bed. Helps me sleep."

He stared at her as if she'd just told him his ears were green. Then he shrugged, obviously forgiving her that flaw.

"That sounds like something Aunt Judith would have said," he told her softly.

"But not what you'd advise, I gather?" she asked with a knowing grin.

"I think you already know the answer to that, Cassie. But in reply I think I'll just quote part of a poem by Ogden Nash that I found in one of Judith's books."

His eyes glittered with anticipation as he met her curious ones across the table.

"Whenever you're wrong, admit it. Whenever you're right, shut up."

"Is that an inscription you want on the wedding cake?" She giggled and laughed out loud at his facial expression.

"I was thinking it might be more fitting inside that ring we're not going to get tonight."

This time she couldn't help it. The laughter burst out and she was embarrassed to see several gray heads nod benignly in their direction.

"My mother always told me to marry a man that makes you laugh. She's going to love you."

"Better than what?" he demanded. He cocked one eyebrow, joining in on the friendly banter.

"Oh, better than marrying some handsome ne'er-do-well, I suppose."

"I think I'll enjoy your mother. Great minds think alike," he told her smugly.

Cassie giggled, shaking her head. "I find that tiny minds think alike, too."

Their waiter showed up just then.

"Anything else, sir?"

Jeff's dark eyes glowed across the table at her in the dim light of the restaurant.

"No," he stated. "I think I've had just about enough."

Cassie hid the smile that tugged at her mouth.

"Tell me about your parents," he prompted, tugging her arm through his as they walked along the brightly lit street.

There wasn't any point in prevaricating. He would know soon enough, if he didn't already.

"They're farmers. They live about an hour away but they don't get to the city very often. Money's pretty tight right now."

He shook his head. "No, I mean, tell me the important stuff. Are they happy together?"

Cassie smiled.

"They've been married almost forty years so I think so," she told him. "I once asked Mom how she and Dad had stayed married so long. She told me that she followed Erma Bombeck's prescription for a happy marriage."

"Erma Bombeck? The humorist?"

Cassie smiled at the surprise in his voice.

"Yep. Mom said if Erma could forgive her husband for not being Paul Newman, she couldn't do any less for Dad."

He chuckled. "I guess that's good enough advice."

"She also told me that she leaves five or six things unsaid each day. According to her, there isn't so much to be sorry for."

"You have three siblings, I understand."

Cassie was about to ask him how he knew when she remembered the security check. Apparently nothing had slipped by and she was probably only regurgitating what he already knew.

"Yes, although one sister is overseas right now. I haven't seen her for two years."

"She works for UNICEF, I believe."

Cassie nodded.

"The pay is very low for such an undertaking," he murmured. "Why would she sign up for a second term?"

Cassie bristled. "Not everything in life is about money," she declared, yanking her arm free of his. "Giselle loves her work and there are other advantages." She glared up at him. "In my family money came way down on the list of our priorities."

"You were lucky," he said gruffly. "In mine it was everything." He slipped her arm through his once more and nudged her onward. "I apologize. I didn't mean to be condescending."

Cassie peered up at him and then decided it was best to get things out in the open now, before this went any further.

"Just exactly how wealthy is your family, Jeff?" she asked, frowning.

"I never took you for the mercenary type." His dark eyes glittered with sparks of anger. His head whipped around to stare at her.

Cassie giggled.

"I'm not mercenary about it." She laughed. "I just need to know what I'm getting into. Are you going to be jetting off to Timbuktu every other afternoon? Will I have to make an appointment with your secretary to speak to you about something?" She stopped laughing when his silence stretched out between them.

"Jeff? Did I say something wrong?"

His face was white and strained when he glanced down. Cassie held her breath as he spoke.

"No," he muttered, "nothing wrong. You just reminded me of something that happened once."

Cassie said nothing, holding her breath lest she break the spell between them. For the first time Jefferson Haddon was going to tell her something about himself. She wasn't going to spoil it.

"My father hated to be disturbed. When I was four, I made the mistake of entering his office at home one time and forgot to knock first. I'd cut my wrist, you see, and it was bleeding. Rory and I were playing, and Mother was away and I forgot all about asking his secretary if it was okay to go in.

"He hated having me burst in like that. Hated that his eldest son was standing there bawling in front of his business associates. I was weak...unworthy of the family name.

He sent me to my room." A hard bitter smile tipped the corners of his lips.

"Yes, but your arm? What about the cut?" Cassie could hardly imagine anyone so cruelly abandoning a child in need. Anger surged through her at the callous treatment.

"Mother took me to the emergency ward after the dinner party was over and they stitched me up. It's fine." He smiled lopsidedly and bared his wrist as if to prove it had been a fuss for nothing.

Gently, softly, Cassie pressed her finger to the faint white scar. Four years old? It was obscene. Tears welled in her eyes at the cruelty he'd suffered and the ugly memory he carried.

"I'm sorry, Jeff. So sorry that you had to be hurt like that."

"It really wasn't that bad. I suppose I was being rather a baby about it." His eyes were wide and full of surprise as he stared at her.

"It was terrible," Cassie disagreed, angry all of a sudden. "Children are supposed to have parents who are strong for them, not the other way around."

"Thank you." It was softly spoken. So softly, Cassie almost didn't hear it.

He helped her into the car and then slid in beside her, letting the motor idle as he turned to face her.

"You're very good with children. Natural and caring. Why don't you have your own?"

Cassie smiled.

"It's rather embarrassing," she told him. "I've always had this dream that I'd marry someone who thought I was the most special person in the world, a prince charming in fact. We would live in a big house and have a huge family." She grinned up at him. "Somehow, here I am at twenty-eight with lots of kids and no house or man."

"Until now," he murmured.

Her eyes flew to his in startled surprise.

"Well, yes. Until now, I guess." She shook her head at him. "Are you sure you know what you're getting into?"

she asked, head tilted to one side as she watched the gold flecks in his eyes glitter brightly.

"Um-hm," he half whispered. "Pretty sure. I'm getting a woman who doesn't mind when someone interrupts her sketches of Bored Boris to get a cookie or kiss a boo-boo better. I'm getting a wife who barely reaches five feet but fights like a heavyweight for the kids she believes in."

His fingers slipped across her hair, twirling several glossy curls round his fingers. The words were whispered in her ear as he leaned over.

"I'm getting a woman who is as beautiful inside as she is out. I think it's a pretty good deal."

His mouth settled on hers and Cassie kissed him back. It was a gentle kiss, a promise. And it was full of possibilities. Maybe that's what had her so flustered.

For as she sat there with Jeff's hands cupped around her face, his own mere inches away, all intelligent thought left her mind. She blurted out the first thing she could think of.

"Don't forget you're also getting a house full of kids."

"More and more like your fantasy, isn't it? Good. They'll get me into practise for when our own come along." He grinned that dangerous playboy grin that did odd things to her tummy.

That flustered her.

"Jeff, I don't really know much about men. I mean, I have a brother, but it's not the same thing."

His finger chucked her chin. "I should hope not."

"Well, no, I mean I'm not very good with the social niceties or dating, or, well, anything." She swallowed. It wasn't easy to tell him all her faults at one go. "I've never been outside Canada while you've probably traveled around the world. Those business associates of yours might be impressed with my ring, but I don't think we'll have much in common otherwise. And I have a terrible temper. I try to control it but..."

She couldn't look at him. Her face felt as if it were on fire and she nervously twisted her hands in her lap.

"Cassie?" His voice was full of rich, smooth laughter,

but he held it in check. A gentle smile tipped his mouth up at the corners. ''Look at me.''

She did.

''You've got this playboy image of me that I can't seem to shake. I'm not. Haven't had time even if I were the type.'' His eyes stared into her, willing her to listen to what hidden meaning lay under his words. ''I'm glad Aunt Judith left the old place to both of us. It needs a big family to make it come to life again. David and Marie make a fine start.''

His voice was like a thick chocolate covering, rolling over her, keeping her snug and safe.

''You don't know much about me and I don't know much about you. Or children. There are bound to be problems. But we're in this together and we can help each other through the tough times as long as we keep talking and trust each other to do what's right. That's what I want from this marriage. Okay?''

Cassie nodded slowly. ''Okay.''

But as she lay in bed later that evening, staring up at the ceiling, Cassie wondered why his touch haunted her. She had never ached to feel a man's arms close around her; never felt bereft when they left. Why now? And why did the touch of those soft, cool lips send her heart rate into overdrive?

This was going to be a marriage of convenience.

Wasn't it?

Chapter Four

Here comes the bride.

Jeff stared at the arched doorway, waiting for his bride to walk down the aisle of the tiny country church. Cassie, once she had given in, had insisted on a church wedding with her family there to see it. First Marie, and then Cassie's sister had sauntered down the aisle and now it was his bride's turn.

He grinned at the thought. Jefferson Haddon was getting married he told himself giddily. Who would believe it? Well, David for one. He'd insisted on being in the wedding party.

"I can be Marie's partner," he told Jeff importantly. And Jeff had accepted that. He knew the boy wanted to fit into their new family. Hmm, he liked the sound of that. Family. He grinned again just as Rory nudged him in the ribs.

"You're supposed to watch your bride come in."

Trust his oh so prim and proper brother to know the appropriate moment for the groom to glance toward the back. Jeff turned his head and then sucked in his breath at the sight of his wife-to-be.

Cassandra Newton looked like a fairy princess. She wore an ankle-length suit made of a gossamer white silk fabric.

The top was a fitted filmy jacket that gave Jeff provocative glimpses of her glowing peach-tinted skin underneath. The jacket ended at her waist where a slim skirt flowed straight down to touch her satin-covered toes. Around the hem a delicate embroidery pattern was woven in silvery silken thread. A tiny white hat perched on her dark curls with just a fluff of veiling at the back. Her only jewelry was the diamond stud earrings he'd given her last night and the pear-shaped diamond solitaire that sparkled on her ring finger.

He felt good about that ring. He'd chosen it himself after Cassie had refused to be drawn into a second trip.

"If it's supposed to be a gift, then I don't want to see it beforehand."

And she hadn't. He'd surprised her with it one afternoon when the kids had disbursed and left them with five minutes of peace.

"From me. To you." He'd held out the ring for her to see and breathed a sigh of relief at the look of delight on her exquisite face.

"Oh, Jeff. It's perfect."

He'd slipped it on her hand and then tugged her into his arms. That was happening a lot lately.

So were those kisses.

His pulse raced as he remembered how she had kissed him back and then flushed bright red when Marie had come upon them.

"Pay attention, Jefferson." That was Rory nudging him in the side. "This is *your* wedding, man."

Jeff came back to earth with a thud.

One slim arm wound through her father's as Cassie walked slowly down the aisle, carrying the deep indigo blue irises she favored over roses. Her fathomless green eyes fixed on him and never wavered until her father placed her hand in Jeff's. Then she glanced at her dad one last time as if to say goodbye.

Jeff squeezed her hand reassuringly before facing the preacher. As he promised to honor and cherish Cassandra

Emily Newton, he made a vow to himself. He would do his best to make their marriage as happy as possible. Perhaps they didn't love one another, but if they worked at it, there shouldn't be any problem they couldn't overcome.

As he glanced down at the diminutive beauty beside him, Jeff thanked heaven they had agreed to take a short holiday together after the wedding.

"I don't want my parents to know all the reasons for our marriage," Cassie had told him. So she didn't have a leg to stand on when he suggested a honeymoon.

"Everyone will expect it," he'd cajoled. "And anyway, it will give us time to get used to each other before we live with the kids. You know teenagers, always on the watch for anything unusual. Then they'll bribe us with it."

Cassie had given in. Finally. But not without some stipulations of her own.

"We are going to take our time getting to know one another. You are not to force me into anything. I want to make very sure we're on firm and solid footing in this marriage, headed in the same direction. We are not going to be the kind of parents who tear each other apart."

The thought of a baby with her bright inquisitive eyes had Jeff's blood sizzling through his veins, but he forced himself to concentrate on reassuring her with some casual response.

Not that he wasn't sincere. He was. But he also wanted his wife to be just that, his wife.

It was funny. In the last two months he'd done a complete turnabout. Suddenly, he wanted a home and a family and all the other normal everyday things men his age had. A relationship between two adults who were friends, who could share things, who cared about one another. A relationship that would benefit both members. A relationship that was nothing like the one between his parents. Which shouldn't be too hard. After all, he wasn't anything like his father.

Was he?

Jeff shook off the ugly thought. Smiling, he slid the wide

gold band onto Cassie's slim finger as he repeated the words.

"With this ring, I thee wed. With my body, I thee endow."

He smiled even more when Cassandra Emily slid her own gold band on his finger. It had been one of her requirements.

"If I wear one, so do you."

Not that he'd argued. It was the reasoning behind her logic that made him smile.

"If women are branded as some man's property, then in this day of equality, men should be branded, too."

"Does that mean you consider yourself my branded property?" he had quipped, knowing she would have a ready response.

"Guess again, pal." Cassie's wide mouth mocked him. "*You* know very well what *I* meant."

He merely laughed at her red face.

Her look had been the severe one he'd seen used on a recalcitrant child. "You'd better clean up your act."

Perhaps it had been a good idea to get married here, Jeff reflected. The well-used church held the perfect atmosphere and the old-fashioned words said precisely what he meant, he told himself as bending, he kissed his new wife. Exactly the sentiments he felt right now, he reiterated, staring at the beauty of her oval face.

As Cassie felt her husband's lips move away, she felt a return of the shakes. She'd had them before. Numerous times over the past few weeks.

What had she done?

Grimly she pasted her smile on and moved through the old church decorated in its Christmas finery of red and green. It was impossible to ignore the terror that gripped her soul.

You have just married a man for money, she told herself. A very handsome, very desirable man, yes. A man who can ignite your senses faster than any man had ever done, it was true.

But still, it was all happening because of Judith's ridiculous will. The shock of it made her hands tremble. Please, dear God, don't let me regret it.

"It went okay, didn't it?" she whispered as they stood in the receiving line at the back of the church.

"It went perfectly, just as you planned."

Cassie watched Jeff surreptitiously. When anyone congratulated him, he accepted their good wishes with a smile but his fingers stayed firmly wrapped around hers during the next few hours, coaxing his strength into her.

And Cassie needed strength. She was so nervous, she felt sick. There was no going back now.

She was married!

Her family had gone all out; to such an extent that their reception housed most of the small town where she had grown up. The tables were beautifully decorated in crimson red and kelly green. A tiny favor wrapped in tulle sat at each place setting. And everywhere there were flowers, fragrant and full of life.

The rent on the hall alone would make a huge dent in her parents' savings account, Cassie acknowledged sadly. She vowed to see about a house in town for them as soon as she and Jeff returned from their holiday.

She refused to call it a honeymoon just as she refused to think about everything else right now. She would manage. Somehow.

Cassie took a deep breath as the tinkling of forks on glassware began.

Not again! Jeff teased her with his kisses at every opportunity. Cassie wondered how long this game of torture would continue.

"Pucker up," he whispered just before his mouth closed on hers.

It was a teasing sort of kiss, featherlight with just enough enthusiasm to whet her appetite. Cassie frowned when he pulled back, chastising herself for wanting more. How could she possibly feel desire for a man she had known such a short time?

The fact was, she knew nothing about Jefferson Haddon.

Oh, she knew he was good with the kids; kind but firm when he needed to be. And he had more than demonstrated his generosity with all of them, acquiescing with alacrity to the many changes she wanted to make at Oak Bluff. He'd agreed to David and Marie's adoption without a qualm.

And when it came to the wedding, Jeff had simply told her what he would like, listened to her views and then helped her make the decisions with compromise on both their parts.

He was fair, she knew that. But she knew only the barest of details about him personally. It was a strange thing to admit about one's husband, she acknowledged.

He had taken her to meet his parents several times but the last occasion was not particularly happy. On that visit, Mrs. Haddon had been generously kind about their plans but it was evident that she, too, felt the atmosphere grow more strained when Jeff and his father disappeared into the library.

Cassie wondered how Jeff's parents felt, seeing their firstborn son marry a small-town nobody. To their credit, they had politely welcomed her into the family, although without warmth or enthusiasm. Mrs. Haddon had graciously accepted her mother's refusal to hold the event in Toronto.

"This is your special day, my dear," she said smiling. "Yours and Jefferson's. You must do whatever you wish. Mr. Haddon and I will help in any way you would like."

"I'm sure there are certain people you'd like to invite. If you'll give me their names and addresses, I'd be happy to send an invitation." Cassie tried to ignore the Ming vase at her elbow and the white kid leather sofa she sat on. If she was to do this, she would have to fit into Jeff's world and learn to relax.

Mrs. Haddon stared at her in surprise before recovering that veneer of composure.

"Jefferson will tell you whom he wishes to invite. We will abide by his decision. As usual."

Since that was settled, Cassie endured a short discussion on the best catering service in the city. Everything had gone smoothly until father and son emerged from the study a scant ten minutes later.

"We're leaving now." Grim faced, Jeff had announced their departure moments later without even bothering to glance his father's way. Jefferson Senior never spoke directly to Jefferson Junior which left Rory to act as buffer between the two men. Mrs. Haddon offered no comments of her own on their short visit.

Jeff had been terse and uncommunicative until they'd arrived back at Judith's home. Cassie had questioned him then.

"What is this family tradition he's talking about upholding?" she demanded, hands on her trim hips. And when he hadn't spoken, she had grasped his shoulder. "Jeff?"

He'd kissed her then, she remembered. With a tenderness that made her heart ache. Made her believe for an instant he truly cherished her as his wife. But that was impossible—wasn't it?

Long moments later she had stared up at his face through eyes glazed with emotion. It was ridiculous to find herself so drawn to a man she had known such a short time, but Cassie made no effort to deny the joy she always found in his embrace.

Her legs wobbled with the effort of standing and she had been glad when he'd whipped her up into his arms to settle into a nearby armchair. Cassie rested comfortably in his arms, bonelessly pliant as he hugged her small body against his.

"What is it?" A tiny frisson of fear coursed through her veins. Jeff had held her gently then, his chin nestled on her head as he muttered an apology.

"It's always bad when I go there," he told her. "But I apologize for taking it out on you. It's not your fault."

His long fingers played with her hair, curling the glossy strands about his fingers as he sat silent and foreboding.

"Why?" She shouldn't have asked it, but Cassie's tender

heart ached at the pain she saw on his handsome face. She wanted to bring back that darkly sardonic grin.

"What's the tradition?" Her tone was quietly insistent and eventually Jeff answered her.

"The firstborn male in the Haddon family is always called Jefferson with the appropriate numeral behind. It's a tradition my grandfather began and my father insists on having it upheld."

Cassie was dumbfounded into blurting out, "How can it be upheld? You don't have any children." A horrid thought crossed her dazed mind. "Do you?" Cassie fixed him with her gaze, her face severe.

He'd laughed at that.

"No, of course not. The old man is just planning for the future."

"Well, I hope you told him he's just the slightest bit premature."

His darkly handsome face had grown stiff then.

"You don't tell him anything," he had muttered, staring down at her hands in his. "No one ever could. It's his way or not at all." He straightened in the chair, the tenseness obvious in his rigidly held backbone. "But I have my own plans. My son is going to be called Robert, Bobby for short."

She heard it, she just didn't believe it.

"Uh, Jeff, don't you think I might want some say about that?"

He had stared right through her for several long moments before a devilish glint lit his dark eyes.

"Well, when the time comes, I guarantee to let you have your say," he'd promised, grinning at her.

It had been a ridiculous conversation, Cassie admitted. Particularly when she didn't even know how this marriage would be played out. She liked his kisses, enjoyed their walks and discussions and they had settled more than one argument with reason. But Cassie also recognized that so much remained unsettled between them. Jeff had agreed that she could take as long as she wished before their marriage would become a real one. Cassie wasn't sure just how long that would be.

"Cassandra?"

She turned to stare into the sparkling pools of dark chocolate and remembered that he was her husband now; she was married.

"Yes," she blinked, staring at him.

"It's time to go," Jeff whispered in her ear, his hand wrapping round hers. "We have a plane to catch."

How could she have forgotten the honeymoon?

Jeff stood then, tall and handsome as he pulled her up beside him and spoke to the assembled group of grinning faces.

"My wife," there was a firm emphasis on the second word, she noticed. A sort of proud stress on the syllable. "My wife and I have to be on our way," he told them, smiling at the various catcalls. "We'll miss our plane if we don't hurry."

Jeff turned to her parents and thanked them again for his bride. The words were a tribute to her and Cassie surreptitiously wiped away a tear from the corner of her eye as she watched the glow of pride on her mother's face.

They moved around the room distributing wedding cake to their guests and thanking each one personally before edging toward the doorway.

"Throw your bouquet, Cassie," she heard her sister call and so she did. Turning her back on the assembled group, she tossed the beautiful flowers over one shoulder and then turned to identify the recipient.

"Good luck." She grinned at Robyn. "It's fitting," she whispered in her friend's ear. "If God planned this, He probably has something up His sleeve for you, too." And then they were out the door and into the car as showers of confetti cascaded around them.

She heard the happy goodbyes from a distance as her glance focused on Jeff. He was watching her, his dark eyes intent on her face.

"Hello, Mrs. Haddon," he murmured before his lips closed over hers.

"Hello, Mr. Haddon," she replied, but it was in her mind. Her mouth was too busy returning his eager caress.

When he finally pulled away from her lips, her new husband buried his face in her neck, drawing in deep breaths of air before his head lifted, dark eyes shining into hers.

"I think we had better drive away." Cassie blushed, embarrassed by her overwhelming response to him.

He nodded and drove off without a word.

It was only after the first five or ten miles that Cassie realized she was still wearing her wedding dress.

"I don't want to show up at an airport wearing this," she exclaimed, suddenly aware of her predicament.

"And I don't have my suitcase. We should go back to Mom and Dad's. We could change there." She tossed a glance at his formal suit and raised an eyebrow. "I expect you would like to get out of that, too."

He grinned that boyish smile that always sent a tiny shaft to the center of her heart.

"Well, I would," he admitted. "But there is no way we are going back to your parents'."

"Why? I thought…"

"Cassie, they think that's where we're going and your brother has a big party lined up. If we go, we'll never catch the plane."

"Well, where then?" She faced him, shifting in her seat uncomfortably.

Jeff stared into the darkness falling around them before pointing to a grove of trees just off to the side.

"I think we can make do there." He smiled easily. "And I put our bags in the trunk this morning before anyone could tamper with them."

It wasn't easy, wiggling out of her wedding finery behind a bush in the chilly middle of nowhere, but it was infinitely preferable to arriving at the airport in it.

Jeff made fun of her shyness when Cassie shielded herself carefully from his interested glance before removing her dress.

"We're married, Cassie. It's perfectly all right. After all, you can't hide from me forever," he mocked, laughingly.

"True," Cassie muttered to herself. "But I can until I pick the time and place."

Jeff helped her fold his suit and her dress into the garment bags Mrs. Newton had thoughtfully provided.

"That should keep them till our fiftieth anniversary," he teased, revving the motor before they drove off down the highway. "That's when we'll take them out and try them on once more."

Cassie marveled at his calm assurance. He seemed so confident of their future together, while millions of doubts swirled around in her own head like sharks ready for a feeding frenzy. She hummed along with the Christmas carols on the radio and ignored them all.

They arrived in Banff several hours later. Cassie unfolded herself from the plane and tried to peer around at the mountains but it was so dark, little could be seen.

"We were lucky," Jeff said, leading her to the waiting car. "If it had been stormy we wouldn't have had nearly such a soft landing." The small cabin he drove them to was several miles away, up a winding treacherous road.

"We'll admire the view tomorrow," he teased her as she stood gazing up at the giant cliffs overhead. "For now, let's get inside and get warm."

It was a charming cottage and she admired the soft glow of wood that lent the inside such a rustic air.

"It was very kind of Rory to lend us his cabin," she acknowledged, watching as Jeff lit the fire in the big stone fireplace.

"Does he come here often?"

"I'm not sure he can get away from Father's demands that easily," Jeff replied. His dark eyes were watching her flit here and there, touching the soft leather of the sofa and the smooth sheen of the log walls.

"Would you like something to eat or drink?" he asked at last.

"Yes! I'd love some coffee."

He frowned. "Rory doesn't drink stimulants. I'm not sure if there is any," he admitted.

"I'll look," she volunteered. Anything to get away from that yawning silence. "I found it. Want some?"

She was surprised to find Jeff standing immediately behind her in the little kitchen.

"I don't usually... Yes, why not? Just not too strong."

Cassie busied herself with the pot and grounds and wondered how she was going to get through the next three days.

And nights.

In fact, it wasn't really difficult at all. They sat by the fire, sipping at their coffee as they discussed their wedding day in minute detail.

"I'd say everything went perfectly," Jeff said with a yawn. "But it was a long day and I for one need some sleep." He nodded to the larger bedroom on the left. "I've put your suitcases in there. Water heater's lit."

Cassie stood awkwardly, feeling strangely out of place. As if something were not quite right.

"Oh. Okay. Well, good night, Jeff." As she turned to leave, his hand closed around her upper arm. She glanced up at him curiously, face flushed. "Yes?"

"Good night Cassandra Emily Newton Haddon. Sweet dreams." His arms closed around her as his mouth slanted down to cover hers. "See you in the morning," he whispered at last.

"Yes," she whispered. "In the morning."

As she lay in the big soft bed listening to Jeff moving slowly through the cabin, banking the fire and locking the door she thought about her wedding day.

"I'll really try," she promised, eyes squeezed tightly closed. "I'll do my best to be the kind of wife you expect. But please, just keep showing me the way, would you? I'm so afraid I'll take a wrong turn."

* * *

"You've taken a wrong turn." Cassie giggled across at Jeff. "This is the third time we've circled in front of the Banff Springs Hotel and even though it is a wonderful old structure, I think I've seen enough for today."

"Smarty-pants," he chided, peering through the windshield at the snowy landscape. "I'm trying to get to the Upper Hot Springs. I am not lost."

"You should have turned right when I told you to," Cassie said with a chuckle. "How amazing—a man who won't admit he's lost."

His dark brows lowered forbiddingly as he stared across the confines of the small car. "I know exactly where I am. You see, there are the Bow Falls." He said it triumphantly, as if they hadn't driven past them several times already this morning.

"I really believe you'd handle this better if you would just stop for a good strong cup of coffee," Cassie muttered, holding her hand over her mouth. "Coffee has wonderfully restorative powers."

"Says who?" Jeff demanded sourly. His eyes glowered at her. "That stuff you made last night kept me up all night. I didn't sleep a wink."

"You're kidding! I slept like a baby. It was wonderful." Cassie stretched her arms over her head and almost purred in the warmth of the bright sunlight flooding through the windows. "I would have had a cup at the cabin but I couldn't find the coffeepot." She watched his face flush a dull red and wondered at the strange tone in his voice.

"I, uh, er, had a, sort of accident with it."

Curiouser and curiouser, Cassie thought, peering across at him as he wheeled the car into a parking spot in front of the town's only McDonald's. The place was buzzing with activity but she made no move to leave the car.

"It was all right last night. What happened?"

Jeff's dark eyes didn't meet hers as he zipped up his jacket and stared through the windshield.

"I, um, thought you might want some coffee when you

woke up, so I put the pot on.'' His face was very red now, she noticed interestedly.

''Yes?'' She tried to sound encouraging.

''Um, er, apparently I forgot to…that is, the top wasn't on. Not properly and uh…'' His voice was muffled in the fur collar and Cassie leaned forward.

''Pardon?''

''It perked all over the ceiling and the counter and the floor. I spent ages cleaning up the grounds and by then the pot had boiled dry. I think it's burned out now. All right?'' He was glaring at her belligerently, daring her to speak but Cassie couldn't have spoken then. She was too busy laughing.

''Well, thank you for the thought anyway.'' She giggled. ''I know you don't like the stuff yourself. It was kind of you to think of me. Perhaps tomorrow you'll have better luck.''

But Jeff was vehemently shaking his head from side to side.

''Don't look at me,'' he denied, holding up his hands. ''I'm totally useless in the kitchen. This proves it. I think we should just eat and drink out. No dishes.''

Cassie smiled at the shudder that crossed his shoulders. Evidently he wasn't a great success in the kitchen. Well, she could manage. Just barely.

''I'm no great shakes myself,'' she told him. ''At home we have the Bennets so that's no problem. But I think I could rustle up a small meal if we wanted to eat in some night.''

Jeff was standing outside, holding her door. As she stepped from the car, Cassie couldn't help the flutter of awareness that rippled through her at the brilliance of his smile.

''That's why there's takeout,'' he whispered conspiratorially. ''For klutzes and newlyweds.'' She couldn't stop the flood of red to her cheeks either as she fingered her shining new rings.

They spent the next few days relaxing, sightseeing and

skiing. They also discussed everything under the sun. Cassie learned of Jeff's affinity for Toronto's SkyDome and the city's beloved baseball team. As they relaxed in the hotel's spa after a day on the slopes, he found out her wish to be taller and her love of football.

He frowned. "You don't look like the football type," he muttered, staring at her size.

"I know." Cassie giggled. "That's why I usually managed to score. Underestimated." She nodded sagely. "Nobody thought I'd carry the ball the whole nine yards." She caught the amused smile that flew across his face.

"What kind of music do you like?" she asked hesitantly, wondering if she should mention her dislike of country.

"Easy listening stuff. Upbeat rhythms that cheer you up. Some jazz." His head tipped backward in the pool as he allowed the warm mineral water to relax the knots of tension in his neck. He turned his head. His eyes opened and fixed on hers. "And you?"

"The same, I guess. Do you like country music?" She waited, praying that he would say he hated it.

"I like some country music," he said, staring off through the wisps of mist that floated from the pool out across the snow-covered valley. "Not the whiny stuff and not the 'dog bit me and wife left me' kind of stuff." They compared favorite musicians for a while and then discussed the view.

"God really knew what he was doing when he created this beautiful place, didn't he?" she mused, staring at the jagged peaks glistening in the bright sunlight.

"Actually, I think most geologists give that credit to the glaciers." He chuckled.

"Well, someone had to create the glaciers," she asserted reasonably. "They didn't just appear from a big bang. I think He made the Rockies specially for folks to sit back and relax. Take a look at the way their lives are going."

"And," Jeff asked curiously, "is your life going the way you wanted?"

Cassie tipped her head to one side as she studied him seriously.

"Just lately it's taken some very odd twists and turns," she confessed. "I didn't even have a husband, much less a home and two children last month. Suddenly I have all three."

He stared down at her. "I thought that's what you wanted."

"I did," she murmured. Her wide eyes studied his muscular form, deciding immediately that Jeff was the best-looking man in the crowded pool.

"Are you having second thoughts?" Jeff's voice was low and serious and full of reservation as his hands closed over her shoulders.

"And third and fourth thoughts." She grinned at him. "But don't worry. I'm not changing my mind." Cassie's eyes remained locked with his in a stare that seemed to search her heart for answers. That intense scrutiny made her nervous.

"Why does that Moraine Lake seem so familiar?" she asked finally, anxious to break the extended silence between them.

"Probably because it's on the back of that wad of twenty dollar bills you handed over at the Christmas store," he teased. "How, exactly, are you going to get that oak rocking horse home?"

"I didn't spend too much, did I?" she queried anxiously. "It's just that I thought it would be so perfect for the wee ones to play on. And it hasn't a sharp edge on it."

Jeff felt his blood begin to simmer as he stared into her bright green eyes. He had a similar feeling two hours later when he saw that she had the same soft, doe-eyed look in her eyes as she tried to talk to a young girl they'd met panhandling in the park. Cassie tried to convince her to go home.

"I'm sure your parents love you very much," Cassie assured her, smoothing her hand over the girl's thin shoulder as she spoke. He'd felt uncomfortable watching but there was no way he was leaving his wife alone at night in the park with that young hoodlum. "They're probably wondering where you are right now, hoping you'll be coming home for Christmas.''

"Naw, they won't," the teen declared as she sat down on a bench. "They don't care about anybody or anything but their stupid old rules. They have a rule for everything," she added bitterly.

"Oh, honey, in real life there are rules for everything," he heard Cassie murmur. "And if you break them, you always have to pay. Sometimes the cost is pretty high." He noticed his wife's quick summation of the girl's thin jacket and lack of boots.

"For instance, society's rules say you have to work to eat. I bet you've been panhandling for a while, haven't you. Trying to get people to give you something for nothing."

The girl had started to nod at Cassie's words and then objected strenuously. "It's not for nothing. I sing and Jack plays. Or he did. He's gone off with another girl now."

"And you're getting pretty hungry, right?" Both Cassie and Jeff watched the straggly blond head nod. "Will you make me a deal?"

"Cassie, I don't think…" Jeff had swallowed his objections when Cassie fixed those glittering emerald eyes on him.

"What's the deal?" the waif demanded, obviously afraid Jeff would talk Cassie out of her offer.

"I'll buy you anything you want to eat if you'll promise to phone your parents first." Cassie met the glare from his eyes evenly, daring him to contradict her offer. "Anything at any place. You name it."

They both watched as the almost-woman struggled with her offer. At last she shook her head.

"No can do," she said in forced gaiety. "No cash for the call." She stood as if to leave. "See ya."

"Wait a minute." Cassie walked beside her, leaving Jeff to trail behind. She deliberately stopped in front of a pizzeria and stared at the youngster. "If they won't accept a collect call, I'll pay for that, too. Deal?"

It couldn't have been easy, Jeff decided, to ignore the

delicious smells of tomato sauce and garlic and fresh yeasty bread wafting on the night air. His own stomach growled in response. At last he saw the blond head nod.

"You have to try, Shelley," Jeff heard Cassie tell her as they hurried to the bank of public phones across the way. "You have to take the first step. After all, you walked out on them. Give them a chance."

As he wondered how she had found out the girl's name, he saw Cassie's hand slip into the younger girl's. She held on the entire time and moved away only when the conversation became emotional. Then his wife slipped her tiny hand into his and held on tight. He heard her breathing a prayer for the troubled child and her family.

They looked up together as Shelley quietly hung up the phone. The girl looked dazed, lost in a haze.

"Are you okay, honey?" Cassie asked, tugging him forward with her. "Is everything okay?" Jeff felt her fingers tighten around his.

"Not yet," Shelley muttered. "But I think it might be. My mom said they've been looking all over for me. They want me to go home. She said we need to work out the rule thing together." Her blue eyes were full of tears. "She said she loves me."

"Of course she does." Cassie hugged the thin shoulders with a laugh. "You're her daughter. She wants the best things she can give to you. It hurt her to have you leave home and live on the streets. She knows how dangerous life can be. That's why she made the rules."

"I guess." Shelley looked around. "Can we go eat? I feel like I'm going to faint."

They had eaten a huge meal at a spaghetti house. Their young charge socked away two large helpings of lasagna, three glasses of milk and a huge slice of chocolate brownies.

"I've never been so full in my life," Shelley groaned at last, her hand fluttering across her mouth. "It feels wonderful." She bent to pick up the scruffy backpack she carried. "But it's late and I'll bet they want to close."

Jeff cast an eye on the short, rotund man who sat sipping something at the counter. Indeed, the place was deserted. They were the last customers in the place. He felt Cassie press against him as she moved, obviously expecting him to vacate the booth and let her out. He decided he liked the feel of her slim shape against him and stayed put.

"Where will you sleep tonight?" he asked curiously.

"I dunno. The park, I guess. It's only for one more night anyhow." Jeff barely caught the shaft of ice-cold fear in her eyes.

"Oh, Shelley, that's not safe! Why, you could be attacked. Anything could happen there." Cassie glanced sideways at him as she spoke, obviously expecting Jeff to add his voice to her objections.

"It's okay. Really." Shelley stared down at her scuffed runners. "If you stay near the others nobody bothers you much." She stared down at Cassie's concerned face. "Thanks a lot, Cassie. Really. I don't know what would have happened to me if you hadn't made me phone my mom."

"It won't be easy, you know," Cassie warned. Her face was serious. "There will be times when you will think that running away will solve everything. You've just got to stick it out and find a solution with your mom."

"I have an idea," Jeff interrupted quietly. He had his doubts about this young girl's sincerity but there was no question that Cassie was trying to help. He offered the words for her sake. "There's a small place about two blocks over. The lady there offers bed and breakfast. Would you stay there as my treat, Shelley?"

Jeff didn't know why he offered. There was no reason. The girl was nothing to him. But something about Cassie's concern for a young girl alone and scared was getting to him.

"No!" Shelley's head shook vehemently. "You guys have done more than enough. I'm not a charity case. Honestly! I'll be fine." She grinned at Jeff impudently. "It'll probably break your budget just to pay the bill."

Jeff stood up, silent, staring at her.

"No," he murmured at last. "I insist. Cassie and I couldn't possibly just leave you alone now. Not when things are about to change for the better. Come on, it's not far to walk. We'll go together."

To his complete amazement, the girl burst into tears. Loud sobs that sent the manager's curious stare to the lone group standing by the door. Jeff stood there, totally nonplussed.

"Why?" she demanded, gulping back her tears. "Why would you want to do this? You don't even know me. Why are you so concerned about me?"

As he watched, Cassie wrapped her arms around the thin pathetic shoulders and squeezed.

"Oh, Shelley," she whispered, a catch in her voice. "You're a human being…a wonderful girl who's in a little trouble right now. Why shouldn't we help you out? Wouldn't you do the same if you found someone in trouble?"

Shelley's troubled eyes studied the smaller woman for many moments. "I will," she promised. "If I ever get the chance, I'll help out some other girl just like you helped me."

They left her moments later, under the gentle ministrations of a round, sunny-faced woman named Mrs. Beedle who was obviously just aching for someone to fuss over.

"Now don't you folks worry about her one little bit," she clucked, hugging the thin body against her own ample chest. "I haven't had a young thing like Shelley to worry about for years. I'm going to enjoy this. Would you like a nice hot bath, dearie? I have some bubble bath my grandchildren sent me."

Jeff and Cassie tiptoed out the back door as the two new friends walked upstairs, chattering madly to each other. They were half a block away when they heard Shelley's shrill voice.

"Cassie! Wait up." She came rushing up and hugged her friend tightly. "Thank you. For everything. And you, too," she added, wrapping her thin arms around Jeff's waist. "I'll write you as soon as I get home." And then she was gone, dashing away in a flurry of white fluffy snow.

"Fresh powder," Jeff murmured, holding Cassie's hand in his own. "Someone's going to be enjoying a good run on Sunshine tomorrow."

"Uh-huh." Cassie peered up into the plethora of stars overhead. "Isn't it a perfect night?" she exclaimed, grinning up at him.

"Mmm," Jeff agreed, pausing a moment to brush her lips with his. "Absolutely perfect."

He stared down at her.

"Why did you do that?" he asked quietly, watching as her face flushed a dull red.

"You, er, kissed me first," she reminded him.

He grinned. "Not that. Why did you go to all that trouble for someone you didn't even know?"

Cassie shrugged.

"Because she was in trouble and I was there. Because I could, I guess." Her green eyes peered up at him. "What would you have done?"

Three days later he still couldn't answer the question as Cassie sank into the airplane seat and whooshed a sigh of contentment.

"It was a pretty good holiday, wasn't it?" Jeff smiled, noticing how quickly she slipped out of her fashionable heels.

"Very good," she agreed. Her eyes studied him. "How do you think the kids have made out?"

"I'm sure that between your parents and the Bennets, they're probably spoiled rotten." He waited, knowing she wouldn't let it go without an argument. It was just a small bit of the knowledge he'd gathered in regard to Cassie.

"Our kids are too perfect," she teased him, grinning with happy abandon. "They could never be spoiled. Just like me. Although you've made a darn good stab at it these last few days."

It was true, Jeff decided. She couldn't be spoiled. Cassie

Haddon was as clear and true as Banff's new snow. He wondered how he'd come to acquire such a perfect wife. And then he wondered how long it would take her to discover all his flaws. And his fears.

Chapter Five

Two weeks later, Cassie wished sadly that she had relaxed more on her honeymoon. There certainly wasn't any time now.

"There will be four of them, Cassie. They could become very important clients and I want to have them in for dinner. Nothing special...just a nice quiet family meal. Okay?"

"Uh, well actually, Jeff, we have..."

"Look, the other phone is going. I've got to go. Talk to you later."

"But Jeff..." Cassie frowned at the hum in her ear and glared at the receiver with malevolence. "Apparently he doesn't want to hear about you guys," she muttered, staring down at the two children at her feet and the gurgling baby in her arms.

"Mrs. Bennet," she called out and then remembered she'd given the woman the day off. "Of course," Cassie muttered slapping her forehead. "Murphy's Law." She glared down at the little boy who'd come into her care several previous times.

"That's your law, Jonathan Murphy. If anything can go

wrong, it will go wrong." The two newest arrivals stared up at her curiously.

"Cookie?" The dark-headed one seemed confused.

"Sure," Cassie replied resignedly. "Cookies and coffee, that's what we need more of in this house."

The table sparkled with good china, delicate crystal and glittering silver. Cassie had set it early, while the kids were napping and unable to touch the delicate things. But what to do for dinner?

"Hi, Cass. What're you doing?" Marie's words came out garbled as she stuffed a granola bar into her mouth.

"I'm trying to decide on dinner. Jeff's bringing home clients and I want to do something special. Trouble is," she mused, one finger twisting her hair in a spiral, "I don't know any meals that don't include burgers, hot dogs and pizza. Kid's stuff!"

"Hey, don't knock it!" Marie was openly laughing at her. "I'll give you a hand if you want. We've been doing some cooking in Home Ec and Mrs. Edmonds gave us this recipe for gazpacho. It's great!"

Cassie tipped her head to one side as she considered.

"That sounds pretty elegant," she agreed. "What will we do for the main course?"

"Well," Marie said as she lifted four chocolate-covered fingers out of the cookie jar and set it back on the counter. "For one meal we fried pork chops and then put them in a casserole in the oven with mushroom soup on top. They stayed there while we made quick rice with peas and carrots in it. It was good. And you can always have a salad."

Cassie grinned, fluffing the girl's long straight hair.

"Marie, you are a lifesaver. Can you watch the kids while I run to the store?"

Marie eyed Jonathan with disfavor.

"That's the Murphy kid again, isn't it?" She frowned at Cassie's nod. "You'd better make it quick then. He's a terror to watch out for." She scribbled out a list and handed it over. "I've written down cheesecake on the bottom. Try and get one of the frozen kind with swirls. It looks fancier.''

Cassie kissed the soft cheek with fervor.

"I love you, do you know that?"

"You only love me for my cooking," Marie quipped with a grin. "Fair-weather friend, that's what you are." Her eyes narrowed slyly. "Otherwise you'd up my allowance."

Cassie left, shaking her head. Children!

"Pssst! Cassie?"

Cassie turned from her discussion with the abrasive woman she assumed was once Jeff's girlfriend. Melisande Gustendorf had her arm wrapped firmly through his and the mere presence of a wife seemed to bother her not a whit.

"Jefferson and I have always been so close," she gushed in a babyish voice that grated on Cassie's nerves. "Why, we were practically raised together!"

"Cassie!"

"Please, excuse me," Cassie murmured and eased away from the gaily chattering group gratefully. It wasn't hard. No one even seemed to notice her absence. "What is it, Marie?"

The kitchen was a disaster area. There were pots and pans all over the floor as two small children amused themselves clanging assorted spoons and lids to produce a piercing clang that defied conversation in a normal tone of voice. Cassie swept across the floor, laundry basket in hand, as she picked up the pans and swiftly replaced them with plastic containers and lids that were much easier on the ears.

"Now that I can actually hear you, what is the problem, Marie?"

Pale and nervously biting her lip, Marie stood in the middle of the kitchen with tears coursing down her cheeks.

"I forgot to turn the oven down," she burst out bawling. "The meat is all dried out and hard. We can't eat that."

Cassie stared at the shrivelled-up darkened mass in the silver container and shuddered. It did look bad.

"You haven't put the mushrooms on yet," she murmured. "Perhaps if we added a little liquid to the soup it would soften them up." She nudged one solid little piece of meat with her finger. "Do you think?"

"I think we should phone for pizza," David offered helpfully. "Jeff's gonna die when he sees that lot."

Cassie scooped the baby's fingers away from the cheesecake on the counter and smoothed the faint indentation they had left on top with the tips of her finger. A huge strawberry helped cover the mark.

"That isn't going to help, David. It's too late to get anything here in time. We'll just have to hope for the best." She watched Marie spread the thick mushroom mixture over the meat and pop it into the oven. "How about your special soup? Do you think it will be okay?"

"Oh, the gazpacho's great," Marie smiled happily. "I changed the recipe a little but if we serve it with those fresh rolls you bought, everyone will be gasping for the recipe."

Gasping wasn't the word, Cassie decided half an hour later. One mouthful of the potent red concoction in her soup bowl had set her mouth on fire. She whipped the babies' soup bowls deftly away and gave them a roll to chew on.

"This is a very different style of gazpacho," the lovely Melisande wheezed, swallowing a huge mouthful of ice water. "It tastes rather like salsa."

"That's our Marie," Cassie gushed, smiling at the blushing girl who sat near the end of the table, right next to two older gentlemen Jeff had referred to as the Remus brothers. They, too, were sipping their water. "Marie learned this recipe at school. Isn't it delicious, Jeff?"

Jeff's eyes bulged in his face as he swallowed a mouthful of stingingly hot spicy liquid. He wheezed for breath several times before gulping down his water. Apparently "Mmm," was the best he could manage. Cassie decided it was better than nothing.

"Just how did you make this stuff?" Melisande asked scornfully, flicking her spoon through her soup as if searching for some hidden poison.

"Well," Marie began softly, "our teacher, Mrs. Edmonds, showed us that if you take hot salsa and add jalapeño peppers, you can achieve an unusual flavor." She frowned, noticing that no one was touching the remainder of their soup. "It's not too hot, is it?"

"It's just delicious, Marie," Cassie reassured her, filling in the gaping silence. "But you know, I imagine these folks all had a large and probably late lunch." She glanced round the table, forcing a smile to her parched mouth. "We eat early in our home because of the babies. We love to have a family meal. Perhaps you'd rather have some salad?"

The Remus brothers and Melisande were nodding eagerly as Cassie removed their soup dishes to the kitchen while Marie served each a small tossed salad. Jeff wasn't saying anything, she noticed, but then that could be because he hadn't known about Marie's cooking lessons.

"This little guy is sure a cutie," Mr. Weatherby cooed, leaning nearer Jonathan's hovering fingers. In a flash, the little boy had fastened his hands on the ends of the man's curling mustache and refused to let go.

"I'm so sorry," Cassie apologized as she pried open the fat grubby fingers. "He's always been curious."

"Children should be seen and not heard," Cassie heard Melisande say under her breath.

"Oh, I'm sorry you don't enjoy children, Miss Gustendorf. I'm afraid that we always have several running around, don't we Jeff? We just love children, you see." The Remus brothers were nodding benignly at her. Cassie looked to Jeff for reassurance and found him staring in horror at the platter of hardened brownish objects which his fork could not pierce. "Allow me to serve you," she offered and whisked two of the pork chops onto his plate.

Cassie moved round the table swiftly, dispensing food generously until the platters were clean. Then she refilled the water glasses before sitting down. The two babies began to fuss then, tired of their ridiculously inedible meal. Actually so was she. Rice was scattered all over the high chair tray tops and some had fallen into her shoes. Since David was merely stabbing at his food, Cassie decided to free him.

"David, dear, would you mind taking the babies upstairs? I think they're tired." She helped him remove the children from their high chairs. As he moved away, she breathed a sigh of relief. At least further disaster from that corner was removed. Now for the meal.

She sawed doggedly at the dried meat, dragging a hunk away to chew on. When it became evident that her teeth would no longer survive the effort, she lay down her fork and knife and stared round the table.

"That is a really excellent meal, Marie. What a lot of work you've gone to. You just keep practising. Some day you'll make a wonderful chef."

A deadening silence greeted this profound lie until Cassie's glare seemed to penetrate even Jeff's blank stare and he also praised her efforts. Gradually, one by one, the others joined in until only Melisande said nothing. At last her words emerged. Cassie cringed in expectation.

"Well, your cooking is certainly the most unusual meal I've ever tasted. Is there coffee?"

"Oh, I'm sure Cassie has coffee," Jeff commented sourly. "She never goes without that."

"Actually, Jeff, Marie also planned dessert. It's strawberry cheesecake." Cassie watched as the young girl proudly served her dessert. Each slice had been artfully decorated with several fresh strawberries and a drizzle of chocolate.

She watched as first one then the next of their guests carefully pressed a gleaming fork through the soft creamy mixture and tasted the smallest bit.

"It's delicious," they exclaimed, their voices a cry of surprise.

"It's really quite tasty," Melisande offered. "May I have another slice?"

Flushed with pride, Marie cut her a huge slice and carefully set it on her plate. "Please excuse me," she whispered softly. "I have homework."

"Certainly, dear. And thank you so much for all your work. We really appreciate your efforts." The others chimed in cheerfully, relieved that there seemed nothing wrong with this course.

Cassie was about to serve coffee when she noticed Jeff's breathing alter. She glanced down and inhaled sharply as her eyes lit on the round rubber ring of the baby's soother where it protruded from under one fat strawberry.

"I...I..." Jeff stuttered his dismay, drawing all attention their way. Quickly as she could, Cassie plunked the coffeepot down in front of him and slapped him on the shoulder.

"Yes, yes, dear. I'm serving coffee right away." She smiled serenely at the assembled group and picked up the silver server as her other hand whisked the foreign object into the napkin on his lap. "Jeff just loves his coffee," she crowed.

Five pairs of eyes stared at her in stunned disbelief. It was obvious they knew better and thought she was nuts.

"But I thought you only drank two cups a day and never after noon," Melisande croaked, peering at him as if he'd grown two heads. "It's after seven."

"Oh, but this is decaf," Cassie murmured, realizing she'd been caught in her lie. "He loves that. Come on, let's take our coffee into the library everyone. Go ahead, dear," she smiled sweetly at him. "I'll be along in a minute."

They trooped out eagerly, anxious to escape the remains of their inedible meal. Well, not totally inedible. The rice was almost gone, the salad bowls were clean and Marie's cheesecake had been a hit. With everyone except Jeff. His slice sat abandoned, an indentation in the center of it testifying to the soother's presence there just moments ago.

"You can't fool us, you know." Melisande's condescending voice cut through her reveries and she glanced over her shoulder to find the older woman glaring at her through narrowed eyes.

"I'm sorry," Cassie began politely. "I don't know what you mean." She squeezed the damning napkin in her fingers and prayed for strength. "Is something wrong, Miss Gustendorf?"

"Yes!" The low seductive tones were tight with frustration. "There is definitely something wrong. You're trying to pretend that you're all one happy family here when everyone knows that you only married Jefferson for his money. What I want to know is what he got out of the deal?" Her eyes narrowed disparagingly. "What in the world would someone like you have to offer someone of Jefferson's status and means?"

Cassie was furious. What right did this condescending person have to come into her home and criticize her marriage? She was about to launch into the attack when she felt an arm curve around her waist warningly. Her nose twitched at the faint hint of woodsmoke on his jacket as she remembered Jeff had called the woman a possible client.

"Jefferson! I was just saying how ridiculous it is to have those children running through this mansion. Why the house simply isn't made to be treated so shabbily." Melisande waved a hand toward the pair of high chairs nestled at the end of the elegant rosewood dining suite. "Your great aunt would turn over in her grave."

"On the contrary," Cassie answered, smiling. "Judith loved to hear the children in the house. She said it came alive with the sound of their laughter." She frowned as she watched Jeff's friend cast a disparaging look at the litter of dishes still covering the table. "Don't worry about this. I'll clean it all up before Mrs. Bennet gets back."

"You see! That's exactly what I mean," Melisande crowed. "She doesn't even know how to handle the servants. Clean up before they come home indeed! They should have been here to serve the meal. Surely they could have managed better than that distasteful display that ragamuffin girl served us."

Cassie bristled at the disparaging tone.

"Now just a minute," she began, tugging her arm away from Jeff's tightening hold. "Marie offered, of her own free will, to help me out on our housekeeper's day off. And she did the best job she possibly could while baby-sitting three small children. So what if the chops were a little overdone. We won't starve. The important thing is that her heart was in the right place.''

"What's important is that Jefferson's business associates were treated to the most abominable meal on this earth! I don't understand your necessity to house these societal strays, my dear. It's simply not appropriate for someone in Jefferson's position.''

"Societal strays!'' Cassie stared. "They're just little children who need love and a place to stay that's safe and warm. We've got lots of that. What's the big deal?''

"It's not fitting,'' the woman continued, staring as David and Marie walked into the dining room, each carrying a crying baby.

"It's perfectly appropriate.'' Cassie cuddled the sweet little bodies to her and buried her face in their softness. "I had a great childhood. I'd like to share that experience with other kids. Is that wrong?''

"Jefferson, speak to her. Surely you understand that this fiasco tonight was…''

"I understand that Marie pitched in when she was needed and I'm proud of her for that,'' Jeff interrupted. "It takes a pretty big heart to cancel your date so you can baby-sit,'' he murmured, looking straight at Marie. "Cassie and I want to thank you for that.''

The young girl flushed with pleasure.

"Oh, that's all right. I'm just sorry that…''

"You have nothing to be sorry about, Marie. It was a lovely meal. And Mel, in regards to money—'' he smiled down at his old friend calmly but with a hint of sympathy "—Cassie has lots of her own money. She doesn't need mine.''

Cassie stared at him in amazement. He cared—he really cared that Marie's feelings weren't hurt by this cold, selfish woman. She would have hugged him but one of the babies started wiggling and she handed one over instead.

"Actually, I just came in to tell Cassie that Mrs. Butterworth and some other ladies from the church are here for a meeting?" Marie raised her eyebrow at Cassie who had completely forgotten the event. "Should I put the coffeepot on again?"

"Yes, please, dear." Cassie sighed. "And if there's any of that cheesecake left, we'll have that, too." She felt Jeff's body move abruptly behind her and turned her head to stare at his suddenly impassive face.

"Yes," he murmured. "If you'll cover mine so nothing falls into it, I'll eat it after I put the babies to bed." He plucked Corky out of his wife's arms and bent to press a kiss against her cheek in front of them all. "You go ahead, dear. Have your meeting. David and I will look after these two. Right, son?"

"Uh, right. I guess."

David followed the happy group, stopping abruptly at the door when Jeff turned to ask, "Coming, Mel?"

A look of extreme distaste marred the beautifully made-up face of Jeff's dinner guest. She glanced around the room once and then straightened her spine with determination.

"Actually no," she told them shortly. "I've just realized that I also have plans for tonight. I have to leave. I'll drop the Remuses off when I go." She cast a second deprecating look around the room before glancing perfunctorily at Cassie. "Thank you for the, er, dinner. It was interesting."

"Oh, you're welcome." Cassie grinned cheerfully. She slung an arm around Marie's shoulders in friendly companionship. "Feel free to come again. Anytime."

They waited until they heard Jeff at the front door bidding his clients good-night before looking at each other and bursting into gales of laughter. And they didn't stop until Amanda Butterworth came marching through the door.

"Cassie Haddon! You know blessed well that we can't start our meeting until the secretary arrives. What is the problem?"

It wasn't easy but Cassie forced her mouth into a prim

line and walked along obediently behind the older woman's plump figure.

"Yes, Amanda. Sorry. I've just had a rather full day. What is it we have on the agenda for tonight? Oh, yes, the Christmas hampers. Well then, let's get down to work." She sailed through the door, prepared to battle through the next challenge. With His help, she determined, she would handle them all. "Good evening, ladies," she called out cheerfully. "Anyone care for coffee and leftover cheesecake?"

Chapter Six

❧

"What in the world possessed you to offer to bake sixty pumpkin pies for those Christmas hampers?" Robyn demanded, lugging another bag of groceries into the kitchen. "Haven't you got enough to do with a new husband, two adoptions in the works, a four-almost-five year old boy, a toddler and a baby?"

Cassie grimaced ruefully. "Amanda talked me into it," she admitted. "I felt so guilty for spouting off to that Gustendorf woman that I didn't have the heart to turn her down."

"Cassie—" Robyn's eyes were wide open "—you don't bake. Trust me, I know this from personal experience."

"Oh, how hard can it be? You buy those frozen pastry shells and the pumpkin stuff in the can and you mix it up and bake it. Hello," she added, snatching up the ringing phone.

"Cassie, I was just checking the balance on our bank account and I noticed a major withdrawal. It's for cash." Jeff's voice sounded oddly uneven as he named the amount.

"Yes, that's right. I wrote it yesterday." She stuffed the foil pie plates into a cupboard and closed it quickly. "Didn't my money come through yet?"

"Yes, of course." She could almost see him scratching his head. "That's a very large amount of money, Cassie. Are you sure...?"

"It's too near Christmas to be asking those kind of questions, Jeff. Besides," she frowned at Robyn's leather-covered back. "It is my money to spend, isn't it? Wasn't that part of Judith's will?"

There was a long pause.

"Never mind. We can talk about it later. When I get home." His voice lightened. "What are you doing?"

"Baking pies. Sixty pumpkin ones for the church Christmas hampers."

"Cassie, you don't bake. Not at all." He snorted with amusement. "Trust me—I know this for a fact."

She glared at the receiver.

"I've already heard that," she muttered. "It seems that everyone's a comedian in this house."

"The comedy was that unusual dessert we, er, enjoyed last night." He chuckled. "It's the first time I've had pineapple upside-down cake that was turned inside out." His voice came softly teasing across the line. "Did I get the part that fell on the floor?"

"If you've quite finished," she mumbled, a flush of red covering her cheeks, "I do have a few things planned for the rest of the day. Unlike some office personnel with their computer toys."

It slid off his back.

"Don't bake," he ordered. When she didn't reply he added, "Please." He chuckled again when Cassie refused to answer. "See you later," he said finally before a click cut their connection.

"Vengeance is mine, saith the Lord. I will repay." She recited the verse with her eyes closed, trying to forget all the nasty things she wanted to do to Jefferson Haddon.

"Cassie, what are you muttering about over there?" Robyn's query cut through her visions of just recompense for the slander on her culinary skills.

"I'm planning my Christmas list," she retorted. "And

don't bother looking because you're not on it. Nor is that sneaky Jefferson Ungrateful Haddon.'' She flicked the grocery bags into a neat pile and pressed them into the drawer. ''But there might be a way you could get back into my good graces, Robyn,'' Cassie suggested, smiling meaningfully at her friend. ''Somehow.''

''I know that look,'' Robyn protested. ''You're going to finagle your way around and I'll end up saying yes to whatever you ask.'' There was a tilt of amusement to the corners of her mouth.

''Not at all,'' Cassie gestured airily. ''I merely thought that as my nearest and dearest friend, you would want to help me plan a day out with my new husband. In the interest of joy, peace and goodwill toward men. You know,'' she cajoled, ''the Christmas spirit.''

Cassie watched Robyn from the corner of her eye as she packed the groceries into the fridge and freezer. Her friend's big blue eyes were wide open as she stared back at her, azure depths sparkling with mischief.

''Do I look like Santa Claus?'' Robyn squeaked helplessly. Cassie knew Robyn was going to give in. ''What exactly do you and hubby have planned?''

''Oh, Jeff doesn't know about this yet,'' Cassie explained with a giggle. ''But I thought it might be fun to go Christmas shopping for the kids. You know, get something special for each of them—something they really want.''

Robyn watched with amusement as her friend's eyes glazed over. It was just like Cassie to go all out at Christmas. She was like a little kid herself reveling in everything from candy canes and Christmas oranges to the carols and decorations.

''Poor Jefferson.'' Robyn shook her head sadly. ''He has no idea of what will hit him on Saturday morning.''

''Then you'll do it,'' Cassie crowed, flinging her arms around Robyn's shoulders. ''You'll baby-sit the kids for us?''

''Oh, baby-sitting.'' Robyn's head sunk onto her chest. ''That's what you want. And you've got that Murphy kid here, haven't you?'' She peered down at Cassie. ''I'll be dead by the end of the day.'' She sighed mournfully.

''Thank you, thank you, thank you. A thousand times thank you.'' Cassie danced around the room excitedly, listing the items she wanted to get on her fingers. ''There's the cutest little pedal car in Sage's...''

''Cassie? Cassie!'' Robyn snapped her fingers in front of her friend's glassy green-eyed stare.

''Yes?'' Cassie answered, but Robyn had a feeling she was drifting off into never-never land.

''How many kids am I baby-sitting?''

''Mmm? Oh, six, I think. The Tyler boys are supposed to be here for the day.''

''Not the Tyler twins?'' Robyn groaned in defeat. ''No wonder you tried to con me. Those two are the worst little brats....''

Her voice died mournfully away. ''You owe me, kiddo. Majorly big-time!''

''You left her with those two juvenile delinquents?'' Jeff stared at his wife, openmouthed. ''And you call yourself a friend?'' He smoothed his ruffled hair and disentangled the yellow sucker from his mohair sweater with resigned disdain. ''No wonder you had to write such a large check!''

''Are we back to that again?'' Cassie grumbled, trying to slip on her jacket and sip her coffee at the same time. ''I told you—it's for a Christmas gift.''

''Twenty-five thousand dollars for a Christmas gift?'' Jeff stood transfixed as he stared at Cassie's blue-jeaned figure. ''Isn't that a little extreme?''

It wasn't any of his business, of course, but he couldn't imagine what she'd spent the money on. And it seemed his wife wasn't talking. Apparently she was more interested in her coffee.

''Well, aren't you going to tell me?'' he persisted. A new idea occurred to him. ''Wasn't it you who said we should share more, work as a team? Team members tell each other the plan, you know.''

Cassie sighed. It was one of those long-suffering sighs that Jeff was learning meant she would give in but she didn't like it. He waited calmly, watching as she sank into the nearest chair.

"You know I don't do well at conversation in the morning," she hedged, staring into the bottom of her now empty cup. "Especially on one measly cup of coffee." Her drooping jade eyes stared up at him tiredly.

"You've had three cups and quit stalling. What is this mysterious Christmas present?" He fixed his eyes on her and watched her squirm. "Cassie?"

"Three? Really?" She stared at the cup with a blank look.

"Cassie!" He roared it out of frustration.

"What?" Her eyes studied his angry face. "Oh, the money." He nodded. "It was supposed to be a surprise and now you're ruining it," she lamented. Jeff refused to look away and she finally relented.

"Oh, all right," she huffed in frustration. "I put a down payment on a house."

He was shocked.

"What!" He eyed her with pity. "My dear woman, you live in a house with eight bedrooms, six bathrooms, a suite over the garages, a television room, a library, more sitting rooms than we need and a huge amount of land." He shook his head dazedly. "What in the world do we need another house for?"

"I knew I should have brought a thermos," she muttered tiredly. "The traffic will be deadly." Cassie picked up her cup and headed for the kitchen. "I'm getting another cup before we go."

Jeff trailed behind her helplessly. She was insane, that was it, he decided. With all these children coming and going, she had finally flipped. It wasn't any wonder really. He'd felt the strain himself when that social worker, Gwen Somebody, had dropped off two more boys on Thursday. And he wasn't home all day with them.

He'd take her away for the day, just as she'd planned.

He hadn't been too hot on the idea when she'd first mentioned Christmas shopping, but now he understood. Cassie needed a day away from this nuthouse.

"Sit down, honey." Jeff pressed her gently down onto a kitchen stool and poured her mug full of black strong coffee as compassion took over.

"Take a big long drink and then we'll talk about this." He watched her sip the brew as his fingers gently massaged her shoulders. "You need a break. I can see that. But we can arrange something here…get some extra help for you or send some of those hoodlums back. You don't have to move out, Cassie."

Her eyes opened wide then—very wide. She stared at him stupidly. As if it were he who had put a deposit on a home they didn't need, Jeff grimaced sourly. He tried more reassurance and ignored the throb of panic that the thought of her moving out brought to his brain.

"It's okay, just relax," he directed. "I'll look after things. I know you wanted Oak Bluff for your kids but it's getting to be too much. I understand, believe me. We don't have to keep taking them, you know." He slid his hand over her black glossy curls as he spoke, hoping his touch would soothe her.

"Just stay. We can work this out together. Isn't that the way we said we'd handle our marriage—by talking out the problems?"

She couldn't move out, Jeff told himself. Not now. Not when he'd just begun to get used to having someone to touch and talk to—even hug sometimes. He didn't want to lose the closeness they were just beginning to build.

"We can change things, if you want," he murmured. "My old apartment is still up for rent. I could…" His voice died away as he thought of those lonely rooms so far from the hustle and bustle of Oak Bluff. And Cassie.

"Uh, Jeff?" She was staring up at him strangely. As if he were the one who was ill. "It's not for me."

"Pardon?" His hand stopped its caress midway as he peered down at her.

"I bought the house for my parents. I got a buyer for the farm and they're going to move into the city sometime in January. It's supposed to be a surprise." Her green eyes studied him as if she were afraid he would faint.

In fact, Jeff felt poleaxed. His knees were wobbly with relief that Cassie wasn't going anywhere.

"Are you sure?" he asked softly. "Things around here aren't getting to you?" He watched the big smile light up her face as she glanced out the window. He could see half a dozen assorted bodies playing in the snow and Robyn's long arm chucking snowballs at everyone.

"Everything around here is perfectly wonderful." She grinned up at him. "A little crazy, but wonderful. Thank you for asking."

Jeff couldn't help himself. She looked so happy sitting there, her eyes glistening with joy as she gazed up at him. He slipped his arms round her waist, leaned down and kissed her. A soft wonderful kiss that lasted for ages and sent his heart rate through the roof.

And Cassandra Emily Newton Haddon kissed him back!

"Ahem! Excuse me, I just need to get a glass of milk." Marie's face was wreathed in smiles as she padded across the room in her stocking feet. "Go ahead with what you were doing," she added and then flushed bright red.

Jeff cleared his throat.

"Uh, thanks, Marie but we can't right now. We've got some Christmas shopping to do. Right, Mrs. Claus?" He held out one arm and felt Cassie's smaller one curve through it immediately.

"Right you are, Mr. Claus. Bye!" She winked at Marie saucily before they sailed through the door together, grinning like children.

Later, as Jeff watched Cassie pour over possible gifts, he began to appreciate the amount of thought she put into each one. It had taken an hour to choose a silly little purple plastic pedal car which Jeff had insisted she have delivered.

"I cannot possibly lug that thing back to the car," he told her seriously.

"I'm warning you. They'll give us one in a box and you'll have to assemble it." The dimples in her cheeks grinned up at him.

"I don't care. I'll pay extra to have it assembled. Anything so that I don't have to walk through this crowd carrying that!"

He'd paid extra. Then they'd tramped from one end of the mall to the other searching for another hour for a telescope for David.

"Nothing too elaborate," she'd insisted. "But something he can study the heavens with." When Jeff had commented she'd turned on him. "It's either that or more rocks for his collection. You want to handle the excavations for that?"

He'd chosen the black medium-range telescope without further discussion. But this two-hour marathon for a metal construction truck was wearing him down.

"Can't we just get the yellow one for Jonathan?" he asked at last, tired of trailing through the Eaton Centre. "He's only four. I doubt he'll notice."

"Of course he'll notice," Cassie snorted. "Didn't you notice when Santa didn't bring you exactly what you asked for?" Her eyes sparkled up at him. "No, don't tell me. You came from one of those families that didn't have Santa, right?"

"Well, actually," Jeff began mildly, somewhat amused by her vehemence, "we did. But we got oranges and nuts and stuff in our stockings. The gifts came from our parents."

"I hate that," she declared loudly, blocking traffic in the middle of the busy mall. "People get so hung up on Santa Claus. As if it were a bad thing for children to believe that there is actually one man in the world who actually gives gifts just because he wants to!"

"Cassie, I don't think..." His voice died away as she poked him in the chest.

"Well, let me tell you, Jefferson Haddon the third, my kids are having Christmas. All of the things and traditions that make it the most wonderful time of the year."

She glared up at him furiously. As if he'd objected.

"They'll know Christmas is about Christ's birth in Bethlehem. But they'll also know that it's okay to do something nice just because it will make someone else feel good."

"Yes, dear. Whatever you say, dear," he agreed softly. His amused eyes met her surprised look. "But we're not doing a lot for the spirit of goodwill by parking ourselves right here in the middle of traffic. Let's have lunch."

He watched her glance around, as if she were only just then aware of the people jostling them and their packages.

"What put the bee in your bonnet about Santa?" he asked carefully as they sat indulging in burgers and fries. Jeff smiled as that rosy color flushed over her face once more. She got flustered so easily, it was almost fun to egg her on.

"We had the most wonderful Christmases when I was a kid. I used to start planning months ahead of time. When I got older, I managed to get an odd job here or there to raise money, but when I was little I had to save every dime. Everybody had to have a gift, you see. And it had to be something really special." She grimaced. "And it had to come from me—not from my parents or with money that I hadn't earned. From me."

Jeff studied her earnest face as he remembered his mother handing him money and a list of items to purchase for each person.

"Just get what I've written on the list, Jefferson. And have the store wrap them. That will save a lot of fuss and bother." She had even chosen her own gift, he recalled.

Cassie seemed to consider nothing was too much bother and he was carrying the huge rolls of gift wrap to prove it.

"My parents believed that it was important for us to learn to give selflessly." She smiled. "I remember one year there was a scarf I really wanted from the catalog. But I couldn't buy both it and the sewing kit I'd picked out for Sam. It was really hard to buy that kit and leave the scarf, but oh, the look on her face Christmas morning!" Her smooth round face glowed with happiness. "It was prob-

ably the same look I had when I found a brand new pair
of figure skates beside my stocking.''

She studied him seriously.

''Every child has the right to believe in wonderful possibilities. There's a magic about childhood that makes kids
so fragile. And yet they can learn from those dreams that
they can do anything they set their minds to. That giving
has its own rewards.''

''But what's that got to do with Santa?'' Jeff asked,
munching on another fry and wondering why he hadn't
ordered adult food when he'd had the opportunity.

Cassie grinned impudently up at him.

''Do you know any adults that still believe there is a
Santa Claus?'' she demanded. ''Well, do you?''

''Not sane ones, anyway.'' Jeff grinned.

''And that's my point. We all come to realize that Santa
Claus is basically the spirit of giving. Some decry it as
consumerism and say it's a 'getting' philosophy and they're
the ones who can't wait to scurry out there and shatter
every little kid's belief in Santa. I think they do that because their own parents handled it wrong. The whole philosophy of Santa Claus is one of giving and I think it re-
flects the Christmas message perfectly.''

''What's the Christmas message?'' Jeff asked doubtfully.
''Peace on earth and all that stuff?''

''That *stuff* and more,'' she nodded. ''Do unto others...to give is better than to receive...but most of all, God
sent his son; his only child. Not because he should have,
or had to, or because we deserved it. But because he loved
us and *wanted* to.'' She frowned up at him.

''So you think giving is the important part of Christmas?'' he asked curiously. ''The gifts and all that?''

''Not just the gifts,'' Cassie denied, shaking her dark
head. ''Giving the love. That's the key. It doesn't matter if
it's a thing or not. The love will far outlast any *thing*.''

Jeff grinned. Gotcha, he crowed mentally.

''Then why don't you just send all the kids a card that
says 'I love you,''' he joked.

Cassie studied him seriously, her beautiful face staring into his.

"I will," she told him. "And I'll hug them and squeeze them and thank God for them. But that red truck is the tangible evidence that I care. And we haven't got it yet." Her eyes sparkled back at him, daring him to deny it.

He groaned, standing slowly.

"I knew it would come back to shopping," he moaned. "And you're like a missile on a search-and-destroy mission. I can barely keep up."

"Must be your age," she teased, piling up their assorted parcels.

"Hey, I'm not *that* much older than you!" Jeff felt about a hundred just then and the mere thought of dragging these parcels about sent his head reeling.

"I'm talking about mindset, not years," Cassie chuckled, grabbing his hand. "Stick with me, buster. I'll show you the way to stay young in spirit forever."

"Or kill me in the process," he grumbled, following meekly behind. He managed to get her to promise to stay in the jewelry store while he carried their parcels out to the car. "Don't leave here," he ordered. "I'll never find you in this crowd."

Cassie was peering through the glass excitedly and seemed not to hear him. He called her name once but her eyes merely passed over him fleetingly before returning to the window. Jeff grinned. There was only one way to get her attention. Using his shoulder to block them from passersby, he bent down and pressed his lips against hers in a soft caress. This was getting to be a habit he could enjoy, he told himself.

"What was that for?" she demanded, but her gaze was fixed entirely on him and him alone, Jeff noticed with satisfaction.

"Just trying to get your attention," he said smugly. "I'll be back in a minute. Don't move."

She stood staring bemusedly at him, her forefinger pressed against her full bottom lip.

"Yes, all right," she agreed bemusedly. "I'll be right here."

He'd learned an awful lot about her today, Jeff mused as he strode through the mall to the parking lot. Cassie was one of the true-blue people who followed her principles with practice. He envied that happy childhood that had given her such a strong foundation. And he understood her desire to pass it on, sort of.

He tucked the boxes and bags away, remembering how she'd hesitated over each purchase except the sweater for Marie.

"She's been coveting this for ages," Cassie had informed him, a smile of pure pleasure tilting those full lips up. "But she's never asked for it for herself. Not once."

He fingered the soft silky fabric from the coolest, hippest or whatever the word was now, place in the mall. That wide-eyed look of delight in Cassie's big green eyes stuck in his mind, tucked away for future reference. Jeff wondered what he could give to her that would make her face glow like that for him. He had a feeling a sweater wouldn't do it.

He stalked as quickly as he could back through the crowds, hesitating near the door of one store where a tall, slim Santa collected for charity in a large black kettle. The unlikely looking Santa jingled his bell, reminding people that there were others less fortunate than they.

Finally Jeff tugged a five-dollar bill from his pocket and tucked it into the slot. As he did so a familiar voice chirped back at him.

"Thank you very much, sir. And Merry Christmas."

"David?" Jeff's voice was a squeak of surprise and he strove to modulate it. "What are you doing here?"

David grinned, motioning to the big swinging bucket.

"Just what it looks like. Ringing the bells. The money goes toward Christmas presents for poor families in the community. Thank you, ma'am," he called to the tiny frail woman who had carefully put her money into the plastic ball. "God Bless You."

"But David, isn't today the day of that game at school? You're going to miss it." Jeff couldn't believe the teenager had willingly abandoned his friends to stand in a crowded mall and do this.

"Naw, I'll see the last half. We only take three-hour shifts. Besides, there will be other games. The charity only does this at Christmas—to pay for the stuff for needy families, ya know. Thank you, sir." A tall distinguished man pushed a fifty through the slot.

"Oh." Jeff didn't know what else to say. "Do you need a ride home?"

"One of the guys is gonna pick me up at three. He's at the other end of the mall. Thanks anyway. See ya later." David jingled the bells a little harder and smiled at the group of kids pushing and shoving their way past. "Merry Christmas," he called.

Jeff moved away, to continue down the strip. His mind whirled with what he had just seen. David was a foster kid. He'd been taken in by Cassie and, if she got her way, he would soon be adopted into their fairly wealthy family. What on earth possessed him to stand in the mall ringing bells for charity?

"Jeff? Where are you going? Jeff?"

He stopped at the sound of Cassie's voice and turned to find her rushing up behind him.

"I've been waiting for ages and then you walk right past. Trying to get rid of me?" she teased. Her eyes darkened as she noticed his expression. "What's the matter?"

"Nothing, really. It's just that I saw David back there." He jerked a thumb over his shoulder. "Took me by surprise."

"David?" Cassie frowned. "What's he doing here?"

Jeff studied her face. She seemed innocent enough—as if she had no idea. His theory that Cassie had put him up to it evaporated.

"He's ringing the bells on one of those charity kettles."

"Oh, how nice. What a kid! And today's his basketball game, too."

"I asked him about that," Jeff murmured. "He said he'd be off in time to see the second half." He searched her face. "Why would he suddenly decide to do this?" Jeff asked. "It's not normal behavior for a teenage kid."

"Well, it should be," Cassie announced firmly, tugging his arm with her own. "There are a lot of people who benefit from that program, and teenagers can help as well as anyone."

When he didn't move, she pulled a little harder.

"Come on, Jeff. We haven't got anything for the Bennets yet. I know just what Mrs. Bennet wants."

As he let himself be led through the throngs of shoppers, Jeff resolved to have a little talk with David later. His mind pricked his conscience.

So what have you given back to anyone lately, Jefferson, my boy? Anything of value?

Chapter Seven

Cassie pushed the tendril of hair off her face and puffed out a sigh as she swished the bubbles over Jonathan's wiggling little body.

"How do the beautiful people stay that way, Johnny Boy?" she asked, catching a glimpse of herself in the mirror. Jonathan gurgled with laughter as she stuck her tongue out at the urchin reflected back. He smacked the water with one hand, sending a tidal wave of water over the edge of the tub and onto her sweatpants.

"Thank you, darling." She smiled. "I needed that dose of reality."

"The beautiful people often aren't very beautiful where it really counts," Jeff's sardonic voice muttered. She whirled around to find him leaning nonchalantly against the door frame.

"Daddy," Jonathan crowed and thrust himself up from the water. Cassie just missed catching his arm at he launched himself at Jeff. The boy's soaking body soon drenched her husband's elegant white shirt and pressed navy slacks.

Jonathan snuggled himself against the expansive chest and pressed his soft little lips against Jeff's neck.

"I wuv you, Daddy."

Cassie watched in suspended animation as Jeff's stern features froze into a mask. He recovered himself moments later to grasp a towel from one of the rods and wrap it around the little boy.

"Well, thank you, Jonathan. I appreciate that."

"I'll take him," Cassie offered. "He's getting you soaked."

But Jeff shook his head. "No, he'll just get you wet, too."

"As if I'm not already." She chuckled. Her eyes glinted with good humor as she pulled the plug and swished the suds down the drain. "Come on, kiddo. Into your pj's."

"Daddy do," he squealed, hanging on to Jeff's hair with his fingers.

"Ah, I think I'd better comply," Jeff murmured, wincing at the tight grip. "I'm too young to be bald." His head cocked to one side as the sound of a baby's cry penetrated the steamy room. "Which one is that?"

Cassie pointed to the Batman pajamas lying folded on the tile counter before moving toward the door.

"We've only got one baby now, remember. Corky went home this afternoon." She moved down the hall, his mumbled response following. "Make sure he gets into bed right away," she told him. "It's way past his bedtime."

She spent a few moments quieting the fussy baby before moving back down the hall to check on Jonathan. When she heard low-pitched whispers coming from his room, she stayed outside the door to listen, allowing only her eyes to peek around the corner.

What she saw startled her. Jefferson Haddon, Esquire, sat on the edge of the bed talking to the little boy who was snuggled under the covers.

"Can I stay here forever and ever Amen, Daddy?" Jonathan's big brown eyes peered up curiously.

"Well..." Jeff began haltingly. "I think this is sort of like a holiday. Your mom and dad might want you to come back to your own house after the holiday is over."

"Will my other daddy take care of me like you and Cassie do?" he queried, tugging at the button on Jeff's pocket. "He doesn't smell nice and pretty like Cassie does. I like that smell." He snuggled down in his little bed. "I like Christmas, too. Are we gonna have a Christmas tree with lights 'n' everything?"

"I don't know," she heard Jeff answer hesitantly. "What did Cassie say?"

"I never asked her." The little boy yawned. "But she really likes Christmas. She was singing songs about Baby Jesus all day today. And she letted me have two ginger-bread boys." He yawned once more. "Don'tcha got no more little boys here, Daddy?" he whined, glaring at Jeff accusingly. "I like to play with the other kids, ya know."

"No," Jeff murmured so softly Cassie had to strain to hear him. "I guess you're the only little boy we have here right now."

Jonathan stared at him for a few moments before he shrugged and let his heavy eyelids fall shut. "Kiss me g'night, Daddy," he mumbled and held up his cheek.

Cassie watched, her heart in her throat as Jeff leaned down to press his lips against the soft smooth skin.

"Good night, son. Have a good sleep."

The chubby arms wrapped tightly around Jeff's neck as Jonathan gave his famous bear hug.

"I love you this much, Daddy," Jonathan crowed, squeezing his eyes tightly shut and grunting with the effort. Cassie thought she saw tears on Jeff's face as he hugged the little boy back and then tucked him in once more.

"Good night."

She realized suddenly that Jeff would be coming out of the room at any moment to find her standing there, eaves-dropping on his conversation. Cassie scurried down the hall and downstairs to the big family room. She was ensconced on the plush overstuffed sofa when he ambled in several moments later.

"Everything okay?" she asked as he sank down in the cushions beside her.

"Well, he's in bed," Jeff offered. "That's the best I could do. He's quite a touching little guy, isn't he? What's his background?"

She stifled the gasp of joy that threatened to overwhelm her. At last! Jeff was finally asking to know more about the children who came to stay in their home. It was a good sign. It had to be, she told herself.

"His mother leaves him here periodically when she goes in for treatment. She's a crack addict."

Jeff stared at her. "And she chose Christmas to get herself cleaned up?"

"Not exactly," Cassie shook her head. Her voice lowered conspiratorially. "They can't find her. She left Jonathan with some neighbors and never came back."

Jeff shook his head sadly.

"And his father?"

"He doesn't have one. At least not one he knows about."

She picked up the cross-stitch bookmark she was working on and bent over it until she felt his hand on her arm. His face was a puzzle.

"But he must have. He talks about his other daddy all the time. He even said he didn't smell good." Jeff's eyes were dark pools of curiosity, but Cassie was more intent on his arm which had flung companionably around her shoulders.

"I know," she murmured, trying to repress the delicious shiver of excitement that coursed through her at his touch. "It's a sort of game he plays. I suspect Jonathan is confused by the different men his mother brings home. To simplify things he just calls them all daddy."

"It's sad," he reflected, fingering the cotton fluff on her sweater. "He seems such a cute kid." Jeff leaned his head back against the sofa. "He even asked me if we were going to have a Christmas tree."

"And are we?" Cassie asked softly, keeping her head bent over her work.

"Cassie," he chided, laughing down at her. His forefinger moved to press her chin up, forcing her to meet his gaze. "You know very well that you'll go hog-wild and insist on the biggest tree there is and then load it down with all sorts of baubles."

She grinned back irrepressibly.

"Oh, I'm so glad you agree. I asked Bennet to find one. I said you'd help get it into its stand." With her eyes, she dared him to back out now. "Think of it as something you'll do for the kids," she advised laughing.

Seconds later, her laughter caught in her throat as he cupped her cheeks between his hands. His eyes were darker now and searching her face intently.

"Okay," he agreed. "I'll set up the tree and help you decorate it for the kids. But this—" his thumb slid across her bottom lip "—this is just for us."

He waited. Long, aching moments until he was sure her attention was fixed on him and him alone.

And then he kissed her.

To Cassie it was exactly right. A tender, but promising kiss that said everything she needed him to say without the words. He cared about her, just the tiniest bit. And he was beginning to realize how much he cared about the children.

She kissed him back, trying to put all the longing that she'd hidden in her heart into her caresses. But she hadn't begun to say half of what she needed to when his head lifted from hers. His eyes were only half aware as he cocked his ear to one side and listened.

She was expecting him to say something romantic, some confession of the heart. What she heard was, "Is that the smoke detector?"

"The child's a pyromaniac!" Jeff's angry voice rose above her explanations loudly.

"He is not. He's just a little five-year-old boy who misses his mommy." Cassie tried to wipe the black soot from her face with one sleeve of her good sweater. At least, it had been her good sweater once.

"An arsonist at the very least! He could have killed all

of us in our beds, not to mention destroying this house you love so much.'' Jeff glared around the master bedroom as if he suspected he would find Jonathan hiding somewhere behind the massive furniture.

"You shouldn't have left those matches lying around," she remonstrated firmly. Her toe kicked uselessly at the huge burn in the rug. "Not when there are children around."

He strode across the room to stand in front of her, his face tightly drawn.

"So now it's my fault? The *children* are supposed to be in *my* room, now are they?" He stared down at her, breathing heavily with the force of his anger. "Maybe if we had a set of stricter controls in place, they wouldn't have this problem."

"Oh, thank you! Now I'm not strict enough?" Cassie grit her teeth. "Maybe you should start seeing them as children who need help and love," she growled. "Instead of little robots who are supposed to do your bidding no matter what!"

"Oh, give it up," he muttered disgustedly. "You're a bigger child than all of them." He surveyed the damage and shook his head. "Who's going to pay for all of this?"

"Ah," Cassie squealed. "Now we come to the crux of the matter. Money. That's always your main concern, isn't it? Money, money, money. Well," she said, dashing the sopping curls out of her eyes as she marched to the door, "don't worry about it anymore, *Jefferson.* I'll pay for it out of my own money."

She cast a scathing glance at the heavy dark wood and thick velvet draperies.

"Believe me, this place could use a face-lift. It's so dark and dingy it looks like a cave." She turned to fix him with her best angry stare. "A cave for a bear."

As she flounced down the stairs, Cassie stopped suddenly as she realized exactly what she'd said. And how foolish it had been. Her allowance had dwindled down to a paltry amount once she'd paid for the house, helped Sam out and found the best psychiatrist for her brother's step kids.

"Ooof!" She hung on to the balustrade with an effort as someone knocked into her from behind. "Can't you look where you're going?" she snapped angrily.

Jeff's eyes peered out at her from above the stack of blankets and pillows he carried.

"No, I can't," he growled. "I can't see a thing. Anyway, you shouldn't be standing on the stairs. You could fall and hurt yourself." He brushed past her, bumping her aside with the soft blankets.

"Especially if I'm pushed," she muttered and then hurried after him. "What are you doing?"

"Finding a nice *quiet* place to sleep," he almost bellowed. "The bedrooms next to mine and across the hall are filled with leftover smoke. I can't sleep there. That leaves here." He fluffed the blankets and quilt out on the maroon leather sofa and dropped two pillows on top. "You might as well have them cleaned and redone while you're redoing mine."

"I can't." She hadn't meant to say it. It just sort of slipped out when she was thinking about ways to come up with more cash.

"Can't what?" Goodness, he did sound like a grouchy bear, Cassie decided. She avoided meeting his black gaze.

"I, er, can't pay for the, uh, repairs," she half whispered and then peeked up. His face was dark and foreboding.

"And why not, might I ask?" His hands hung on his hips in a question mark, ready to castigate her for her frivolities.

"I haven't got enough left. My money's almost gone," she told him softly. She turned away at the hiss of disgust.

"It can't be," he said incredulously, the blankets suddenly forgotten. "What on earth did you buy? Another house?"

"No, I didn't," she replied angrily. "I made a small loan to my sister and brother, that's all. They'll pay me back. When they can." Cassie didn't even flinch as she told the white lie. She no more expected repayment than to fly to the moon. "Anyway, I'll do what I can. You don't have to worry about it. It's my fault it happened, anyway. I should have warned you."

He sighed heavily, raking his hand through his dark hair with reluctance.

"It's nobody's fault, Cassie. And don't worry about the rooms. Insurance will cover all that." He peered down at her through the gloom. "Why didn't you tell me about Jonathan's *little* problem with matches?"

"I don't know." She shrugged, avoiding his eyes as her toe scuffed the beautiful Persian rug. "I guess I thought you'd make him leave and I want Jonathan to spend this Christmas here with us, in Judith's house."

It bubbled out in a torrent of words that brought a rueful grin to his craggy face.

"What is it about this house?" he muttered. "It's as if you're totally captivated with it."

Cassie stared up at him.

"Oh, it's not the house," she assured him. "It's what I want to happen in it." She watched him frown.

"What exactly do you want to happen here?"

"Love. And joy. And peace and goodwill." She enumerated them for him with arms outstretched. "I want it to fill every corner and every person."

"For Christmas, you mean?" he asked, obviously trying to understand.

Cassie smiled softly as she walked from the room.

"That would be a good start," she acknowledged. She retraced her steps to poke her head back into the study. "By the way," she informed him. "The Christmas tree decorating is scheduled for tomorrow after church. You are going to help, aren't you? After all, you're the boss!" She ducked when he threw the pillow at her and ran racing up the stairs.

"Now, if You could just get him to go with us to the service tomorrow morning," she prayed softly. "That would be the best possible start to the day."

And the good Lord seemed to hear for when Jeff came into the kitchen for breakfast the next morning he was telling Jonathan that he could sit on his knee during the service.

"But only if you promise to behave," Jeff said sternly. "We can't have any more fires or Cassie and baby Steve and all the rest of us will have to move out. It's too dangerous. Is it a deal?"

"Thank you, Daddy," Jonathan chirped happily and promptly spilled the baby's cereal all over the floor.

As they sat together in the solemnity of the church later that morning, a child in each lap, Cassie let herself join in the singing wholeheartedly. After all, she had the best of all possible worlds, didn't she?

Not quite, her conscience reminded. She had the house and the children and she was married to Jeff. At least in name. She stuffed away the rest of the silly notions that filled her head at inappropriate times. Unlikely things like his sweet kisses, his arm slung around her waist as he told her how much he loved her.

She felt a hand tugging on her skirt and glanced down to note that Jeff was seated. So was everyone else. She sank onto the hard wooden pew hastily and tried to hide her face in the baby's neck. Which was impossible given the stench emanating from that small being. Jonathan picked that particular moment to kick up a fuss, too, and Cassie prayed for strength as she reached for the diaper bag.

"Trade you," muttered a frustrated Jeff. He picked up the baby and the bag with one motion and left the bench and Jonathan as everyone bowed to pray. Cassie was pretty sure that's when the odor hit him because he turned to frown fiercely down at her before heading reluctantly for the nursery.

"Wanna go wif Daddy," Jonathan squeaked. She hushed him, mentioning the words *Junior Church* which always worked magic on the little boy's demeanor. He sank onto the seat as quiet as a church mouse and closed his eyes reverently.

"And bless us Lord as we enter the season celebrating your birth. May we feel that peace and goodwill toward men flood our hearts with joy. Amen."

"Ahhhmen," Jonathan repeated loudly. His big eyes opened wide as he glanced around and noticed the other children stirring. "Church time," he crowed, earning a laugh from the small congregation.

"Kids are frighteningly straightforward, aren't they?" Pastor Jake remarked, watching as the children filed out haphazardly. "That's why we love them so much."

Jeff slipped in beside her again. Cassie noticed that his lovely navy tie seemed damp. And there were spots on his jacket and shirt, too.

"What happened?" she asked, leaning over to whisper in his ear.

"This kid is a little too accurate with his aim." When she still looked puzzled he continued. "Especially without a diaper to hamper him."

She couldn't help the small giggle that escaped her at his disgusted look. "Just keep repeating 'I love kids' to yourself over and over," she whispered.

She thought she heard him mutter, "I'll get Cassie," but the offertory ended just then and she didn't want to ask him to repeat it.

Jeff had just gotten comfortable in his seat when the minister launched into his sermon.

"I've chosen the topic of love for a pre-Christmas series," the smooth eloquent voice began. "As we read in first Corinthians, there are many faces to love. Let's read that passage together."

Love. He was sick and tired of hearing about it. But the way the man spoke, his attitude that nothing mattered if love wasn't involved, twigged some bit of curiosity in his mind.

"If I gave away everything I have, but didn't love others, what good would it do?"

Harrumph, he felt like saying. That must be the law Cassie operated on. It seemed to him that she was determined to give away every last cent she owned.

"Love is not selfish or rude. It doesn't demand its own way." The minister continued his discussion, enumerating the qualities of love. "You see folks, when we were children we acted and reacted like children. But now that we're adults we need to stretch our thoughts far beyond childhood and embrace the world around us."

The words chewed at Jeff's mind, repeating themselves over and over. Put away childish hurts and move on. But how? How could he forget the deep-seated pain and anguish of those days—just let them roll off his back?

"No," he told himself firmly. He wasn't going to just forget about all the heartache and anguish he'd carried for so long. He would remember it so that he never allowed it to happen to him again.

Pastor Jake was winding things up now. Jeff's ears perked as he listened to the closing remarks.

"When everything else is gone, folks, there are only three things that will remain. Faith, hope and love. And the Bible tells us that the greatest of these is love. Let's spread a little around this Christmas, shall we?"

Jeff rose with everyone else and sang the old familiar hymn from memory while his mind worked overtime. He wasn't a heathen. He could be as charitable as the next guy. His wife wanted a big happy Christmas; fine. He'd see that she got one. And in the process he'd make darned good and sure that no child under his roof ever had cause to complain about his treatment.

But love?

That was something he couldn't afford. It cost too much.

Chapter Eight

"**I**t's a little lopsided." Cassie giggled as Jeff wired down the pine's sticky trunk. "No, the other way. That's better." She picked the pine needles out of his hair with a laugh. "You're really getting into this Christmas business, Jefferson," she teased.

Jeff grinned. She always called him that when she was up to something. Usually something sneaky.

"Well, that looks steady," he joked heartily, smacking his hands together. "Now the rest of you can take over while I relax and watch." His rear end had barely touched the sofa's cushion when he found her standing over him.

"Great! You can watch Stevie." She dumped the burbling baby on his lap and moved to free the lights from the new kid's fingers. Jeff could never remember the little girl's name.

"After the indignities he subjected me to in church? I don't think so." Jeff placed the baby on a nearby blanket on the floor and handed him a ring of plastic keys.

"I've been meaning to ask you about that," Cassie murmured faintly. Jeff could see the twitch at the corner of her mouth. "The janitor said you asked him for rubber gloves?

And when I changed him just now, his diaper was on backward." She gazed across at him innocently. "Well?"

"It seemed the best solution to the problem of getting wet again," he told her. "I just put him on his stomach and put the diaper on. I forgot the little animals would be marching across his backside." He made a face. "I would have asked the guy for a face mask if I thought he'd have one. That's disgusting!"

He heard that full-bodied laugh burst out and ring through the room. The children stopped what they were doing to stare at her as she doubled over in hysterics.

"Aren't you the guy that wanted his own son?" she chortled. "How were you planning on handling the diaper business?"

Jeff glared at her, feeling like an idiot. Trust the old codger to go blabbering his business, or rather Stevie's, to the whole church!

"My kid isn't going to descend to that disgusting level," he told her shortly. When she burst into renewed hysterics he bristled with frustration. "Are you going to decorate that tree or not?"

"Come on, guys," she called, still chuckling as she called in the children. "It's tree-trimming time."

It was more like a day at the loony bin, Jeff grinned, surveying the mess in the family room later. There were bits of packaging and torn pieces of paper littering the carpet, and empty red tumblers sat here and there about the room, evidence that everyone had enjoyed Mrs. Bennet's egg nog.

"Doesn't it look magnificent?" Cassie exclaimed behind him, her eyes as wide as the baby's. "They did a fantastic job."

He glanced at the heavily laden tree with its twinkling white fairy lights and combination homemade and store-bought decorations. It was a family tree. Not fancy. Not overdone. Just decorated with something from everybody.

Everybody except him. Apparently Cassie had noticed that, too.

"I popped the popcorn for the ropes. Marie made the angel. David did those clove spice ball things. Jonathan glued the paper chains and Stevie—" she paused, thinking "—Stevie licked most of the candy canes. The ones hanging toward the bottom, anyway," she cried triumphantly. Her big green eyes studied him seriously.

"What are you going to add to our family's Christmas tree, Jeff?"

He stared at her.

"Me? Why…nothing. I told you, I'm not really good at Christmas." He felt an irrational anger at her for pointing out that he didn't fit in here, either. "What?" he barked, noticing her shaking head.

"That's a cop-out you don't get to use here," she told him, sinking down onto the fluffy cushions. "I'll just wait here until you think of something. Go ahead."

He glared down at her and wondered anew how less than one hundred pounds of femininity could be so aggravating. He crossed his arms stubbornly.

"Jeff, we agreed that we'd share things in this family. You have to do your part." She frowned at him. "You're not even trying. Come on."

"All right," he muttered, giving in to her bossiness. "What do you suggest I do? Pick cranberries in the woods and string them up? Or cut boughs off another tree and decorate the mantel?"

She had that glint in her eye again!

"Hey, that mantel idea is a good one. I wonder…"

"Kidding," he hollered, frustrated by her intransigence. "I was kidding." He crossed his arms once more and smiled down on his petite nemesis smugly as a new idea occurred to him. "Anyway, I've already contributed."

Her eyes flew to the tree and he watched them flick swiftly over the baubles and lights.

"I don't see anything."

"Of course you don't." He laughed, pleased at his little joke. "Can't see the forest for the trees, can you?"

"I don't get it. What are you talking about?" His wife

stood there in her stockinged feet, glaring at him balefully. "I was here the whole time. You just sat there and watched us put all this stuff on."

"Which you wouldn't have been able to do if I hadn't set the thing up in the first place." He smirked. "So my part in this, er, decoration, was completed first."

She laughed good-naturedly.

"Sneaky," she grumbled. "Very sneaky."

"You haven't seen the half of it," he drawled, slipping the mistletoe from his pocket and holding it over her head. "You're so big on Christmas—do you know what this tradition is?"

He watched delighted as that pretty rose flush suffused her neck and face, forming bright circles of color on her cheeks.

"Jeff, there are children present in this house."

"I know," he murmured. "So what? We're married. It's allowed." She didn't even try to move as he tipped her face up toward his, Jeff noticed. Matter of fact, she even leaned in a little, in anticipation.

He'd barely even touched her saucy little mouth when the phone rang.

"Oh, for Pete's sake! This place is like Grand Central Station at rush hour. Hello," he barked into the phone and then modulated his voice as Pastor Jake's friendly tones intruded. He kept his arm wrapped around Cassie anyway, just in case it wasn't another minor emergency.

"She's right here. Just a moment please." He handed her the phone with resignation, allowing one finger to wrap around a fat glossy curl that fell forward onto her cheek. "Pastor Jake. Something about angel costumes."

"Oh, good grief." She sounded as frustrated as he felt, Jeff decided. He kept his arm right where it was, wrapped around her waist as she spoke, and let his other hand brush over her shining head.

"I'll be there right away," he heard her say before she hung up the phone. Her head tipped forward on his chest as she leaned against him tiredly. "I have to go to the church. Apparently Sue Ellen Withers forgot to finish the costumes for the Sunday School's Christmas pageant tomorrow evening.'' She sighed as his hands massaged the knot in her shoulders.

"Not that you can blame her."

Jeff couldn't have cared less about Sue Ellen Withers or the angel costumes or anything else just then, but he felt compelled to ask.

"Why?"

Cassie's big emerald eyes sparkled up at him.

"She went into labor last night and just gave birth to a ten-pound baby boy. I think she's entitled." Her voice sounded misty, full of daydreams.

Jeff bent and pressed a kiss against her glossy head.

"Go ahead," he mumbled. "I'll look after the kids."

"Are you sure?" She frowned at him assessingly. "Marie's out baby-sitting and David's working in his lab. There will be just you, Jonathan, Alyssa and Stevie."

When that soft, caressing look fixed on him, Jeff felt a new energy surge through his veins. He could do this, he told his quivering insides. He could manage.

"I'm sure we'll be fine," he answered. "You'd better get going."

All the screaming denials his subconscious was pushing forward died an instant death when Cassie smiled her special smile and stood on her very tiptoes to press her lips against his cheek.

"You're a sweetheart," she whispered. "Thank you." And then she scurried from the room just before his fingers tightened to hold her back.

Jeff heard a gurgle of sound and glanced down to see Stevie sucking on some tinsel.

"Okay kid, it's just you and me. And you're not eating any more of that stuff. Strictly dairy products from now on."

All of a sudden, Jonathan left the toy train he'd been vrooming round the track and ran over to cling to his leg.

"I want a story, Daddy. The one about the baby who came to bring love."

As he stared down at the two innocent faces, Jeff felt the same old pangs of loneliness strike once more. Was this how a father felt, he wondered, when his children asked for something? Did all men get this mushy feeling inside their gut when a little kid snuggled against them? Had his father ever felt this strange feeling when he smelled the soft dewy skin of his own freshly bathed baby?

A short time later, Jeff pushed the traitorous thought away as he snuggled Stevie against his shoulder and burped him. He concentrated on the baby's sweetly powdered skin as he laid him in his crib and turned out the light.

Kids were so forgiving he noted as he scrubbed down the bathroom before starting Jonathan's bath. They didn't care where the love came from, as long as somebody took the time and effort to listen and care for them. And if a parent wasn't prepared to put in that time and effort, why should they be entitled to care for that little life?

Jeff refused to dwell on the things his father had missed out on. Things that he was sharing now with Jonathan. Things like bath time with a zoo of plastic animals that had specific names. Things like toothbrushing—Jeff had never known how truly complicated that simple operation could become. And other things like bedtime stories and prayers.

"But how does God get to hear everybody's prayin'?" the little boy demanded. "Does he have lots and lots of ears or something?"

"Something like that," Jeff answered, hoping he wasn't agreeing to something sacrilegious.

"Oh." The eyes scrunched closed once more as Jonathan started on the God blesses. They popped open seconds later. "Did God bless you, Daddy?" his little voice chirped.

Jeff thought about that. The truth was he was very blessed, Jeff decided. He had a wife and a wonderful sort of hodgepodge family around him that he'd done nothing to deserve. And he had this little boy. For a while anyway.

A tiny bundle of curiosity and innocence that made him long for his own son more and more.

"Daddy?"

Jeff stared down at the angelic little face and thought about his current life.

"Yes, Jonathan. I think he really did bless me. Good night now."

"You have to kiss me." The little imp grinned. "Cassie always kisses me good-night."

Jeff leaned down and pressed his lips against the downy soft skin. "Is that right?" he asked. "I don't know very much about bedtimes."

Jonathan nodded thoughtfully.

"It was pretty good," he decided. "But you have to hug, too. Like this." He wrapped his eager little arms around Jeff's neck and held him in a stranglehold.

And Jefferson Haddon the third reveled in the discomfort as he hugged the little waif back again.

He thought about that hug long after Cassie returned from the church and questioned him intently about each child. He thought about it as she kissed his cheek and bade him good-night. And he thought about it many minutes after he'd retired to his charred lonely room.

How could any man reject what was so freely offered? How could a father reject his own son?

Cassie fidgeted with the bright red velour suit she had chosen to wear to the children's Christmas pageant, tugging the tunic down as she admired its clean straight lines. She peered at herself in the floor-length mirror and wondered if it wasn't a little too showy, a bit too bright.

After all, the children were the feature attraction this evening she told herself severely, as she brushed her glossy curls into some semblance of order. And just because she wanted to attract one man's attention in particular didn't mean she had to spoil the evening for them.

"Well, he can hardly miss me in this outfit." She chuckled and turned away to put on the shiny gold star earrings and matching star brooch. "And red is my favorite color."

She cast one more doubtful look at her image and shrugged. For better or for worse, she had promised. Well, tonight was definitely going to be for the better. She was adamant on that.

"Wow!" Marie flashed her huge shy grin as she stood in the doorway. "You look great."

"Thank you, my dear." Cassie curtsied, taking care not to overbalance on her new black patent heels—three-and-a-half-inch heels. She would have worn higher ones, but shc had enough trouble staying upright on these. "You look pretty hot yourself."

Marie's straight blond hair gleamed brightly against the black velvet jacket and lace-edged white blouse. In her matching slim-cut pants, she looked exactly what she was. A beautiful young teenage girl.

"It's not too much is it, Cassie? I'm supposed to meet Nate after the service. We're going to exchange gifts and I wanted to look special."

Cassie hugged the tall slim girl against her and brushed a kiss against her head.

"You are special, Marie. You're a very beautiful daughter."

Marie flushed with pleasure, her eyes downcast.

"Not quite yet," she whispered hopefully, her tone eagerly wishful.

"The papers don't say it," Cassie agreed, tipping the girl's chin up to stare straight into her eyes. "But I do. And no judge in any court could make it more official than it feels right here." She tapped a finger against her heart. "Okay?"

Marie nodded, grinning from ear to ear. "Okay."

"Don't spend too long saying goodbye to Nate. He'll be back in a week, remember." Cassie fluffed her black locks once more and then picked up her small beaded bag. "And we have carolers coming around afterward."

"I know," Marie agreed softly. "I'll be here to help."

Cassie frowned. "I don't want you to be there to help, Marie. I want you to be here as part of our family as we welcome people into our home." She grinned. "You've done more than enough helping lately."

Marie smiled back, taking no offense at the words. "Well, you have to admit that I'm better at baby-sitting than I am at wrapping oddly shaped gifts."

Cassie rolled her eyes in agreement. "I'll say."

They walked down the staircase giggling like young girls as they joked back and forth. Jeff stood waiting at the bottom, little Stevie cradled happily in his arms and Jonathan standing beside him. To Cassie's surprise the little boy was dressed in a tiny black-and-white tuxedo that exactly matched Jeff's.

"Wow," she whistled. "Don't you guys look great!"

Jonathan grinned and puffed his chest out proudly.

"Daddy buyed me a new suit for Christmas," he told her smugly. "That's 'cause we're the men in the family."

Cassie swallowed the lump in her throat as her misty eyes met Jeff's. "Well, good for you, Daddy," she whispered softly, placing her hand on the soft smooth wool of his white sweater. "You look pretty good, too. For an older man." She couldn't help the little joke, praying that it would take away some of the tension that had suddenly fallen in the room.

"Ha-ha!" Jonathan chortled with glee, pointing upward to the sprig of mistletoe hanging in the archway above their heads. "Now you have to kiss Daddy, Cassie."

"Do I?" she whispered softly, staring into the dark chocolate depths of Jeff's clear eyes. She could no more look away than remove herself from the circle of his arm as it curved around her waist.

"Yes, you do," Jeff murmured, dipping his head down.

"Well," she breathed on a silky sigh of delight. "If I have to, I have to."

Jeff kissed her. Thoroughly, completely and to her great satisfaction. And she kissed him back until the chuckles of several assorted children brought them back to reality.

"We do have to get to the church," David mumbled, red faced with embarrassment as he tugged at the brown housecoat that enveloped his spare form and rearranged the white dishtowel held on his head by a thick cord. "This shepherd outfit is the pits," he muttered finally. "I'll probably die of heatstroke."

"No one in this family is dying tonight," Jeff declared, squeezing Cassie's waist in a gentle caress. "Let's go everybody." He handed Stevie to Marie and held out Cassie's white lamb's wool jacket with a flourish. "Madame?"

Cassie tried to curtsey and nearly toppled over on her brand-new spiky heels. She reached out to press against his chest for support. And promptly lost her breath as his dark, amused eyes sparkled down at her.

"It's not necessary to throw yourself at me," he murmured so quietly no one else could hear. "I'll be available later tonight, in front of the fire. Care to join me?"

She got lost in those smooth, liquid chocolate depths and forgot to answer until his fingers closed around her upper arms, setting her back on her own two feet. His fingers slid upward to brush through her hair.

"Cassandra?"

"Hmm? Oh, later. Yes, later," she chirped brightly and slipped her arms into the coat.

As he lifted it around her shoulders, Cassie thought she heard him whisper, "Just the two of us. Alone."

That promising thought stayed with her on the short drive to the church where they met and greeted their friends. It haunted her as she stood beside him, singing the same Christmas carols she'd sung for years and hearing Jeff's low voice join in. And it nagged at her subconscious while she watched the children's presentation of the age-old Christmas story.

"Doesn't Alyssa look sweet?" she leaned over to whisper, her shoulder rubbing companionably against Jeff's.

"Who?" He stared at the stage with a frown on his face, trying to figure out who she was talking about.

"Alyssa, the littlest angel." She nodded toward the stage

and watched his eyes search out their newest addition. The little girl stood silent in her gleaming white robe and crown of tinsel, the frills at the top of her little socks bobbing as her feet tapped rhythmically against the floor.

"Oh, her. Yeah, she looks cute. I forgot her name." He grinned back at her with that smile that tugged at her heart and made her want to hug him. It was almost as good to feel his fingers thread through hers as he held her hand.

"Here comes Joseph," he whispered. "I sure hope Stevie behaves." He smirked, lips twitching at he watched Mary place the squirming child in his makeshift manger. "I wonder if he knows he has the most important role in the whole play."

"I doubt it. He only knows when it's feeding time and that's getting pretty close now." Cassie inclined her head to the diaper bag at her feet and smothered a smile. "He's a true male—his brain is connected directly to his stomach."

Jeff's arm curved around her shoulders, drawing her more tightly against his side. She could smell the fresh clean scent of the soap he used as his head bent close to hers. "Look—Jonathan's about to sing," he whispered excitedly, his breath stirring the strand of hair over her ear.

Cassie smiled at the gleam of pride in his eyes, but before she could reply, the soft, clear tones of Jonathan's childish voice as he sang "One Small Child" filled the air. The pure treble notes rang to the rafters with joy, bringing a tear to many eyes in the small, cozy church. For a moment, Cassie felt suspended in the wonder that God had cared enough to send his only son to earth as a small defenceless child who, at one time, might have looked much as Jonathan did.

Then there was much clapping and laughter and Jeff removed his arm. But the joy and pleasure stayed, hidden snugly under her heart as she thought eagerly of the evening ahead.

An hour later, Judith's old brick house was full to the brim with excited squealing children, embarrassed teenagers and adults of all ages. They gathered around Judith's baby grand in the brightly lit conservatory and blended their voices together in songs of worship, celebration and joy. Then the children were bundled up for a sleigh ride through the softly falling snow in an old-fashioned sleigh drawn by two fine horses that Bennet had borrowed for the evening. And through it all, Mrs. Bennet scurried around, replenishing glasses, offering pastries and beaming with happiness.

"Isn't it wonderful to see the old house alive again, Mr. Jeff?" The housekeeper glowed, refilling his glass with her special raspberry punch for yet another toast. "Your aunt would have loved this sight. She always wanted people to enjoy her home."

Cassie's tinkling laughter rang through the room just then and, if possible, Mrs. Bennet smiled even wider.

"That's a rare young woman, Mr. Jeff," she whispered. "Knows exactly what she's about bringing happiness back into people's lives. Miss Judith did right to try to keep her here."

Jeff grinned. "I think so, too, Mrs. Bennet." He leaned over and kissed her wrinkled cheek. "And I think Aunt Judith found a real treasure when she found you, too. Merry Christmas, Mrs. Bennet."

"Now what are you doing kissing the likes of an old lady like myself?" Mrs. Bennet gushed, her white skin tinged a faint pink. "'Tis your wife you should be kissing tonight, Mr. Jeff." She winked and scurried away after directing a pointed glance at the mistletoe hanging just above them.

"Isn't it a wonderful night?" Cassie exclaimed, threading her arm through his. "The happiest night of the year."

"Mmm-hmm, wonderful," she heard him murmur and looked up to find his gaze locked on her lips. "I've just received some wonderful advice from Mrs. Bennet. Older people are sometimes very wise."

Cassie stood transfixed as he bent his head and kissed her soundly in front of a houseful of people. Her face flushed as red as her suit when their guests began clapping merrily.

"I think that's our signal to leave you newlyweds alone." Pastor Jake grinned. He tugged his wife's hand. "Come along, Sara. Let's get home to our own mistletoe."

"Jake!" His wife protested, but it was a weak one and her face glowed with happiness. "Merry Christmas, Cassie. And you too, Jeff."

One by one the families drifted out the door until no one was left but the two of them, Marie and David. Jonathan lay curled up near the fire, sound asleep in his brand-new suit. Maryann Craven had handed a sleepy Stevie to Cassie before she, too, went out the door.

"Good night," they called out into the brisk night air. And heard the resounding "'night" echoing back.

"Come on, big guy." David grunted, lifting Jonathan's slack body. "It's time to go to bed."

"But I hafta get my stocking ready for Santa," Jonathan mumbled, barely awake.

"We did it before church. Remember?" David laughed down at the little boy. "Everything's all ready for Santa."

"But I wanted to change socks," Jonathan protested wearily. "I was…gonna use—" he yawned hugely and settled into David's arms with a sigh "—a bigger one," he finished as his eyelids drifted down.

"Good night everyone," David said, smiling as he moved toward the stairs. "I'll put him in bed, Cassie. Don't worry."

Cassie walked over and brushed her hand over his dark head.

"Thank you, David. Merry Christmas, dear." She brushed a featherlight kiss over his cheek. She watched tenderly as the boy moved up the stairs with his precious bundle.

"Mom! Look!" It was the first time that Marie had ever called her Mom and Cassie felt a pang clench and unclench in her breast. She turned toward the girl, misty eyed as she cradled the sleeping baby. "It's a promise ring. From Nate."

"Honey, that's lovely. Really lovely." With a worried smile she fingered the thin gold band that held Marie's aquamarine birthstone. "But, Marie, don't you think you're a bit young to be promising anything to Nate?"

"Here, give me the baby," Jeff said. "I'll put him to bed while you two talk." He glanced down at Cassie with a glint in his eyes. "I'll share some punch with you in front of the fire. Later."

Cassie couldn't say anything around the lump in her throat. But she smiled in what she hoped was an encouraging way and agreed. "Later."

"Love can't be wrong, Cassie." Marie's voice broke through her musings. "You always say God wants us to love people. Well, I love Nate. And someday I'm going to marry him."

It was the first time Cassie had heard defiance in the young girl's voice and she realized suddenly that Marie had chosen Christmas Eve to challenge her authority.

"Come and sit down, sweetie. Let's talk about this." She guided Marie to the sofa in front of the crackling fire and sank down onto it with relief. "I've got to get these shoes off. I don't know how anybody wears the things for more than five minutes."

"That's because you're not used to them." Marie giggled. "They're new and cool, but they're not your usual style."

Cassie wiggled her toes and groaned. "You're not kidding, kid," she agreed with heartfelt enthusiasm. Her face softened as she looked at the girl who would soon legally be her daughter.

"I know you're excited that Nate gave you such a lovely gift, Marie. But please try to hear me out," Cassie began softly. "Nate's a wonderful boy. And I can see why you're attracted to him. He's kind and considerate and a wonderful friend." She watched Marie nod and then continued, choosing her words with care.

"Sweetheart, you're just starting out on your journey of life. You are getting to know and understand boys in a new and different way than you did before and that's perfectly normal. But just because you meet someone you like right now doesn't mean that you can plan your whole life around that person."

"But Nate loves me," Marie broke in angrily.

"Of course he does! You're a very lovable girl." Cassie smiled as she searched for the right words. "But there are all kinds of love and you and Nate have years and years ahead to plan for. You told me you want to travel, to visit France where your grandmother came from. Does Nate want to go there? And what work will you choose while you are there? What will you do?"

She smoothed the blond hair with a shaking hand and prayed for guidance as she searched for the words to help Marie see the possibilities ahead.

"You and Nate are changing every day. You're finding out new things about one another and the world all the time. Enjoy that. Go places and do things with all your friends. See the kinds of things that make people happy and then set out a plan for yourself."

Cassie sighed softly, staring into the fire as she wondered if she was being hypocritical in her advice.

"You and Nate have a whole future lifetime to be friends. Don't rush anything. Enjoy being young and carefree. Make it a time to remember."

Marie stared down at her ring, twirling it round and round on her finger. At last her head tipped back, eyes meeting Cassie's concerned ones.

"Okay," she agreed. "I'll tell Nate that this is our friendship ring and that no matter what, we'll always be best friends." Her forehead furrowed as she searched Cassie's face. "But I am going to marry Nate," she insisted. "Sometime."

"Maybe," Cassie temporized. "Sometime in the future. When you've both decided to make a commitment that will last the rest of your lives. That's a pretty serious thing to decide at fifteen, Marie."

"Like the commitment you and Jeff made so you could keep the house and adopt David and me?" Marie queried.

Cassie stared, unaware that the girl knew so much about their private affairs.

"Well, yes," she admitted. "Although, everyone makes their own decisions about what they want out of life. I wanted you and David to live with us for as long as you want," Cassie said softly.

Marie nodded. "Just like Jeff wants his own son," she murmured.

Cassie gaped, her mouth hanging open in surprise. "H-how do you know about that?" she asked.

"He talks about it all the time," Marie informed her. "But only when he's with Jonathan." Her forehead puzzled in thought. "That's what the meeting in front of the fire's about, isn't it?" she asked, smiling.

"Sort of," Cassie admitted, flushing an embarrassed pink.

"Well, go get fixed up then," Marie chided, glancing around. "I'll clean up this place while you're gone."

Cassie stood, smoothing her slacks and picking up the heels with one finger. Her mouth stretched in a wide smile.

"Thank you, Cupid," she quipped, tongue in cheek.

Marie merely winked and set about picking up glasses and discarded napkins. It was clear that she was all in favor of a romantic evening for Cassie and Jeff.

The very thought of it made Cassie's knees shake.

Chapter Nine

"Mmm, this coffee is delicious," Cassie murmured, sipping from the porcelain cup once more. She wiggled her toes and basked in the warmth from the crackling fireplace. "We did fill all the stockings, didn't we?"

She glanced around the dimly lit room and smiled at the bulging felt stockings she'd sewn so carefully. Her grin grew as she realized Marie's idea of romance was to light a zillion candles and turn off the lights. An assortment of stringed instruments softly played Christmas carols in the background. She had to admit, Cassie decided, it was a darn good idea.

"We filled the stockings, we wrapped the gifts, we put out Santa's lunch, which I hope you didn't make," he teased, brown eyes glinting. "The Bennets and all of the kids have gone to bed and it's just you and me." He handed her a huge sheaf of crimson red roses. "Merry Christmas, Cassie."

"They're beautiful," Cassie gasped, burying her face in the fragrant petals. "Thank you!" He was staring at her in a way that made her feel strangely uncomfortable. Cassie contemplated the wisdom of escape. "I'll just get a vase." His hand on her arm prevented her from moving.

"Already done." He handed her a crystal vase half filled with water. "Courtesy of Marie."

"Oh. Well. Thank you again."

"You're welcome again." He grinned. "You've done a great job with the house," he added, glancing around at the surfeit of decorations on every window and wall. "And the kids are certainly looking forward to tomorrow. Or today, rather." He held up his watch. "It's after one."

"Mmm," Cassie answered, sipping her coffee slowly. "I hope tomorrow or today, whichever it is, goes as well." She tipped her head up to glance at him. "Are you sure your parents wouldn't come for dinner? There will be lots of food that I didn't cook and you know I'd like to have both our families present."

He removed the cup from her hands and set it on a nearby table before clasping his big palms around hers.

"Cassie. You have this idealized version of my parents that is nothing like the reality. They don't like children. They like perfection, order, neatness. Watching Jonathan slop around with his mashed potatoes and gravy would drive my father nuts."

"He can be well behaved," Cassie protested. "Sometimes."

"That's not the point. My parents aren't like yours. They don't think in terms of sing-alongs and board games and popcorn. Father's more like Melisande in his view on children. They're tolerable if they are kept at a safe distance from him." He peered down at her, a set smile on his lips. "You can't fix this Cassie, so leave it alone. We'll manage."

Cassie heard the note of pain in his voice as he laughed dryly. "Maybe they would loosen up if they saw other people relaxing and having fun," she offered quietly.

He moved a little closer to her on the soft, plushy cushions and put his arm around her shoulder.

"I do not want to talk about my parents tonight," he whispered quietly, pressing his mouth against her ear. "Surely we can think of a more interesting topic?"

Cassie sat motionless as his hand threaded through her hair.

"Like how beautiful you look tonight." His eyes slid over the red velour. "Red is definitely your color. I remember you were wearing it the first time I saw you. I thought it suited you then."

Cassie's eyes widened. "You did not think any such thing," she protested, laughingly. "You thought I was some money hungry woman who had latched onto your aunt for all the freebies I could get." Silently, she dared him to deny it.

"Okay, maybe I didn't see it right away," he allowed as one fingertip slid down the pert tip of her nose. "But I can see it now. And I like what I see." His hands came together around her neck, cupping her face. "You're a very beautiful and giving woman, Cassandra Haddon." His lips nibbled on her earlobe. "I'm very glad I married you."

She couldn't say anything then because his mouth moved to cover hers as he told her without words exactly how much he thought of her. Of their own volition, Cassie's arms lifted and wound themselves around his neck as she shifted a little closer, returning his caresses with gentle touches of her own.

"I'm glad I married you, too," she whispered when his mouth finally moved away. His hands smoothed over her back slowly, cradling her closer. "Did you hear something?" she asked a second later, dark headed tilted to one side.

Jeff's mouth was buried in the curve of her shoulder, his lips nuzzling the delicate white skin there.

"Mmm-hmm," he agreed. "Bells."

"No, it's more of a whirring," Cassie whispered and then forgot about it as his lips moved to her ear. She heard his words with an acute ache in her heart even as she thanked heaven for them.

"I think you'll make the most wonderful mother," he confided softly. "You've got so much warmth and love to give. Give a little bit of it to me," he begged in a muffled voice just before his mouth moved over hers.

And Cassie did. She poured out as much of her love as she could, only realizing then that she loved him more than she'd ever thought possible. Her love was overwhelming, powerful. And it demanded expression.

With a light delicate touch she fingered the collar of his shirt, slipping her fingers upward through the soft, silken strands of his hair. One finger traced the smooth dark eyebrows and thick full eyelashes around his eye. It moved down his aquiline nose and traced the sensuous outline of his lips before lowering to press against the dent in his chin.

Her lips followed a natural progression down to where her fingers had left off. As she kissed him on the mouth, and felt his immediate response, Cassie wondered how she could tell him of her love.

"Cassie, honey, I want…" There was a definite whirring sound now and they both glanced up at the same time, staring into each other's eyes. "What was that?" he demanded quietly.

"I don't know." Cassie studied her hands. "One of the kids maybe?"

"I don't think so." Jeff set her gently away from him and stood. The sound penetrated the silence of the room clearly. "It seems to be coming from behind the Christmas tree," he muttered, striding across the room.

Cassie watched as he peered through the branches and jumped nervously at the loud curse. "What is it?" she asked curiously, standing just in time to see him remove a video camera fastened on a tripod from the corner.

"Now, how in the world…?" her voice trailed away in stupefaction at the recording device that had obviously been set up to record them both.

"I'll tell you how it got there," Jeff stormed. "It was planted there. To film us. And I know exactly who did it."

Cassie frowned. "You do?" She thought for a moment and then gave in to curiosity. "Who?"

"Your soon-to-be daughter, that's who. Of all the prying,

sneaky, underhanded..." She let him spout off for a few minutes while she tried to sort things out.

"You think Marie set this up to record us?" she asked at last.

"That's exactly what I think. No wonder she was so accommodating," he griped, snatching the cassette out of the camera. "She wanted to set things up exactly right so she could tape us."

"Marie would never do that." Cassie shook her head. "She's much too thoughtful to intrude on us like this."

"I know you think they're all perfect," Jeff muttered, shoving the camera and tripod into a closet. "But somebody set us up and then recorded it. I'm going to find out who."

Cassie trailed up the stairs behind him, recognizing deep inside that it had to be Marie. Everyone else had long since gone to sleep. Only the young girl was awake, sitting cross-legged on her bed with her headphones on, humming quietly to the music playing in her ears.

"Marie!" Jeff barked her name only to be shushed by Cassie. Marie stopped the player and slipped the earphones off her head in surprise when she saw them.

"You'll wake the whole house, Jeff," Cassie admonished, pushing the heavy fall of hair off her forehead. "And frankly I'm not up to that." She stared down at the young girl. "You and I and Jeff need to have a serious talk, Marie. Now." She saw the trace of fear threading through the girl's troubled gaze before she nodded and headed for the stairs.

Marie was sobbing by the time they reached the family room, great gulping sobs that shook her thin body.

"I'm sorry," she wept, twisting her robe between her fingers. "I didn't mean to hurt anyone."

"How could you not mean to hurt anyone," Jeff demanded, towering over her. "You deliberately invaded our privacy and set up a camera to record it. What were you planning to do—sell copies?"

Cassie heard the frustration and embarrassment in Jeff's

tone. And she felt exactly the same way. But right now they had to put their own feelings on hold and deal with a mixed-up young girl who had her first crush and didn't know how to handle it.

"Why, Marie?" She asked it softly, letting her disappointment show. "Why would you do such a thing?"

"I wasn't going to show anyone," Marie promised tearfully. "I never meant for you to find out."

"But honey," Cassie said with a sigh. "It was still wrong."

"And underhanded, too," Jeff added. "How would you like it if we spied on you and Rick?"

"Nate!" Cassie and Marie said the name together.

"Whatever! How would you like it if we videotaped the two of you out on a date and then sat here and watched your private conversations?" Jeff looked as if the very idea of watching young love at work made him cringe.

"I wouldn't. But I didn't mean any harm. Honestly."

"Okay, sweetheart. I believe you." Cassie patted the wringing hands. "But I want to know why you thought you had to do such a thing."

"I had to know about love," Marie whispered.

Cassie swiveled her head up to stare at Jeff. He shrugged, obviously without the answers she wanted.

"What about love did you need to know that you thought you'd find on a videotape?" His voice was soft with steel edges as he stared down at the girl. His eyes glittered with anger.

"You remember I told you Nate gave me a ring?" She looked to Cassie for confirmation. At Cassie's nod she continued. "And you said that there were all different kinds of love. Well, I want to know what they are." She stared up at Jeff, dashing the tears from her eyes as she spoke.

"I want to know about the love between you and Cassie so that I'll know it's the real thing when it comes to me."

Cassie sat on the cushions with her mouth hanging open. She couldn't say a word. Well, really, what could she say?

Jeff doesn't love me, Marie, but I married him because I needed this house to continue with my work? Not likely.

She started in surprise when Jeff sat down beside her and curved his arm around her shoulders. She felt the squeeze of his hand as his words came out slowly, as if he were feeling his way.

"Marie, people all experience what you're calling love differently. You can watch someone else and admire what that emotion has done for them, or you can appreciate the difference someone's caring makes in another person's life. Do you know what I mean?"

"You mean like the difference Cassie's love made in David's and my life when we got to live here permanently?" Marie asked as she nodded slowly.

"Yes," he agreed softly. "Exactly like that. But you can't just spy on other people and then try to take what you think works for them and apply it to you. I think love probably means something different to you than it does to either Cassie or me."

Cassie didn't utter a word. She was too amazed to hear Jeff's interpretation of love. Up until now, he'd refused to even use the word.

"You see, I think when you meet someone and you think that you have fallen in love with them," he continued softly, "you'll know if that's the person you want to spend the rest of your life with. You might think you know it right away or it might take you a while to sort it all out."

"Sort of like you two," the girl snickered mockingly. "It's taken you forever to sort things out."

Cassie stared, amazed that this soft-spoken, quiet girl had seen through their pretense. She felt Jeff's hand tighten on her shoulder once more and decided to let him finish the job.

"We haven't sorted everything out *yet*," he told her honestly, staring down into Cassie's bright eyes. "I think our marriage is going to be about continually sorting things out." He grinned a self-deprecating smile. "But that doesn't mean yours will be."

"What I'm really saying," he advised, "is that you can't use someone else as the yardstick for your life. You have to decide what it is you want out of life and hold out until you get it. You're not me and you're not Cassie. You're you—Marie. And your experiences are going to be totally different from ours."

"And Marie?" Cassie couldn't help but add the last word. She remembered those turbulent teenage years too well not to tell the whole story. "There will be all kinds of love along the way. A gentle, tender first love. A friendly kind of love for the date at your prom." She smiled and brushed her fingers over Marie's bent head.

"A stronger love for someone you meet in college who seems like the answer to your prayers and makes you cry instead. And the one man who makes you feel special and beautiful and a whole lot of other miraculous things. Only you can decide which one will last a lifetime. But don't sell yourself short by grabbing the first one that comes along or by trying to make your life into someone else's. Okay?"

Marie nodded, standing straight and tall before them.

"I owe you both an apology," she said softly. "I know you'd respect my privacy. I'm only sorry I didn't respect yours. I hope you'll forgive me?"

Cassie hugged her close. "Of course we do," she whispered. "Now go to bed. It's almost Christmas."

"Good night," she murmured, heading for the stairs.

"Good night," they answered in unison.

When the door to her room closed with a soft thud, Cassie met Jeff's bright gaze with a shrug.

"Well, that was interesting." It was not the right thing to say.

"It could have been," he muttered, moving to place the fire screen before the fire. "I was hoping we might get some time to ourselves for once."

Cassie felt the same disappointment. Right to the end of her toes. She had been on the verge of discovering something wonderful; anticipation of some understanding or personal communion had hovered for a moment and then flown away. Now she just felt tired and drained.

"We'll manage it," she promised weakly. "One of these days."

His head tipped to one side as he studied her. Carefully, without touching her anywhere else, he leaned over and placed a soft kiss on her lips.

"Promises, promises," he drawled. But when she studied the dark expressive eyes, she could find no clue to his meaning. "Who is it that makes you feel special and wonderful and all those other things, Cassie?"

But he didn't wait for her answer. He merely snuffed out the candles and walked her to her door. "Good night," he murmured, staring down at her.

"Good night, Jeff. Merry Christmas."

"Yeah. Thanks."

From the corner of her eye, Cassie caught just a glimpse of the gold foil box he slipped surreptitiously into his pants pocket. It had been a gift, she was sure. Something personal he'd chosen especially for her.

Then why hadn't he given it to her? she asked herself sadly.

Chapter Ten

"**I**'m telling you, Rory, it's positively hair-raising. To think that a kid would do something like that." Jeff smacked his hand against the counter and glared at his brother. "It could have been very embarrassing, you know."

Rory grinned back at him, obviously pleased at the sight of his uptight elder brother. "But nothing happened, did it?"

"No!" Jeff glared across the room, wishing he didn't feel so stupid.

"Well, then," Rory asked reasonably, "what's the problem?"

"She's my wife and I'm getting tired of never having a moment alone with her." Jeff barely contained his anger. He forcibly restrained himself from kicking the solid wood table leg as he explained.

"There's always another child to cuddle or some emergency job that needs handling. It's like she's constantly running away from me." He glared at his chuckling sibling. "It seems like the only one who wants me around is Jonathan."

"Well, there's a consolation for you." Rory smiled. "Why don't you take that ball and run with it?"

"I don't just want a child. I want my wife!" Jeff heard himself bellow the words. His eyes opened wide as he realized what he had just said. Rory wasn't slow on the draw, either.

"Now there's a switch." His brother grinned. "It was always 'my son' this and 'my son' that. Are you saying you're giving up that lifelong dream of the perfect son in favor of a new dream named Cassie Haddon?" He shook his head. "Hard to believe, big bro. Hard to believe."

"I'm not giving it up. Not completely," Jeff protested. "It's just that I'm married now, and I would like to make a go of that before I introduce any more children into this madhouse."

He whined plaintively about the past week's activities and added the fact that he'd been awakened today at five-thirty a.m. by a small child jumping on his midsection.

"It's pretty hard to get romantic after that," he muttered.

"Are you in love with Cassie, Jefferson?" Rory peered at him seriously, his glasses dipping low on the end of his nose as he stared over the top of them.

"You know very well that I don't believe in love." Jeff dismissed the question with a wave of his hand. "I'm attracted to her, yes. Who wouldn't be? We share some of the same interests and values. I feel a fondness for her and of course, I want her to be happy. But love?" He shook his head. "It doesn't exist. Except in the movies and fairy tales."

Rory rearranged the test tubes littering the basement workshop as he considered his brother's words. His eyes were intent when they focused on Jeff's.

"Yeah," he muttered to himself. "Love exists. Especially in this house."

"What?" Jeff demanded, straightening the bottles back in a neat row. He frowned at the strange look covering Rory's handsome face.

"Never mind." Rory shoved his hands into his pockets. "So, what do you want from me?"

"I thought, maybe, just once, the great Rory Haddon might have the answers." Jeff infused his voice with biting sarcasm as he glared at the smiling face.

"I probably do. What's the question?"

It was a terrible thought, this being Christmas day and all, but Jeff decided he'd really like to plant his fist on that smugly grinning countenance.

"How can I get Cassie to spend more time with me? Alone." Jeff bit the words out from between his gritting teeth. If his brother had set out to annoy him purposely, he couldn't have burrowed under his skin more.

Reginald Thomas Haddon, Rory for short, smirked at his elder brother in delight.

"Perhaps a date? A little fun and frolic. A carefree night of pleasure? You remember dating, don't you, Jefferson? That couples pairing thing all the other people did in college?"

Jeff frowned. "A date?" He tossed the idea around in his mind before glancing up at Rory. "Doing what?" he queried.

"How do I know what old married people do for fun? I'm the youngest brother. Dinner and a movie, maybe. Bowling? I don't know." His eyes widened as a new thought occurred to him.

"Maybe you could get her interested in your work. If you slaved together over the computer, who knows what could happen?" He grinned with delight.

"Work together?" Jeff frowned. "I was thinking of something a little more…imaginative."

"Hey, don't knock it till you've tried it." Rory laughed. "And speaking of knocking…" He motioned his thumb upstairs.

"Not another hour of one-sided chitchat while the parents sit there glowering," Jeff groaned at the series of thumps on the stout basement door. "Cassie's so big on this family thing, you'd think she'd notice that they're not into it."

Rory frowned. "I think you're misjudging them, bro. Dad held the baby for ages earlier on."

"Yeah." Jeff grinned sardonically. "About six inches off his knee in case anything got on his cashmere pants."

Rory was shaking his head.

"No, I meant after that. Later on, once he got used to him. He was dangling the kid on his knee and babbling away like a regular grandfather. It was amazing."

Jeff climbed the steps wearily. He laughed harshly at the tender picture his brother painted of the hard-nosed, acrimonious man he'd spoken with earlier.

"In your dreams," he muttered.

In fact, he'd actually been surprised when his parents had accepted Cassie's invitation for brunch. They'd shown up with a carload of gifts and a giant bouquet of flowers for his wife. Cassie had been almost as excited about that as she had been about his roses, he grumbled silently.

"Oh, Jeff. Good." Cassie slipped her hand into his arm and dragged him over to where Stevie sat in a brand-new walker. "Did you know your father picked this out himself?" she asked softly.

"Really?" He tried to infuse a modicum of warmth into his voice while keeping his eyes averted from that familiar white head.

"And your mother says he searched all over to find that crane to match Jonathan's truck." He winced at the nudge she directed to his ribs.

"They're very nice," he muttered dutifully, feeling less than grateful. "Thank you both."

Jeff watched as his stiff, austere mother, whom he had known as a cold, unapproachable woman for the entirety of his life, leaned over and pressed a kiss on little Stevie's head.

"Nonsense, Jefferson," she murmured softly, staring at the babbling baby. "It's our right as grandparents, isn't it, Jeffie?" She looked to her husband for confirmation.

"Yes, dear," he said staunchly, obviously daring his son to contradict him as he jiggled Jonathan on his knee.

Jeff looked from one to the other of them with astonishment.

"They're not your grandchildren, Mother," he said clearly. "They're not even our children. They're just here for a short while."

"But that doesn't mean we can't love them," Cassie countered from her place at his side. "It doesn't mean they can't have a grandma and grandpa whenever they come here, does it, Jeff?"

As he stared down into her lovely face, Jeff couldn't stop the words from coming. Who could deny her anything when she looked like that?

"No," he agreed, his voice strangling as it came out. "I suppose it wouldn't hurt for them to pretend for a little while." He glared over at his father who was slowly getting to his feet. "Better a little affection than none at all, I suppose."

He heard Cassie gasp and winced at the pointed elbow she embedded between his ribs.

"That was mean," she hissed angrily. "They're trying to be nice. Maybe you could try, too?"

"Cassandra, my dear, thank you for a lovely afternoon." Jeff watched his mother regain her composure. Her face was white with strain and she didn't look at him, but kept her eyes fixed firmly on his wife. "I enjoyed meeting the children again. Perhaps you could bring them over one afternoon."

"I'd like that," he heard Cassie agree. "How about next week sometime?"

He left them discussing dates and walked Rory to the door.

"Can you believe it? They want *kids* running around that mausoleum? A little late isn't it?" he mused bitterly.

"Jefferson." Rory's voice was soft and hesitant. "Maybe you haven't realized it, but Mother hasn't been well. She's..."

"Probably worn out from the old man ordering her around," Jeff finished angrily.

"Oh, shut up for once, will you," Rory snapped, shrugging into his jacket. "Can't you just once let go of all that anger and accept that our parents are human beings? Maybe they did make mistakes. Get over it. They're not going to be around forever, you know." He stamped his feet into his boots and glared at his brother angrily.

"Find a little forgiveness, would you? You might need it yourself some day when kids like Jonathan or David come back to you with complaints."

Jeff stared after him as Rory strode down the driveway and then raced away with a grinding of the gears in his fast sports car. He had never seen his brother stand up for his father like that. Not once in thirty years. As he stood in the cold, brisk air, staring down the road, he heard a voice clearing behind him.

"You and your wife seem very happy here, Jefferson," his father observed. "I'm sure Judith would have enjoyed knowing you've put her home to such good use." Jefferson Haddon, the second, thrust out his hand.

"Merry Christmas, son."

Jeff stared at him bitterly. He thought he could just wash it all away, did he? Years of pain and heartache, self-doubt and recriminations? Not very likely.

"Yeah," he muttered angrily, refusing to take that outstretched hand. "Merry Christmas." His voice was full of bitter recriminations.

"Why did you have to do that to them?" Cassie asked softly, when everyone had left the room. "They really tried and you slapped them in the face." Her eyes studied him sadly.

"Is it worth it to hang on to all that bitterness and anger?" she demanded. "Does it make your life better to know that regardless of how hard they try, you're never going to let your parents off the hook? Will that even the score?"

* * *

It should have ruined the day, Jeff decided hours later. But somehow, with the advent of Cassie's excited parents, her sister and brother and all of their children, the rest of the day had passed happily. The new house had obviously been a fantastic idea since her parents couldn't stop talking about it.

"If that isn't just like our Cassie," her father announced happily, throwing his arm around his daughter's shoulder. "Always planning some wonderful surprise."

Jeff had watched their interaction carefully after that, curious about the obvious rapport between the two. In fact, he noticed that the whole family giggled and laughed and teased one another. He could learn from them, Jeff decided. For the benefit of his own son.

He had just decided to question Frank Newton when Mrs. Bennet announced dinner and the family gathered around the table, still jostling one another until her father had called a halt to say grace.

"Father, we thank you for this day, the day you sent love to this earth in the form of your only son. And we thank you for Cassie and Jeff and their family. Help us to share together now with full hearts for the peace and goodwill you've brought to us this day. Amen."

"Ahhhmen," Jonathan repeated happily.

It was a noisy evening, bordering on riotous as the mob of laughing children clustered round, trying every toy they'd been given. The adults spent their time playing board games and talking after the dishes had been cleared away.

Jeff found himself sitting next to Frank later on as they sipped Cassie's unusual Christmas punch.

"You've done a wonderful thing here, my boy," Frank congratulated him. "These kids couldn't have had a better experience than Christmas day filled with love."

"It's not so much my doing," Jeff denied. "Cassie's the one who insisted they stay here."

"Yep." Frank grinned. "She's got a big heart. I can see how much she loves you, too."

There wasn't much he could say to that so Jeff let it go.

"How'd you like her gift?" Frank's bright eyes gleamed with happiness. "I'll bet you were surprised. Cassie spent a long time on that."

"Actually, we haven't gotten around to exchanging gifts yet," Jeff told him, the gold foil box in his pocket burning a hole. "With the kids and everything, there just hasn't been time." His face flushed a dark red at the curious look in his father-in-law's eyes.

"I think it's time you did, my boy. Christmas is almost over. Edna," Frank called, hoisting himself from his comfortable chair. "It's time for us to go. These kids need some sparkin' time to relax." His eyes sparkled down at Jeff. "Alone."

They were all gone within a matter of twenty minutes, leaving the house quiet—or at least as quiet as it ever got, Jeff decided. Cassie disappeared to put the excited kids to bed with Marie's help.

"Jeff?" David stood before him, holding a small box in his outstretched hand. "I know I gave you that tie already. But this is your real Christmas gift. I made it for you."

A lump the size of a mandarin orange rose in Jeff's throat as he read the small burned-wood plaque nestled inside.

A Father is someone who is there when you need him.
Someone who doesn't need to be asked for his help.
A Father knows kids make lots of mistakes. He does too.
Fathers forgive and forget about them and move on.
Fathers include their kids in the important things.
Real fathers are hard to find.

"It's wonderful David," he managed to say. The tears in his eyes were embarrassing and he tried to blink them away as he stared at the young boy who had come to depend on him. How could he let him down?

"It's oak from the front yard. See, I routered the edges

and sanded it myself," David told him proudly. "Since you're going to be my official dad, I thought you wouldn't mind hearing my views."

"I don't mind at all," Jeff whispered. He stared at the tall gangly boy and felt the weight of his responsibilities land heavily on his shoulders. It was an awesome obligation. And he had no practise. "I just hope I can live up to all this," he uttered.

"I'll help you," David offered. "And if it gets too bad, we can always get Cassie to be the tiebreaker." David grinned.

"Thank you, David. This is the best Christmas gift I've ever had." He hugged the boy and then quickly let go as David glanced around. "It's okay, son," he teased. "I think hugging between fathers and their kids is okay. Maybe even cool."

David's eyebrows rose at that but he grinned anyway.

"I guess so. G'night."

"Good night, David."

Jeff tucked the little board into his briefcase carefully. He'd post it on a wall at work, he decided. Where he would see it every day and remember his new job as a parent. As he left the study, Jeff glanced out the window, his eye caught by a movement outside.

It was Cassie. His fingers curved around the gift in his pocket. There were only a few more hours left. He'd give it to her out there, Jeff decided. Where no one could interrupt them.

He found her sitting in the garden on a weathered bench Judith had always favored. Her face was tilted toward the sky as she stared at the navy-blanketed heavens with pinpricks of rhinestone bright light flecks scattered here and there. Jeff sat down without making a sound, content to watch her.

"Isn't it beautiful?" she breathed, the warm air leaving her mouth in a cloud that was soon whisked away by the light wind.

"Beautiful," he agreed, staring at the pure clear outline of her face.

"Just think of the changes that occurred on this earth on this very night a little less than two thousand years ago," she whispered. "Can you imagine the love it must have taken to let your only son leave home and come to a place where you knew he would be mistreated? Even killed." Jeff saw the tears sparkling on her cheeks as she turned to look at him. "Sometimes I can hardly believe in so much love."

Jeff sat silent, contemplating her words solemnly as he, too, stared at the wondrously lit sky. There it was again. Love. It was like a mantra, chanting constantly in his mind.

"Oh, look," Cassie cried happily. Her outstretched arm pointed to the heavens. "The northern lights. Aren't they magnificent? So bright and yet they change constantly. It's kind of like our world," she mused quietly.

"Everything's always shifting, altering. And yet God remains constant in His heaven, directing our actions if we let Him." She smiled, a wide, delighted smile that stretched her mouth in its joy. "I love Christmas," she said, laughing.

In her happiness, she hugged him. A friendly, outgoing hug that begged him to share in her pleasure. And Jeff hugged her back because for once, he also liked Christmas.

"What's this?" she murmured, picking up the small gold package off the snow where it had slid from Jeff's hand. "Is it for me?" she asked wide-eyed, a smile tugging at the corners of her mouth.

He nodded.

"But you've already given me a silk blouse and a new jacket and those books I wanted."

"I know." Jeff picked up her hand and fingered the rings he had put on her hand short weeks ago. "This is for this Christmas and next Christmas and all the ones to come. Go ahead, open it. You'll see what I mean."

She did. And breathed a sigh of delight as she lifted the delicate gold links from their bed of cotton. Dangling from one gleaming circlet hung a tiny angel, its wings out-stretched ready to fly.

"It's lovely," she breathed, studying him with her bright eyes.

Jeff fastened the tiny clasp around her wrist and fingered the angel with his thumb.

"It's sort of like Marie's promise ring, I guess," he said, embarrassed that he'd even thought of getting something so personal for her. "The angel reminded me of you." He grinned, hoping to ease the tension. "Next year I'll get a star."

Cassie smiled, a radiant look of pure joy lighting her features as she leaned over and kissed his cheek.

"Thank you," she said softly. "It's the most lovely gift I've ever had."

Jeff twisted his head to brush his lips against hers, want-ing to deepen the kiss and yet afraid to spoil the sweet sense of wonder between them. But he kissed her anyway, with all the pent-up longing he felt. When at last Cassie moved away, he noticed her hands trembling.

"I have something special for you, too," she murmured, eyes downcast. "It's still under the tree."

Together, arm in arm, they walked slowly back along the snow-covered path to the house and made their way silently through the dimly lit hall to the family room. And there, tucked away behind the tree, Jeff saw the large flat package. She handed it to him and he read the attached card curi-ously. "Judith helped make some of your dreams come true. My wish is that you realize the rest of them in the coming years. God bless you, Jeff. Love, Cassie."

He studied the second last word with interest. There it was again, he mused. Love. But then, coming from Cassie that was normal wasn't it? She was full of what even he had to admit was what he thought of as love. He wondered what she meant.

"Open it," she demanded, dancing from one foot to the other. "Quickly."

With a laugh, he tore the paper open. The mirth caught

in his throat as Judith's smiling face stared up at him. Her tired blue eyes sparkled out through the acrylic daubs that Cassie had used to portray his aunt so accurately. Her mouth tilted at the corners in that old familiar way, chastising him for some long forgotten misdeed. Her image was so lifelike that he could almost hear Judith's voice chiding him for waiting too long to visit.

Tears squeezed out of his eyes and rolled down his face as he stared at the wonderful woman who had taken such good care of him all those years ago. The woman who had continued to keep her guiding hand on his life through the years.

And he had never said thank you. Not properly. Not in a way that expressed the thankfulness he felt for her care, concern and yes, maybe even love in his young life. A pain tightened in his chest. A pain that told him he would never have the opportunity again.

"Jeff," Cassie touched his shoulder gently. When she saw the tears in his eyes, she gathered his head gently against her and held him tightly. "Oh, Jeff."

"I never told her," he moaned sadly, wrapping his arms around her waist and leaning into that soothing touch. "I never said how much I loved her."

Cassie brushed the dark strands back off his forehead and kissed it tenderly. Her words gently soothed the gnawing ache in his chest.

"She knew, Jeff. Judith always knew."

Chapter Eleven

"I can look after three small children every bit as well as you can, Cassandra. I'm not totally incompetent." Jeff stared at her with the light of battle in his eyes. "After all, Marie and David will be nearby to lend a hand."

Cassie frowned.

"Yes, but you wanted me to help you with that new program you're working on and instead of helping you, I'm landing you with more work." She glanced around the kitchen once more. "I'll try not to be too long although his mother did tell the social worker that Greg's pretty sick." She hesitated. "Are you sure..."

"Just go will you," Jeff bellowed. "We'll be fine."

Cassie tugged on her jacket and strode to the door.

"All right, I'm going. I'm going." She yanked open the front door. "Come on, Robyn. I can tell when we're not wanted."

Robyn raised her eyebrows, staring behind her with curiosity. "What in the world's gotten into him?" she grumbled. "Has he been working in that lab for too long or what? First he can't stand kids and now he wants to be alone with them. Yikes!"

"I know," Cassie nodded. "He's been like this ever

since Christmas. It's as if he's trying to make up for lost time or something. He, David and Jonathan are like the Three Musketeers. When Jonathan goes to bed, Jeff buries himself in the basement.''

"What are they working on?" Robyn asked, steering confidently into a skid and then out again. "It must be something pretty big."

"Search me." Cassie shrugged. "It's something to do with David's science project that's due the first week of January. My guess is they're going to make some spectacular presentation that will, hopefully, impress the teacher."

"What is it for anyway?" Robyn demanded. "Physics, biology, chemistry?"

"Robyn, you know I hate all three of those terms," Cassie grumbled, shuddering. "Why are you asking me?"

Robyn laughed and gave her friend a sly sidelong look.

"I figured things must have changed if you're helping Jeff with his computer programs," she said dryly. "You never used to know a hard drive from an autoexec bat."

Cassie frowned. Robyn was teasing her, that was it. She could tell from the tone of her voice. But she had absolutely no idea what her friend was talking about. She decided to change the subject.

"How bad is Greg?" she asked instead. "Sondra didn't say much when I called the agency."

"Not much to say," Robyn frowned sadly. "He was beaten up pretty badly." She risked a glance across at Cassie, taking her eyes off the road for just a second. "It's those teenage gang thugs," she explained. "He made the mistake of saying no to them and they didn't like it."

Cassie's heart sank as she saw the twelve-year-old boy swathed in bandages in the intensive care ward at Sick Children's hospital. Greg's face was a mass of cuts and bruises but thankfully the doctor had said his eyes had not been damaged. He did have internal injuries that were causing problems and it would be touch and go for the next twenty-four hours.

Cassie folded the pale hand with its IV infusion tube

gently into hers and sank onto a nearby chair. Silently, with her eyes staring at his poor battered face, she began to pray for Greg's recovery.

"Cassie?" She opened her eyes to find Greg's mother, Nina, standing nearby. There were tears on the woman's cheeks as she stared at her son.

"Hi, Nina." She hugged the frail woman gently, smoothing the tears from her thin, haggard face. "How are you?"

"He was a good boy, Cassie. He didn't get into drugs and he kept going to the youth group like you said." She stared down at the still figure. "Why didn't God keep my boy safe, Cassie?"

It was a tough question and Cassie didn't have a ready answer. She hugged Nina close and whispered a prayer for wisdom.

"Honey," she said softly, feeling her way along. "Maybe we're looking at this all wrong. God did keep Greg safe. He kept him out of the gang and off the drugs. I don't know for sure, but maybe he had to go through all this so the boys who did this to him could see his faith."

Nina still wept softly.

"God always has a purpose, Nina. Maybe we can't see it right now, but we can know that He didn't keep Greg out of the bad stuff just to abandon him. We can't stop trusting Him now."

"I know," Nina sniffed. "And I'll try to keep strong. He was so happy when he came back from your place in August. He was like a new kid." She grinned. "No, he was more like the old Greg."

"And he will be again." Cassie smiled. "You just wait and see."

They sat together until Robyn came in to take a turn. Cassie agreed to meet her later in the cafeteria and had just sat down with a cup of rank black coffee when Jeff's father walked in.

"Why Mr. Haddon," she greeted him, smiling happily, "what are you doing here?"

Jefferson Haddon looked bone weary, she decided. His

eyes were sunken into his head and his whole body seemed to sag under the expensive suit.

"We were visiting a friend," he told her. "And Glenda fainted." His eyes were listless. "They don't want to move her until they know what's wrong."

Cassie drew in a deep breath and steadied herself. Not now, she prayed. Please God, don't take her now.

"Can I do anything for Mrs. Haddon, sir?" If there was anything to be done, Cassie knew that Jeff's father would have spared no expense for his wife. Still she had to offer.

"No." He shook his head sadly. "I don't think..." His eyes brightened suddenly. "Well, maybe if you wanted to stop by for just a moment," he ventured. "I know she'd like to see you."

"Of course I will," she agreed. "What floor is she on?" Jeff's father agreed to take her himself after they had finished their coffee.

Cassie barely stifled the gasp that rose involuntarily when she found Jeff's mother lying on a narrow cot half an hour later. The woman was gaunt and gray, her ashen face drawn in haggard lines of pain.

"I'm so sorry you're not feeling well, Mrs. Haddon," she murmured, grasping the outstretched hand. "Do they know what the problem is yet?"

Glenda Haddon's white face turned toward the wall.

"I've known I was ill for some time now, dear," she whispered. "I was supposed to begin treatments last week but I wanted to wait until after Christmas." Her eyelids slipped closed with a sigh of weariness.

"That's why we've been so anxious to try to restore our relationship with our son," Mr. Haddon murmured. Tears pooled in his eyes. "I know we've had some problems, but I thought maybe the time had come to settle things. I'm afraid I was wrong." He stared at her sadly. "My son will never forgive me for not being the father I should have been to him."

Cassie wrapped her arms around the bowed shoulders and hugged him tightly.

"Don't you dare give up now," she ordered tightly. "Don't you dare. Jeff will come round. It's just going to take some time, some prayer and a lot of love. And I've got lots of all three."

Mr. Haddon smiled tiredly. "I think you do, Cassie. You're very good for my son. He's changed since he married you."

"So have I," Cassie managed to respond through the lump in her throat. "I've come to understand another side to God's love. With His help, I'm going to help Jeff to see it, too."

"Good for you." Jefferson Senior clamped his hand on her shoulder. "Just promise me that you won't give up on him. No matter what. You're all he has left." His sad eyes dropped to his wife's sleeping form. "We spoiled our chances with him. And now it's too late."

"It's never too late," Cassie told him firmly. "God can work through the biggest mountains. Just keep praying for him."

"We will, dear. And thank you. I don't know how we would have gotten through these past few months without you."

Cassie stood in the elevator thinking about his words. In truth she felt like a fraud. What right had she to promise that sick woman that her son would find it in his heart to forgive her before it was too late? She saw Jeff every day. Ate her meals with him and raised children with him. She loved him more than any person on earth and yet even she couldn't force him to lay aside the old bitterness.

"Father, I need your strength now," she prayed. "Lead me in the right direction. And help me to follow your leading."

Robyn was waiting in the coffee shop, grinning from ear to ear.

"Greg woke up," she informed her cheerfully. "He said his whole body ached like a bad tooth." She grinned. "It was worth every misbehaving moment he spent in my Sunday School class just to hear those words."

They made a swift detour so Cassie could congratulate the boy on his firm stance before she directed Robyn to take her home.

"Missing hubby already, are we?" Robyn teased. Her eyes widened at the solemn look on Cassie's face. "What's the matter?"

As she related her chance meeting, Cassie dumped the whole burden on her friend. "He's just got to come round, Rob. I don't know how much longer Mrs. H. has."

Robyn patted her shoulder.

"She has as much time as God wills. You can't change that. Just keep on keeping on."

It was good advice, Cassie decided as they turned up the driveway to her home. It was a good feeling—home. She stepped out of the car and stopped abruptly as she spied the little crowd gathered on the front lawn. In the middle she could see the bright blue of Jeff's ski jacket. He seemed to be lying on the ground.

"What's going on?" she demanded, racing over to the huddled group and sinking to her knees beside Jeff's still body.

Jonathan wailed as he grasped the still hand. "I didn't mean to hurt him. Please God, make my daddy all better." His little mittened hands patted the dark head tenderly.

"What happened?" Cassie asked David, who stood nearby holding Stevie. As she talked, her hand smoothed the hair away from Jeff's forehead and brushed over the lump at his hairline.

"We were having a snowball fight. All of a sudden he just toppled over." David's eyes were weaving back and forth from hers to Jonathan's small crying figure. "This is what hit him."

Cassie peered down at the snow-encrusted ball of ice.

"But Jonathan couldn't have thrown this hard enough," she murmured, trying to piece events together.

"I threw it for him," David admitted, his face pasty white as he stared at the big man lying in the snow. "I didn't notice the ice."

. "His pulse is strong," Robyn observed, kneeling beside Jeff's other side. "I think he's coming round."

Cassie cupped his cold cheeks in her hands.

"Jeff," she called softly. "Jeff!" His eyes blinked open slowly. "Oh, thank God!" she exclaimed, wrapping her arms around him and pressing little kisses all over his face. "Are you okay?"

"I'm getting better by the minute," he assured her, drawing her head down to his. "Just keep doing what you're doing. I'll be in heaven."

Jonathan started wailing again. "I don't want my daddy to go to heaven."

David shushed him with a grin. "I don't think he's going anywhere right now," he teased. "He's too busy kissing Cassie."

Cassie heard them all laughing and pressed Jeff's hands away as her cheeks flushed an embarrassed red.

"Come on, faker," she muttered. "Let's get you upright."

"Aghhh," he breathed, one hand fingering the skin on his brow. "What hit me, a Mack truck?"

"No, a snowball." David moved to support him with one arm under Jeff's broad shoulder. Cassie noted the care with which David helped him stand. "I'm afraid I threw one I shouldn't have."

"Yeah, he throwed this one, Daddy. He's a bad, bad boy." Jonathan frowned at David fiercely. "Don't hurt my daddy anymore," he ordered.

"Who gave David the snowball, Jonny?" Cassie eyed the child sternly, daring him to deny it.

"We were playing. I didn't mean to hurt him!" Jonathan's voice was full of indignation.

Cassie bent down and faced him squarely.

"I know you didn't. But we have to be careful. Some things that are hidden inside can hurt other people very badly." She risked a glance up at Jeff and found his dark eyes fixed on her. Cassie continued her reprimand, averting her face from that searching look.

"Covering that piece of ice up with snow just disguised it," she said softly. "But the ice was still there underneath and it still hurt Daddy. We don't throw ice at people, Jonathan."

"I'm sorry, Daddy. I didn't mean to hurt you."

Jeff nodded, patting the child's covered head. "I know you didn't Jonathan."

"Do I have to go to my room now?" Jonathan sobbed, tears pouring out of his eyes.

"Have you learned a lesson?" Cassie asked, brushing the tears away.

Jonathan tipped his head to one side, a mittened hand under his cheek as he thought about it. One foot tapped silently on the packed snow.

"Yes," he crowed at last. "Don't try to hide bad things."

"Good." Cassie smiled, patting his head. "I think you've all had enough snowballing for one day. Let's go have hot chocolate."

When everything had settled down once more and Robyn had gone her own way, Cassie cornered Jeff in the study.

"I still think you should have a doctor check out that lump," she said frowning.

"I've already told you," Jeff complained, holding the ice pack to his aching head. "I'm not going to any emergency room for a dinky little bump on the head." His eyes glowed mysteriously. "If," he added teasingly, "you should feel the desire to continue what you started outside, however, that might help with my cure."

Cassie frowned. "What I started?"

He smiled, flicking his finger against her cheek. "Yeah. You were kissing me and calling my name like you really cared whether or not I was dead."

"Of course I care." She brushed his hands away and took a step backward, flushing a deep dark red. "But I certainly wasn't kissing you," she argued. "You must have been dreaming."

Jeff shook his head. "Liar," he whispered. "Come

here—" he beckoned to her "—I'll show you what I saw in my dream."

"Jeff!" Cassie protested weakly, wishing she could just relax and snuggle into the circle of his arms, feel them support her. She needed that just now. But to what would it lead?

"I came to help you with the computer stuff. If you don't want my help, I have other things to do. David's youth group is coming over after their tobogganing party tonight, you know."

"Cassie, honey," he drawled, "you can help me anytime. And I mean that from the bottom of my heart." He kissed her lips with a laugh as she flushed a dark red for the second time.

"Sorry." He grinned unrepentently. "I couldn't help kissing you. You're so irresistible." He kept his arms around her waist. "And I do think it's quite normal for married couples to exchange these pleasantries from time to time." His lips touched her temples. "If fact," he whispered, "I think we should do it more often. Much more often."

Cassie pulled herself away with difficulty, moving slowly toward the door. "I guess you don't want my help."

"Yes, I do. Really." He had that little-boy look that Jonathan used so often. She couldn't help giving in.

"Fine. Then let's get to work."

He waved a hand at the chair behind his desk. "Be seated and I'll explain."

It seemed simple enough to Cassie. She just had to type in some funny little symbols in between those short abbreviated words. She'd never actually done it before, she reminded herself an hour later, but it really wasn't that hard. She studied her work with a proud smile and then glanced at Jeff who sat at his laptop, punching madly at the keys.

How would she tell him, she wondered sadly. How could she explain that it was time to forget the old hurts and get on with the future? A future that his mother might not have.

Her fingers punched in the key commands he had listed.

Suddenly there was a squeal from the computer that hurt her ears. Then everything went black.

"What in the world was that?" Jeff demanded, frowning as he strode across the room. "Cassie," he inquired softly, a forbidding look on his face. "Where is the stuff you just inputted?"

Cassie punched several buttons on the computer but nothing happened. Not a thing. Everything stayed black, totally unresponsive to her panicked state.

"I don't know. I was just going along and suddenly everything went black. Did you hear that squeak it made before it died?"

"Don't punch in anything else," he ordered, turning her chair around. "Let me in, please. Don't touch that!" he yelled as she hit the reboot button once more.

Cassie scrambled out of the way, shrinking from his angry face.

"You don't have to holler," she huffed, watching him try a combination of different keystrokes. Finally the screen lit up in its usual bright blue. "You see, I didn't do anything wrong."

Jeff just kept muttering as he punched in a variety of access codes. The screen remained blank for ages while Cassie held her breath.

"Come on! Come on," he implored, fingers flying over the keys. Finally a bright white message flashed onto the monitor.

Bad file name. No such path exists.

"I don't believe this," he groaned. "Come on, baby. Where's the backup?"

No backup for that file. Do you want a search?

"Yes," he bellowed angrily. "I want you to search and find my program." He typed in another message.

No existing files. Do you wish to create a file?

Cassie stood helplessly by as he punched key after key, searching for the missing program. And as she did, she listened to his voice grow angrier by the minute.

"What did you do?" he growled finally, standing and

towering over her. "Six months of work went into that program and in one fell swoop you've deleted every bit of it." His face was dark and menacing as he advanced on her retreating figure. "What did you do to my program?"

"I didn't do anything," she squeaked. "I just keyed in what you told me to type from those notes."

"The notes," he hollered, a light brightening his glowering face. He turned toward the desk and then stopped dead in his track. "My notes," she heard him whisper as he stared at the desolation in front of him.

Jonathan sat cross-legged on the floor with the small metal trash can in front of him. A plume of smoke rose from inside it as the child clapped his hands excitedly, dropping in the last bit of yellow lined paper she'd been working from.

"Look, Daddy. Garbage all gone."

"My notes," Jeff yelled, grabbing the can and blowing on the flames with gusto. Bits of ash and blackened paper fell on the carpet around them, but only one piece of the yellow paper remained. Unfortunately, Cassie saw, it was blank.

Quickly she snatched up Jonathan in case any of the ashes were still hot and held him on her hip. Jeff turned at the sudden movement, his eyes black with fury as he glared at her.

"Get that little pyromaniac out of my sight," he stormed, his teeth bared. "And do it before I warm his bottom so hot he'll never touch a match again. He's a danger to society."

"Oh, Jeff," Cassie protested hugging Jonathan close. "You don't mean that. He didn't mean…"

"Nobody seems to mean anything around here," her husband shrieked. "I get knocked out, but no one means it. My designs are ruined and you tell me you didn't mean to erase everything off my computer? Thanks a lot! For nothing!"

Cassie walked to the door and handed Jonathan to a gaping Mrs. Bennet. Then she quietly closed the door and turned to face the ranting man in front of her.

"Just calm down," she advised smoothly. "There's a way around this. There always is."

He glared at her, teeth gritting.

"Oh, really Miss Peace and Goodwill. Well, here," he thrust the rolling chair toward her. "Be my guest. Magically restore my software designs again." When she simply stared at him in amazement, he grasped her arm and led her to the desk. "Well, go ahead, lady. Wave your magic wand and make everything okay."

"Stop shouting," she ordered in her best no-nonsense voice. "There are children in this house and they deserve a calm, stable environment."

"This is my house and I'll yell all I want." He raked his hands through his hair in frustration. "There are always children around," he barked angrily. "From the moment you wake up and even after you go to bed, there are children. They squawk and bawl in the middle of the night, they muck up my clothes and they try to do me bodily injury. Yesterday I found a dog in my sock drawer."

His voice had risen proportionately with each complaint, Cassie noticed. She wondered about tossing a glass of ice water at him and then decided to tough it out. He obviously needed to blow off steam.

"Oh, that's not staying—it goes when Stevie does. I know it's been busy these past few weeks—" she began placatingly. She didn't get further.

"Busy? This place is worse than a zoo. I can't even wear my clothes anymore because they either smell of smoke or baby spit or worse." He scowled at her, eyes narrowing. "I've had three hours of sleep a night for the last three weeks and when I get up, you're prancing around dispensing peace and goodwill like some nauseatingly sweet fairy godmother. It's disgusting."

Cassie tried to swallow the smile but she just couldn't do it. Unfortunately Jeff saw it and turned on her.

"Don't you laugh," he ordered in savage tones. "Don't

you dare! I've had it up to here with this nuthouse." He sank down onto the sofa and then jumped up again in agitation. "Do you know how ridiculous I felt at that parent-teacher interview? How many men do you know who are married one week and show up the next carrying a set of twins through the local high school?" He snorted. "Not to mention the mess they made!"

"They were only here overnight," Cassie reminded him. "It didn't hurt us to take them along. Anyway, I couldn't find a sitter for everyone."

"That's the problem," he shrieked, throwing his hands up. "There's never time for anybody but these kids. I thought we might spend some time together this afternoon and now look!"

Cassie sighed as her glance encompassed the messy desk, the bits of ash scattered across the floor and the look of defeat on Jeff's handsome face.

He stared at her from under his eyebrows.

"Why don't you spend a little of that boundless energy on me?" he whined sourly.

"I tried to," Cassie defended herself. "I'm not good with computers but I tried to help you out because you asked me to. I know it's been hectic and I thought that maybe if we were to work as a team on this then, well…" She nodded at the mess. "I guess it wasn't a very good idea."

"What do you mean you're not good with computers?" he asked softly, advancing to stand directly in front of her. "You do know how to type in a program, don't you, Cassandra?"

She hated it when he said her name like that—low and sort of threatening. Her chin tilted up defiantly.

"I just know how to put in exactly what you told me to. Sort of."

He gripped her elbows in his hands, forcing her to meet his flinty gaze. "Put what in where?"

"Put those squiggly things into whatever file it was in

when I took over. How should I know? I'm not the computer genius. I thought it was all set up and ready to go.''

Jeff let go of her and forcefully stepped backward two paces before speaking. His face was hard and set in rigid lines of fury.

"You deliberately sabotaged my program," he asserted clearly. "You sat there and tampered with something you knew nothing about purposely to ruin me."

Cassie was aghast.

"I did no such thing. Jeff, I didn't know…"

"And you have the nerve to talk about love," he snarled scathingly. "How could someone so full of *love*—" he spat the word out "—intentionally do that?"

She had held on for as long as she could; Cassie simmered furiously. There was no way she was taking this sitting down.

"If you would shut up long enough to listen to me, you'd know that I didn't do anything on purpose. I was trying to help."

"Gee," he muttered hatefully. "Don't help me anymore, okay? You'll kill me with all this kindness."

"Listen," she stressed, squeezing her fingers into tight fists. "If you weren't so self-involved you might be able to see that the people around you really do care about you. Believe it or not, we're trying to help you in spite of yourself."

"How?" he demanded silkily, leaning back on the desk. "By making my company go under?"

"I wasn't trying to do that," Cassie enunciated clearly. "I was trying to help. You know—assist, aid, support. But, you know what?" She brushed the tears from her eyes and turned toward the door. "Forget it, okay? Just forget it. You don't need anybody. You're doing just fine on your own." She pulled open the door and turned to face him.

"Tell me, Jeff," she asked softly, "if you're doing so well in this solitary world you've built for yourself, why do you need me or Rory or David or anybody? Why don't you just dump us like you dumped your parents? We're only gonna mess things up in your perfect world. You see,'' she swallowed the sob in her throat and spoke clearly. "That's what humans do—they make mistakes.''

She stepped through the opening and pulled the door shut behind her. But not before she whispered the last words remaining on her tongue and in her heart.

"You don't need any of us, Jeff. You're much better off on your own.''

Chapter Twelve

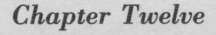

"There isn't a whole lot more that could go wrong, Robyn. We're not even speaking to each other at this point. I don't dare tell him about his mother." Cassie sighed as she took another swallow of the fresh coffee Mrs. Bennet had just made.

"Where is he now?" Robyn asked, trying to hide the smile on her lips.

"Downstairs with David. Tomorrow's the big day for their presentation, you know. They're trying a test run tonight." She made a face. "The rest of us have strict orders not to set foot in the basement. Hah! Who'd want to?"

"What, exactly, are they building?"

Cassie shrugged. "Who would know? Not me."

Robyn looked around the empty family room with curiosity. It looked sort of stark and bare without the Christmas decorations.

"Where is everyone?" she asked.

"Alyssa's gone back to her father for now. Stevie's with his grandparents. Jonathan is asleep and Marie's out with Nate." Cassie frowned. "I don't know exactly what to do about those two." She glared at her friend. "And don't say leave them alone. I'm worried about her."

"Why? Marie is a perfectly lovely girl. She loves living here with you and Jeff." Robyn grinned. "Separately," she added softly. "Anyway, she would never do anything to hurt either of you."

"It's not me I'm worried about," Cassie admitted. "It's her. She's fifteen and she's convinced herself she is in love with Nate. She's talking about marriage, Rob. Marriage!"

"I thought you believed in marriage, Cassie." Robyn's tones were full of smug humor. "Doesn't look quite so rosy now, does it? Changed your mind, girl?" She patted Cassie's knee with sympathy. "Tell Auntie Rob all about it," she whispered in commiseration as big fat tears rolled down Cassie's face.

"I do love him, Rob. More than I ever thought I could love anybody. And I want so much for us to be close, like a husband and wife should be." She sniffed, tucking her legs up under her.

"But..." Robyn encouraged.

"But he won't let me in. He thinks love is just a silly emotion that wears thin after a while. Just when I think he might really be learning to love me, he throws a fit and shuts me out again." She sniffed sulkily.

"And then there's his family." She groaned. "I can't begin to talk to him about that. He won't even sit in the same room as me anymore let alone talk about his parents." Cassie blew her nose, staring into the fireplace.

"How is his mother?" Robyn's face was sad. "Has she started the treatments, yet?"

"Uh-huh." Cassie nodded. "She's actually had several chemotherapies. The doctors seem quite hopeful about her chances if she can just get her spirits up. I talked to her on Monday, you know." Cassie swallowed another mouthful and then pushed her cup away. For some reason coffee didn't fill the same gap it once had, she decided ruefully.

"She desperately wants to settle things between Jeff and herself. And I said I'd help, but with this cold war on, what can I do?"

Robyn shook her head doubtfully. "I'm not sure it's a

good idea for you to get involved, Cass. If what his father said is true, Jeff has good reason for his painful memories. You can't blame him for feeling hurt when his own father treated him like a visitor in a military academy. But he is going to have to confront it for himself. You can't do that for him.''

"I know." Cassie nodded. "I wish I could. And I don't have to tell you not to breathe a word of it, do I?" A tremor of uncertainty ran through her. "If Jeff knew I had been seeing them, I think he'd be so angry he'd never forgive me. Not that he will anyway," she finished sadly.

They sat silent, staring into the fire together, each busy with their own thoughts.

"He watches you all the time, you know," Robyn told her, smiling at the sparkle that rose in her friend's eyes. "Whenever you come into the room, when he thinks you're not looking, his eyes are on you with this pathetic sort of wistful look. I think he loves you."

"I'm sure," Cassie mumbled.

"I mean it. I think he is genuinely attracted to you and wants to do something about it. He just doesn't know what yet." She patted Cassie's hand. "Give it some time, kiddo. Jefferson Haddon will come round eventually."

A sudden boom resounded through the house at that moment, shaking the pictures on the walls and rattling the dishes.

"What in the world...?" Robyn exclaimed, but she was talking to herself for Cassie was already running barefoot toward the basement door. Robyn caught up to her as she ripped the door open and bounded down the stairs.

Thick gray smoke hung in puffs in the brightly lit room. The assorted test tubes were all knocked over, gray powder spilling from some of them. Cassie, however, had eyes only for Jeff's blackened face.

"Jeff, what happened? Are you hurt? Is there a fire?" The words stopped suddenly. He grabbed her as she descended to the bottom step and swung her round and round.

"It worked," he gloated triumphantly, soot-covered face

wreathed in smiles. "We actually did it. David's going to get a double A plus for this one." He grinned at her jubilantly before his lips closed over hers suddenly, drowning her response.

And Cassie did feel as if she were drowning as she exulted in his embrace. Without thinking, she wound her arms around his neck and gave herself to that kiss, wishing it could go on forever. Unfortunately, Jeff quickly came to his senses and swiftly set her down.

"Sorry," he murmured, averting his eyes. "I guess I was a bit excited. Isn't it fantastic?" He couldn't suppress the grin that stretched his mouth wide.

"Way to go, Dad!" David high-fived him in a complicated ritual of thumbs and fingers that gave Cassie time to regain her composure. She stared at the series of duct-taped loops, twists and turns that descended in an intricate pathway from the ceiling to the floor.

"What is this?" she asked, catching sight of several dominoes, pieces of Jonathan's plastic building set, six paper tubes and two pulley systems. There were also bits of racetrack, miles of string, marbles and a host of other articles she didn't recognize.

"It's a Rube Goldberg machine," David told her grinning. "We set it up so that once you let the marble go it takes twenty-two steps to light the firecracker that we manufactured at the other end. Each step illustrates an example of one of the principle laws of physics—like the law of gravity. Isn't it great!"

He looked so delighted with his invention that Cassie didn't have the heart to mention that his teachers surely wouldn't permit him to set off a firecracker in school. She would have never allowed him to do such a thing at home if she'd had any idea what they were up to down here.

"David, you're a genius," Robyn declared, studying the intricate machine as if she knew something about it. "How are you going to get it to school?"

As he explained his plan for transporting the fragile device, Cassie looked toward Jeff's still figure. He was staring straight at her and for once, Cassie did not avoid his eyes but held his gaze steadily, searching the dark brown depths for an answer.

"I should probably go get cleaned up," he muttered at last, glancing toward David. "We've got a lot of work to do to pack this thing up for the morning."

"Yes, I imagine so." Was this stilted conversation the way they would always converse? she wondered sadly. "David called you Dad," she remarked softly.

Jeff's face lit up with an inner glow that made him look boyish and carefree.

"I know," he admitted. His eyes held hers. "I like it."

"Well, good," she murmured, turning to move up the stairs in order to hide the ache she was sure must be in her glance. "I'm going to make some tea if you want some. I need something hot to calm my nerves after that sonic boom."

She had only taken three steps when his hand on her arm stopped her.

"Tea, Cassandra?" he asked quizzically, his chocolate eyes melting as they moved slowly over her black leggings and long red sweater.

"Yes, tea," she breathed, loath to tear her gaze from him. "Peppermint, I think. Coffee just doesn't taste right tonight." She held her breath and asked the question uppermost in her mind. "Want to share some?"

Oblivious to the other interested spectators, Jeff lifted one hand and brushed his fingers over her smooth cheek with the lightest caress imaginable.

"Yes," he whispered. "I think I would." His eyes shone into hers. "Thank you."

"You're welcome," she answered automatically as she turned and walked up the stairs on a cloud of air. "You're very welcome."

What does it mean? Cassie wondered later that evening as she lay in bed thinking about the past hour the four of them had spent eating David's favorite chocolate cake and sipping peppermint tea in Mrs. Bennet's sparkling clean kitchen.

That strange, funny look—what does it mean? Could it be that Robyn is right for once? That my husband really is falling in love with me?

"Please, Father," she prayed softly. "If this is your will, let it happen. I love him so much."

The Bible verse she'd read this morning came back to mind just before she drifted off to sleep.

I will be with you in trouble and rescue you and honor you. I will satisfy you with a full life.

"He can't go," Jeff said in a low harsh voice. "Not now."

Cassie glanced from the young girl crouched nervously in their family room to the bulky form of Selma Bay, her social worker.

"Surely you knew that Jonathan was not intended to stay here forever, Mr. Haddon. His mother had to leave him but she is more than ready to care for him again. We have to give them every opportunity to be together, to renew their bond."

"What bond?" Cassie heard the anger in Jeff's voice. "She abandoned him to go make a hit!" His scornful eyes raked over the young girl. "She's a drug addict and heaven knows what else. How can you say she's fit to care for an innocent child like Jonathan?"

Cassie's heart ached for him. She knew how he felt. He had become Jonathan's daddy in every way but one. The months had passed so quickly. It was almost spring and now the little boy was being ripped away.

"There's no point arguing about it, Jeff," she soothed, tightening her hold on his hand in sympathy. "We only get them for a little while and during that time we try to do whatever we can for them. Then we have to let them go and let God take over."

"And where was He when she—" he jutted one finger at Jonathan's mom "—left him alone?" He turned to the social worker and glared. "How do you know she won't do it again?"

The girl burst into tears.

"I won't. You have to believe me, I won't. I've spent weeks now worrying and wondering about him while I've been in treatment." She swiped a hand across her eyes and met his angry gaze head-on. "I never even knew I'd left him alone," she admitted tearfully. "I needed a fix so bad I couldn't think of anything else."

Jeff's dark eyes raked over her scornfully. "So what's changed?" he demanded.

"If Lisa leaves him again, Mr. Haddon, the courts will consider taking Jonathan away on a permanent basis." Selma looked sternly at the rake thin form of the young mother. "This is your last chance, Lisa. Jonathan needs his mama but if you can't handle it, we have to find someone who can."

Lisa stood and walked over in front of Jeff. Her voice was soft but full of courage.

"I want to thank you and Cassie, Mr. Haddon. I know you've taken good care of Jonathan for me." Her voice dropped. "And I can see that you really care about him. But so do I."

Cassie watched Jeff's eyes harden to pieces of black coal.

"Prove it," he said at last. "Give him to me. I can take care of him, give him the things he needs."

"Oh, Jeff, no," Cassie cried, but it was all in her mind. She knew there was nothing she could say to remove that look of misery from his hard, bitter features.

Jonathan came racing through the door then on his fat stubby legs. He stopped short at the sight of the thin, tear-faced girl on the sofa.

"Mama," he cried, holding out his arms and running toward her happily. "Hi, Mama."

Cassie watched as Lisa swung her son high up in the air

and down into her arms. She hung on tearfully, kissing his cheeks and his hair as she slid her hands over his soft, pudgy body.

"Oh, baby! Mommy's so glad to see you. Are you all right? Did you miss me?" Lisa's voice was filled with love as Cassie watched the young woman's eyes beam down on her son.

"I got a new truck, Mama. Daddy buyed it for me." Jonathan grinned at Jeff brightly, but when his 'daddy' didn't grin back, he climbed down from his mother's lap and scurried over to pull on Jeff's pantleg with one sticky hand. "Daddy sick?" he asked softly, pressing his head against the black wool pants.

Cassie rose and went over to Jeff, picking up Jonathan in one arm and then wrapping her other arm around her husband's waist as she spoke to the little boy.

"No, sweetie. Daddy's not sick. He's just a little bit sad that you're going home with Mommy. Remember we talked about that?" Jonathan nodded. "Daddy loves you very much, you know, and he's glad that your mommy's going to look after you."

Jonathan nodded again, sinking his head onto Jeff's shoulder. Cassie felt his weight lift as Jeff took the little boy into his own arms.

"I wuv Daddy, and I wuv Mama, and I wuv Cassie." He beamed as he pressed a big smack against Jeff's cheek. "Daddy doesn't like matches," he informed his mother. "I sorry."

He looked mournful and Cassie decided they'd had enough sadness. A child returning to his family should be a happy event. At least for the child.

"I know you are, darling," she reassured him. "But I'm very happy you're going back to your own house with Mommy. She's all better now but she needs her little Jonny-boy to hug her at nighttime and read stories to her and kiss her good-night. Do you think you can do that?" she asked softly.

"But I want Daddy to come to my house," Jonathan sniffed on the verge of tears.

"I can't, Jonathan. I have to stay here and help Cassie with the other boys and girls that come for a visit." Jeff's voice came at last, low and gravelly, but he held on to his control. His eyes were huge pools of sadness as they gazed at Jonathan.

Cassie felt her own throat clog as she watched the two size each other up.

"Okay," Jonathan agreed at last. He scrambled down and went to sit on his mother's lap. "Will I come to visit again, Mama?"

Cassie broke in before anyone could say anything.

"You have to come and visit Jonathan. Every week. Daddy will need to make sure you're eating all your vegetables." Her eyes shone as she watched Jeff kneel down beside the little boy.

"And you remember, no playing with matches. They hurt people. And no ice, either." She noticed Jeff's hand shake.

"I know." Jonathan smiled his generous wide smile at them all. "Jonny's a good boy," he crowed.

Quickly, Lisa bundled him into his new winter jacket and pulled his tuque on his head. Cassie stopped her as Jeff carried the little boy to the car.

"Lisa, please bring Jonathan for a visit soon. We're going to miss him so much and we'd like to keep in touch. Please?"

"They really bonded, didn't they?" Lisa smiled as she watched her son kiss Jeff's rough cheek. "I can see your husband is a very loving man. Congratulations. We'll be around next week and every week after that until you're tired of us." She squeezed Cassie's hand. "Thank you," she whispered as the tears flowed down her cheeks. "Thank you for caring for my baby."

"You're welcome, but now it's your job," Cassie answered, watching Jeff stride back toward the house. "Don't let us down."

"I won't."

They stood together for a long time after the car rounded the bend, staring at the empty, barren landscape. Winter's end always seemed so lifeless, Cassie decided. Dead and dirty and worn as it waited for new life to spring. She felt Jeff move and turned to go inside the house with him.

"Don't ever do that again," Jeff ordered in a hard cold tone.

Cassie wheeled around in surprise. "Do what?"

"Don't bring another child into this house and expect me to look after it, care for it and then hand it over when the time is up." He moved jerkily toward the study.

"Jeff?"

He stopped but refused to face her. Cassie prayed for the right words to ease his turmoil.

"That's exactly what my work is all about. I only have the children for a short time—an interval in their lives. I know that. It's why I try to pour as much love and caring in their little hearts as I can. Hopefully it makes them stronger and better equipped to face the future."

The silence yawned between them starkly, full of pain and torment.

"He called me Daddy," she heard him whisper, heartbroken.

Cassie moved silently over behind him and placed her hand gently on his shoulder. Jeff flinched but did not move away.

"And to him that's who you are. So be there for Jonathan whenever he needs you. Let yourself be his refuge, his touchstone of stability in a mixed-up life."

He turned to face her and Cassie felt her heart shrink at the awful agony in his dark eyes.

"I can't," he groaned. "It hurts too much."

She reached up and cupped his cheek with her hand, smiling gently as she tried to ease his sorrow.

"Then focus on the happy times you had together. Fix your mind on the wonderful things you gave to Jonathan at a time when he most needed you." She smoothed his dark hair back, speaking gently as she caressed his face. "Remember the way he looked at you with that great big grin, and those funny little hugs he insisted upon. And know that you gave that security of trust to him, Jeff. Treasure those memories and be prepared to be there when he needs you again."

Jeff straightened at that, drawing himself rigidly erect as he glared down at her.

"And he will need me again, won't he? He'll be abandoned again, left out in the cold or something worse." He scowled at her fiercely. "Why, Cassie? You tell me why he should have to leave here and go back to that kind of a life with a woman like that. Tell me why?"

Cassie breathed a prayer even as the words slipped through her lips.

"Because Lisa is his mother, Jeff. She's his mother."

His smoldering embittered eyes tore at her heart. Suddenly he wheeled away from her and strode out of the room. Cassie barely heard him speak.

"I thought he was mine," he whispered on an agonized sigh. "He should be my son."

"Yes! Yes! Yeees!" Cassie thrust her arms toward the heavens in a yell that brought Mrs. Bennet running up the stairs at top speed.

"Is everything all right, Miss Cassie?" The older woman's chest heaved with her sudden exertion as she stared at her mistress with a frown. She rubbed her apron over her glasses before settling them back on her nose.

"Everything is absolutely, positively, fantastically glorious." Cassie laughed, grasping her by the hands and dancing her around the room.

Jeff came striding into her bedroom moments later to find the two of them laughing hilariously as they flopped onto the side of the bed. His eyes widened in shocked disbelief as he gaped at the two of them.

"Uh, is there a problem here?" he asked slowly.

Cassie burst into fresh paroxysms of laughter and

bounced across the room, standing before him huffing and puffing.

"Today," she announced giggling, "there will be no problems at Oak Bluff."

"Oh?" He quirked one dark eyebrow curiously. "And that is because…"

"That is because…" Cassie dragged the moment out for all it was worth. "Because Bored Boris and I have just landed an interview with an editor who likes my work and wants to talk to me about a possible publishing date!" She let the rest of it flow out in a rush, too excited to hold back as she grinned up at him. "Isn't that fantastic?"

"Congratulations," he said, staring down at her. "You've worked hard for this."

"Yes, but it's such an opportunity," she babbled, not even noticing Mrs. Bennet had left until the door closed behind her. "Just listen to this, Jeff." Cassie sank onto the side of the bed and sighed.

"They had a children's book slated for publishing in October but the work hasn't yet been completed or they don't like it or something. Anyway—" she beamed "—mine is finished and the woman said they really want to use it."

"So what comes next?" Jeff asked, sitting on the velvet chair she kept in the corner. "Do you have to hire a lawyer or something?"

His face creased in a frown as he stared at the assortment of small pictures decorating the walls. Cassie saw his eyes rest on Jonathan's snapshot for several moments before he jerked his head away.

"Well, not quite yet." Cassie laughed, pretending she hadn't seen the slash of pain cross his face. "I'm supposed to go in Monday for a conference." She danced a little jig at the excitement of it, stopping suddenly as she noticed his clothing.

"Where in the world did you get those?" she gasped, staring at the same ragged jeans and tattered shirt he'd worn to the wiener roast so long ago. "Don't tell me you kept them all this time?"

His face flushed as he glanced down at himself.

"I didn't, Bennet did. He resurrected them when I started building the playhouse."

Cassie frowned. "You are building a playhouse," she repeated, unable to picture it. "Where?"

"By the creek, in the elbow of that big old oak tree. It's a fantastic setting." His face lit up with excitement as he spoke, Cassie noticed. "Come on, I'll show you."

He held out his hand companionably and there was no way she was going to refuse such an offer, Cassie decided happily. Wasn't this just what she'd been praying for—time to spend with her husband? An opportunity to open up the lines of communication once more? A chance to get closer?

They strolled through the lawns and gardens to the back of the property where a bubbling little creek roiled past. Everything looked fresh and green, sprouting with life in the warm spring sunshine.

"Isn't it wonderful how much difference a few weeks can make?" Cassie sighed, breathing deeply of the fresh, fragrant air. "It seems like only yesterday it was Christmas."

"That's because you and Boris have been buried in the library," Jeff teased. He held out his hands. "Ta-da!"

Cassie stared at the lopsided structure tilting forward crazily from the boughs of a sturdy oak. The tree seemed the most secure thing about Jeff's tree house as it swayed in the gentle breeze, but she wasn't going to admit that.

"It looks very nice," she offered generously, patting one new board suspended from the base. "Did you do all this by yourself?" she asked curiously.

"Well, Bennet helped me with the floor," he told her stamping on that part firmly. "But the rest I did myself." He swung down and barely missed scraping his head on the jagged end of a protruding two-by-four.

"I see." Cassie peered intently at the firmly anchored

floor. Bennet, she decided, must have a better grasp of construction methods.

"Look out," she heard him yell and then felt herself pulled sharply back from the tree. A board which moments ago had formed the top section of the window, toppled to the ground a mere six inches from their bodies.

Jeff lay on the ground facing her. "Are you all right?" he wheezed, breathless from their sudden tumble.

"I think so." Cassie giggled, brushing off her shirt and jeans.

He sat up, hugging his knees to his chest as he stared at his work. "I just can't seem to get the nails to stay put," he told her seriously. "And just when I think I've got one part of the thing stable, something else comes loose." His dark head tipped to one side as he considered the problem.

"Can I help?" she offered, trying to hide her smile. It was obvious that tree house construction was not Jefferson Haddon's best hobby. In fact, the whole thing reminded her of a edifice built by preteenage boys in her hometown years ago.

He stared down at her for a moment and then shook his head.

"No, thanks. I want to do this myself, with my own hands. You see," he explained, his head averted from her, "I always wanted a tree house when I was a kid. I thought it would be so wonderful for Rory and I to have our own little place where we wouldn't bother anyone."

"And did you get it?" she inquired softly.

"We tried." He grimaced, standing to dust off his pants. His face was hard and bitter. "My father had it torn down and hauled away. He said it ruined the value of the property and the look of the trees."

"Well, it's certainly hidden away back here," Cassie observed, glancing through the dancing leaves overhead to the bright clear sky. "You have to really look to even find it."

"I know." His chest puffed with pride. "That's why I chose this place. It's kind of like—" he paused, thinking.

"Oh, I don't know. The secret garden, maybe. A secluded little oasis for kids to come and think things over." His eyes were fixed on something far away in his imagination that no one else could see.

"What kids?" Cassie probed gently watching his stare swivel and focus on her. "Kids like Jonathan who come to us for a break?" she murmured softly.

His shadowy eyes searched hers as he stood beside her. Cassie felt the tension melt away between them as his mouth curved in a tiny mocking smile.

"Or our own kids," he amended speculatively, his eyes lighting up as she flushed a bright pink. "They might enjoy a picnic out here or a place to play their music as loud as they want. Hey!" His face brightened. "Maybe we could send David out here with his boom box."

Cassie let the moment stretch between them, waiting for him to make the first move. Her heart thudded with love as she stared into his dear face. How she wanted him to love her! She ached for that special closeness that she knew could grow between them. If only he would let go and let love in.

As he made his way over to the pile of lumber stacked haphazardly nearby, she felt a pang of regret for what could be. And wasn't now. But she wasn't giving up, she told herself. God had sent her to Judith, given her a chance to stay in Oak Bluff and continue her work. Surely He hadn't done all that to leave her alone, aching for a love that would never be?

"Jeff," she said hesitantly. "Soon Marie and David will legally be our children. Are you ready for that?" He turned to examine her with a questioning look.

"It will be permanent, Jeff. For the rest of our lives. There won't be any going back. Are you ready to commit to that? Can you accept that they'll grow and change and move away from us whether we want it or not?" She hesitated. "Can you love them and let them go?"

He studied his boots as she spoke, giving them an intense

scrutiny she knew they didn't merit. When at last he lifted his head, she studied his serious face.

"I don't know," he said. "David and I, we're very close and he means more to me than I ever thought he would. But love?" He pressed the drooping curls off her forehead and cupped her chin in his hand. "I don't know if I can do that."

It should have depressed her and yet Cassie found herself full of hope. For the first time Jeff hadn't openly denied love's existence. He'd merely said he didn't know if he could deal with it. That was all right because she had more than enough faith for both of them.

"That's okay," she said, holding his hand between two of hers. "Caring enough to give them a home and a future is a start. We'll take it one day at a time."

His lips joined hers in a seal of promise that left her heart fluttering madly. Thank you, thank you, thank you, her heart whispered fervently as she relaxed in the warm comforting circle of his arms. Just keep your spirit working in him.

"Can I help you build?" she asked when he finally moved away to pick up his hammer once more. She flushed at the mocking grin on his face.

"Do you know any more about building tree houses than you do about baking?" he asked, tongue in cheek, his eyes flicking over her shining eyes.

"Well, no," she admitted. "I've never built anything before." An idea surfaced and she giggled with delight. "I am quite good at painting, though," she offered.

He sauntered over to her and flicked an amused finger across her cheek before bending to kiss her cheek.

"Especially dinosaurs and dragons." He grinned. "Okay, when I'm done this thing—" he jerked a thumb backward at the odd assortment of boards "—you can paint it. Anything but pink," he qualified. "Is it a deal?"

Cassie thrust out her hand. "Deal," she agreed happily.

Jeff worked all Friday evening at the tree house. Cassie ventured out several times but found very little progress in the construction, although his stock of nails and pristine lumber had seemed to diminish rapidly.

He came in three times on Saturday. The first time Cassie nearly lost her breakfast at the gash on his head.

"It's nothing," he muttered. "Just a little cut."

"But how on earth did you get it?" she demanded, dabbing the damp towel gently against his black hair as she tried to staunch the blood. He winced at the sting of the antiseptic, jaw tightly clenched.

"One of the boards didn't stay exactly where I put it," he told her. Cassie watched in the mirror as his eyes narrowed. "I think the nails they sold me are an inferior grade," he complained suspiciously. "They don't seem to hold at all."

She averted her face and mumbled a reply.

"By the way," he said, hesitating on his way out. "I think we should celebrate your success. Let's go out for dinner tonight, someplace fancy." He glanced around. "Are the kids away?"

Somewhat amazed, Cassie agreed.

"Yes, they're both on school trips for the weekend, remember." She stared at him. "What time were you thinking of?"

He thought for a moment, studying her relaxed figure in the slim blue jeans and matching shirt.

"We should leave around seven," he said matter-of-factly. "I thought we might go to that new play at the Pantages after dinner."

"Fine." She stared after his disappearing figure with shock widening her eyes. A date—they were going on a date. Just the two of them.

"Cassie, do you know where there are another pair of gloves I can use?" That was the second time; right after lunch.

She looked up from her watercolor sketch of the patio and stared at the single glove he wore on his left hand.

"I thought you had a brand-new pair on this morning,"

she frowned, trying to remember. For some reason his face grew red at that.

"They were new. But now I need another pair."

Bennet came through for them, digging out a shabby, threadbare pair of gardening gloves from the shed.

"May I help you, Mr. Jefferson, sir?" he offered hesitantly, his eyes widening at the grass stains and tears covering Jeff's already filthy garments. "Two often make the load lighter."

"No, no. Thanks, Bennet," Jeff waved airily. "But I want to do this myself. And please call me Jeff," he replied. Cassie grinned as she heard her stiff, formal husband casually use the nickname she'd given him last fall. It seemed a long time ago now.

The third time he came in, Jefferson Haddon was steaming mad.

"I'm going back to that ridiculous lumber yard and demand they replace this second-rate material with the premier grade I paid for," he stated angrily. His eyes blazed into hers. "Is it okay if I take your car? Bennet's cleaning mine for tonight."

"Of course," Cassie said, clearing her throat. "It's almost five, though."

"I know," he called over his shoulder. "I'll be quick."

Once he'd driven down the driveway, Cassie gave in to the urge and walked out to see the progress he'd made. As she stared at the mess of broken and multinailed boards, her mouth curved in amusement. It was obvious that Jeff had tried very hard to create something. She just wasn't sure what it was.

Oddly cut lengths of lumber hung here and there at strange angles forming a sort of peekaboo wall that wouldn't have stopped a flea. One white glove was nailed between two boards and that was the only solid nail Cassie found. She walked around the entire thing several times, without finding the entrance.

"Probably best if you don't go up, Miss Cassie," Bennet suggested from behind her, his face held in its usual stern facade. "I don't believe Mr. Jefferson has quite completed his work."

He pressed a hand on one wall which immediately dismantled before their eyes. Cassie could see the marks of nails which had been partially pounded in and then removed. There were innumerable amounts of the shiny green nails all over the ground, partially hidden in the grass. She picked several up. They were bent, most had their heads flattened. None could be used again.

"Begging your pardon, Miss Cassie, but I don't believe the children will be safe playing in such a thing unless some changes are made." Bennet cleared his throat as they stared at the short, rough-cut ends that were nailed fan style to the side of the oak tree.

Cassie grinned at the older man when he pointed to the pile of splintered and now totally unusable clean white spruce headers that had been hacked into a useless mass lying in a heap by the creek bank. On top Jeff had written, Firewood.

"It might not hurt to get Jonathan down for a visit," she agreed, laughing. "He could light the place on fire. But not now. I don't want Jeff to know we've been here. It was a good idea. Just leave it for now."

"As you wish," he agreed, walking back beside her. "But I do hope the next group of children that come to Oak Bluff don't find it until it's been, er, reinforced."

The smile left Cassie's lips.

"There won't be any more," she whispered sadly. "Jeff won't allow it."

"I'm sure he'll change his mind, my dear," he told her, giving her a gentle pat of commiseration on the shoulder. "He'll begin to miss them as much as we do."

"Thank you, Bennet." Cassie smiled tearfully. "And may I say how much I've appreciated Mrs. Bennet's and your help these past months. I know it has been rather unusual for you to have so many children here."

"Mrs. Bennet and I have never enjoyed ourselves more." Bennet smiled widely. "It's the little ones, you see.

We never had any of our own and Mrs. Bennet dearly loves children.'' He grinned. ''Spoils them rotten, she does.''

''So do you.'' Cassie grinned back. With a return of sadness, Cassie thrust away pangs of mourning for her loss. The children would come back. After all, it was only temporary. It had to be. Carefully she began preparations for the evening ahead. An evening with just the two of them.

Is this what you want, Lord? A time for Jeff and me to relax with each other? Alone. It was a scary thought for a woman who was as much in love as Cassandra Haddon was with her husband. Would she give herself away? Would he realize that she loved him and feel embarrassed by it?

Cassie tossed the thoughts out of her mind and concentrated on what to wear. She wanted to look her best after months of caring for small children without a moment to herself. Tonight she intended to make up for all that slovenliness and wow him with pizzazz.

She only wished she had been given more notice. Cassie grimaced as she stared at the clothes in her huge closet. If a wife only got one chance, she should make the most of it.

Chapter Thirteen

CASSIE was curled up in the sunroom enjoying the last weak rays of the spring sun when her husband finally came through the door. He was covered from head to toe in mud, but his face wore a huge grin.

"Sorry," he apologized. "I got a flat tire and had to change it on Cordouvan Road. It hasn't dried up there yet and some kids splashed me." He swung around, his brown eyes opening into huge round 0s as he stared at her in her finery.

"Wow!"

She stood and curtsied, enjoying the look of admiration on his surprised face. She'd chosen a silk vest and matching pants in palest peach with an even paler chiffon blouse underneath. In her ears were the diamond studs he'd given to her and a thin gold chain hung around her neck. Her only other jewelry was the delicate gold bracelet Jeff had presented to her on Christmas night.

Cassie glowed as his eyes widened at the black hair she had piled on her head. It had grown longer over the past few months and she'd only managed the intricate style with Robyn's help.

"Ten minutes," he promised grinning and raced up the stairs like a boy to a baseball game.

Actually it was closer to twenty but Cassie didn't mind. It gave her time to practise in the spindly spikes Robyn had persuaded her to buy with the suit.

"They match perfectly and so does that bag. And they're on sale."

Cassie stumbled haphazardly over the thick plush carpet and prayed that wherever they were going she wouldn't land on her face. Or her rear.

"Are you sure you want to spend another night with those things on your feet?" Jeff stared at the strappy leather sandals suspiciously. "Aren't they a little, er, extreme?"

"On purpose," she told him glowering. "They give me height. And when you're this short you need all the height you can get."

"I think you look perfect, with or without stilts." He grinned. He held out one black-clad arm. "Shall we, Mrs. Haddon?"

Cassie drew in a breath of air for courage and linked her arm through his. "We shall, Mr. Haddon." She whispered a prayer as he escorted her into his gleaming car. *Lord, please...*

Jeff wanted it to be an evening of laughter and fun. The restaurant was very haute elegance and he hoped Cassie would enjoy it. It was certainly a change from the places they'd taken the children and he watched her eyes grow huge as she stared at the beautiful crystal and shimmering silverware. He suddenly realized that her lack of pretence and sophistication didn't matter anymore. He felt comfortable with this woman wherever they were.

A number of people stopped by their table to speak with him, obviously curious about Cassie. He introduced her proudly, pleased with the way she spoke to each. A surprised Melisande stopped dead in the middle of her grand entrance to stare at them openmouthed.

"Jefferson, my dear. Had I known you would be dining here tonight..." Her voice died away as Cassie spoke up.

"How wonderful to see you again, Miss Gustendorf. Jeff and I have been intending to have everyone over again one evening but things have been so hectic."

He felt like crowing with delight. At last, Cassie was assuming her position as his wife. He wondered how far this new bravery extended.

"May I join you?" Mel asked, motioning for a waiter.

Jeff choked on his ice water. No way, he decided. Not tonight. But Cassie was way ahead of him.

"Oh, I'm so sorry, Miss Gustendorf." She shook her head imperceptibly at the waiter. "But Jeff and I are celebrating a special occasion tonight. Just the two of us. Aren't we, dear?"

Her fingers closed lovingly around his and Jeff held on. It was the first time in ages she had touched him of her own accord and he savored the sensation.

"Yes, darling," he murmured. "A very special occasion." He kissed her fingers softly and folded them back into his own.

"Celebrating what?" Melisande demanded rudely. "Taking on yet another homeless child?" Her tone was spiteful and Jeff watched Cassie flinch.

"Well," he murmured softly, staring her down until her face reddened. "That would be something to celebrate but this is much more personal. You see…"

Cassie's voice cut across his.

"Jeff! Darling," she admonished, covering her surprise. "It's a secret." She smiled at the interloper. "We're not telling anyone just yet."

Melisande's spiteful blue eyes opened wide as she stared at Cassie in disgust.

"Don't tell me…" Her voice was full of disdain.

"Oh, we won't," Cassie replied. She smiled intimately at Jeff, who leaned back in his chair and let her do the work. "We'll share it for just a while more before we tell the world."

Jeff motioned to the waiter surreptitiously. In microseconds the black jacketed youngster was at Mel's elbow.

"Your table is ready, madame."

With one last malevolent dagger-piercing glare, Mel slinked off to her own table. Jeff watched as Cassie snapped her napkin into her lap and sipped her fruit punch mixture.

"Old nosey parker," she muttered angrily. Her eyes glared at Jeff as he sat there grinning.

He pretended to clap. "Bravo, Mrs. Haddon. You are a very good defense for a poor helpless male."

Cassie blushed and then burst out laughing.

"I'm sorry," she apologized. "I shouldn't have done that." Her eyes were downcast as she refused to meet his. "She'll probably go around telling the world that I'm pregnant, you know."

Jeff nodded calmly. "Probably," he agreed. He lowered his voice to ask the next question. "Would that bother you?"

He watched as she stared off into space, the lights of the lovely crystal chandelier reflecting in the emerald depths of her eyes. Her whole face softened tenderly as he watched.

"Cassandra," he murmured finally, and watched her eyes move back to him hazily. He didn't need to ask anymore, Jeff decided. From the look on her face, he knew exactly how she felt about having her own children to care for.

"Hmm," she whispered softly, still half involved in her daydream as she looked at him.

Jeff moved over to stand behind her.

"I asked if you wanted to dance," he drawled into the smooth shell of her ear.

As Jeff guided her around the tiny floor to the light, delicate notes on the piano, he wondered at the beauty of his wife. They had been married for, let's see. His eyes opened wide.

Four months! And in four months this was the first time he'd held her for any length of time. His hand pressed on her back, coaxing her a little nearer as he caught the faint hint of her perfume. It was a light, delicate scent that seemed to cling to her. The smell of flowers but with an underlying hint of spice.

"I like your perfume," he whispered, allowing his lips to move slowly down the curve of her neck. "What is it?"

"Soap," she murmured, smiling into his shirtfront.

"Oh." His fingers smoothed over the sheer sleeve of her blouse to the bracelet he'd given her. "Well, I like it anyway."

"Thank you." It was a whisper and he watched as she closed her black lashes and swayed against him to the music.

"You have beautiful hair," he told her, fingering the tendril that lay against her long smooth neck. "So soft and shiny. It looks like sable."

Cassie tilted her head back to peer at him with amusement. "You're comparing me to an animal." She chuckled. "That's original."

They moved several more steps together before he heard her whisper into his ear.

"It's all held up by hair spray. If you touch it, it will come down."

He grinned, tightening his hold on her narrow waist as he nestled her against himself.

"I'm not touching your hair," he avowed softly as his fingers curved round her waist. Her wide-eyed stare acknowledged the truth with a tiny shiver. Jeff felt it to his toes. And was blissfully happy.

At least she wasn't indifferent to him.

He heard her soft musical voice through a fog.

"Jeff?"

"Yes, my..." He caught himself in time, glancing down to peer into her face. "What is it, Cassie?"

"Could we sit down now?" she asked plaintively.

A wave of frustration hit him as he realized she wanted to get away from him, wanted to break this wonderful contact they had finally achieved.

"Certainly," he agreed harshly, drawing away as his arms fell to his sides.

She leaned over, wrapping her fingers in his as she whispered softly, "My feet are killing me."

Jeff grinned and slid his arm back around her waist.

"I did warn you." He smirked, suddenly thrilled with life. "Vanity, thy name is woman."

"Hah!" She glared at him, glee sparkling in those turbulent green depths. "And I suppose you wear that bow tie because you like being trussed up?"

They sparred laughingly all through the delicious meal of salmon steaks and fresh spring potatoes. Jeff noticed Cassie eyeing the dessert cart and looked at his watch with regret.

"We'll miss the opening curtain if we stay too much longer," he advised softly.

"Maybe later," Cassie agreed. "I'm satisfyingly satiated now anyway." As he drove to the theater she studied him oddly. "What is this show we're going to see?" she asked curiously.

Jeff grinned as he guided her inside the theater.

"Afraid of my taste," he teased.

"I think your taste is wonderful," she told him seriously. "You always seem to know exactly the right thing to say and do."

"Thank you, although I think you're flattering me just to get dessert." He chose to make it a joke rather than dwell on what, exactly, she meant. Besides, he might be way off base tonight. "It's a return of *The Phantom of the Opera,*" he told her, watching her face for a response. "You've probably seen it before but…"

"No, I haven't, but only because I've never been able to get here when it was on," she cried, clasping his arm in delight. "How wonderful! Thank you."

She was an appreciative audience, Jeff decided later. She had laughed and cried and clutched his arm at intervals throughout the musical production. And as the end neared, she only snuggled a bit nearer when he dared to wrap his arm around her shoulders.

After the houselights came up, Jeff smiled as she pawed through her tiny leather bag for a tissue.

"I'm sorry," she sniffed. "I'm such a mess. It really was a great show."

"Come on." He smiled soothingly, folding her hand in his. "Let's go have dessert."

Her wide eyes more than made up for his efforts, Jeff decided later as they sat by a window at the top of the CN Tower watching the brightly lit Toronto skyline slowly revolve past.

"This is excellent," she proclaimed, closing her eyes to fully savor the texture and flavor of her cappuccino cheesecake.

Jeff grinned. He might have known she would choose a coffee-flavored dessert, he decided. Coffee was like a trademark with her. As if on cue, the waiter returned with her espresso cup once more.

"Are you sure you won't try this?" she cajoled, sipping the rich potent brew.

"Cassie, you know very well that coffee and I do not mix." He flicked his finger toward her empty plate. "And I daresay there was enough caffeine in that to put me on a high for a week. I don't know how you can pack away that much and not be up at least all night."

She tipped her head back and smiled. "I believe they do have decaf," she said, staring out at the sparkling night lights. "Thank you for a wonderful evening," she murmured, staring at him with a soft wide-open look. "It was a fantastic way to celebrate. Although, technically—" she giggled "—I'm not sure if I have anything to celebrate."

Jeff closed his hand around hers and squeezed. He felt a gentle protectiveness for this small delicate creature that urged him to shield her from the problems of the world. What would she say, he mused, if he kissed her. Later on. At home. In the dark?

"You'll do it," he assured her. "If anyone can do it, you can. And when you sign that contract, we'll celebrate again. Is it a deal?"

She stared at him silently for a moment.

"Yes," she whispered at last. "It's a deal."

It was a quiet drive home. Neither of them felt inclined to talk and Jeff was content to ride along in the smoothly purring car with her hand threaded in his. As they pulled into the driveway and he helped her out, Cassie stood staring at the starlit sky.

"It was wonderful way up there in the tower," she murmured, eyes huge as she gazed at him. "But I think we have the best view of God's heaven right here." Her hand lifted up and Jeff followed it, hugging her close in the cool air as they stared at the constellations.

"Maybe you're right," he replied finally, lowering his eyes to stare into hers. "But I think I've got the brightest new star right here."

Slowly, tenderly, he drew her close and wrapped both arms around her snugly.

"I'm going to kiss you," he whispered. "Any objections?"

Cassie shifted just a bit, sliding one arm around his waist and the other over his shoulder to touch his hair.

"Just one," she answered so softly he had to bend his head to hear. "What took you so long?"

Jeff stared, unable to believe he'd heard it. Cassie actually *wanted* him to kiss her? Had even been waiting? He laughed at the absurdity of it. Talk about mixed signals!

"What's so funny?" Cassie complained, tilting her head back to study him. She had to look way up because she had long since removed her heels in the car.

Jeff grinned.

"All you had to do was ask," he stated dryly. Her fingers nudged his head a little lower.

"I'm asking," she confided.

"I'm kissing," he whispered back. And proceeded to do just that.

"Oh what a beautiful mooorning. Oooh what a beautiful day!" Cassie slipped on her new silk stockings with a smug little curve to her lips. "I've got a wonderful husband—I wish he would make up his mind."

She smiled at the little poem. Very little, she decided wryly.

Stick to kids' stories, Cassie, she told herself. Robert Louis Stevenson you will never be.

It felt good to know that Jeff had as much difficulty pulling away from her as she had from him Saturday night. And yesterday they had spent the entire day together; attending church, picnicking in the park with Robyn and her friend and later bicycling to the ice-cream store for a treat. All in all, the weekend had been a giant step forward in their, well, unusual relationship. Best of all, Jeff hadn't uttered one single protest when the social worker had dropped by unexpectedly last night with two preschool children. He'd merely helped her bathe and prepare them for bed, a funny little smile curving his lips.

And today, wonder of wonders, she was actually going to talk to someone about publication of her book. Publication! Her heart rate accelerated at the thought.

She slipped the silk blouse Jeff had given her for Christmas over her shoulders and buttoned it up with a gleam in her eyes. The man had taste, she decided.

"Cassie?" A rap of knuckles alerted her to Jeff's presence outside her door. Good heavens, she hoped he hadn't heard her singing. She cringed.

"Just a second," she answered, zipping up the creamy wool skirt of her suit. Yes, she told herself jubilantly. Smart, elegant, not too dressy.

"Good morning!" She tugged the door open and found him standing on her doorstep. Her eyes widened at the delicate purple blue irises he held out.

"For good luck," he told her. "With my best wishes."

"Thank you!" Cassie leaned over to press her lips against his cheek and found his mouth pressed against hers instead.

"Now that's how we say 'good morning' in this house," he teased, grinning at the flush of color in her cheeks.

"I'll have to remember that when I see Bennet," she retorted smartly. She twirled in front of him. "Do I look all right?"

"You're not wearing those, are you?" Jeff's dark eyes remained fixed dourly on her pale spiky high heels. "I thought you'd learned your lesson about those ridiculous shoes."

Cassie frowned.

"I need the height," she told him seriously. "I want to look professional and businesslike."

"You look great," he told her sincerely. "Knock 'em dead."

"Thanks." Cassie beamed up at him, willing her heart to slow down its ridiculous pace.

"Well, uh, I've got to get going." He turned to leave and then glanced over his shoulder. "Phone and tell me how it went," he said. "I'd like to know."

Cassie smiled softly. "I will," she promised.

Monday mornings were always the pits for traffic on the 401 into Toronto. It seemed that no one took public transportation on that particular day of the week.

"Including me," she muttered, grinning in spite of herself.

For the hundredth time, her glance moved over her portfolio as she checked to be sure her drawings were intact. They sat there, just as they had five minutes ago, waiting for her proud presentation.

Cassie thought once more of Jeff's thoughtful gift. Even now the flowers lay beside her on the seat, filling the car with their faint odor.

He'd remembered that irises were her favorite. She grinned to herself. After all this time, he'd still remembered. What a guy!

She pressed the accelerator to ease past a semi when the steering suddenly jerked to one side.

Not now, she prayed fiercely. Please not now.

But apparently the car didn't hear, for it veered drastically as she tried to stay in her own lane. Slowly, carefully, she signaled right and eased past the other vehicles into the caution lane. Her heart sank as she stared at the flattened tire on the driver's side.

"Why today?" She moaned. She knew a tow truck wouldn't make it through until well after the throng of cars had dissipated. There was nothing for it but to change the tire herself.

She wished desperately for the trench coat she'd left at home, even though the temperature was well above twenty degrees Celsius. It would at least have protected the cream-colored fabric of her suit.

"There is absolutely no point groaning about it, kid," she told herself, lifting out the jack. She might just as well spend her time working.

It took a little over fifteen minutes to work the tire free and the effort cost her four fingernails. Thankfully she had a spare pair of panty hose, Cassie thought glancing down and grimacing. The ones she had on were history. Sweat beaded her brow as she rolled the mulish tire to the rear of her car. She just knew her makeup would be a write-off.

Five more minutes lapsed while she strove to figure out just exactly how one undid the carpet covering the spare and lift it out of the trunk. With a grunt of satisfaction Cassie finally lugged the tire free and whooshed a sigh of relief as it thunked on the ground.

"Thank goodness," she groaned, rolling it along. That was when she noticed the huge grease mark across her skirt. Her heart sank as she realized there was no way she could disguise it. Her only hope lay in arriving early enough to make a quick purchase someplace near her appointment, she decided, glancing once more at her watch. She brushed her hand across her face and realized that she had just smeared the black sticky stuff from the hub all over herself.

"Oh, Lord, I need help," she prayed, shoving the wheel into place with a sudden burst of energy. She had almost finished fastening the last nut when she noticed the time. "I really need help," she thought again, whisking the tire iron round once more. There was mud all over her clothes and grease covering her hands, but Cassie ignored it as she rushed. Quick as a wink she had the jack down and out and was walking around the fender when she noticed the tire.

It was absolutely flat! How in the...

Like a movie camera, her mind rolled the film of Jeff arriving home on Saturday. "I had a flat," he'd said.

Anger, white-hot and steaming rose in her as she realized just what this meant to her future career. She would miss her appointment with the editor. She would lose the once-in-a-lifetime opportunity to have her book published. She would never have a chance to autograph Bored Boris or his friends.

Cassie snapped the car door open, uncaring that she lost another fingernail on the door handle. With one hand she grabbed the car phone and punched out Jeff's private office number.

"Jeff Haddon," he answered brightly.

A tide of red cast a film across Cassie's eyes as she heard his voice. That he would purposely do this to her was...

"Hello?"

"You wanted to hear how I did," she snarled, clenching the phone and gritting her teeth.

"Cassie, love. Yes, I did. Isn't it a little early—"

"No, *love*," she yelled, frustrated beyond endurance. "It's far too late."

"I don't understand...."

"I don't imagine you could," she snapped. "After all, you've got it all, haven't you, Jeff? The house, the money, me stupid enough to promise you a son. And I haven't got anything!"

It came out on a wail that started the rush of tears from her eyes.

"She didn't like it?" Jeff queried in a puzzled tone. "But I thought you said..."

"She hasn't even seen me yet," Cassie screamed. "I'm sitting on the 401 with a flat tire and no spare." She lowered her voice. "A spare that you used and deliberately didn't have repaired."

"I didn't…"

"You had the nerve to accuse me of sabotaging you," she accused in a cold, hard voice. "You tried to insinuate that I would deliberately spoil your designs." She sniffed and brushed the tears away with the back of her hand, noticing anew the scratches left from the sharp metal on the fender.

"Well, I would never deliberately do that to you, Jeff. I have never tried to hurt you and I can't believe that you would go to these extremes to ruin something that is so important to me. My suit is ruined, my nails are ripped, not to mention my stockings. I've got oil and grease and goodness knows what else covering me and my heels are broken." The tears started afresh.

"I trusted you," she sobbed. "I thought you were…I'll never forgive you for this. Never."

Disappointment overwhelmed her as she wept for the chance of a lifetime that was gone. She forgot she was even holding the phone until Jeff's voice bellowed across the airwaves from the general direction of her filthy skirt.

"Cassie, pick up that phone and talk to me," he ordered in a no-nonsense voice.

"I have to go," she muttered sadly. "I have to call a tow truck." She reached out to hang up and heard his voice once more.

"Cassie!" It was a loud, peremptory order.

"Yes," she whispered, staring mournfully at her portfolio.

"I can get a truck there faster than you can. Tell me exactly where you are."

She told him in dull, uncaring tones.

"Okay. Stay put and lock the doors. Cassie?"

"Yes, all right," she answered, returning the phone to its rest.

She didn't know how long she sat there until the red-and-white flashing lights in her mirror drew her attention.

The tall handsome officer jumped out of his car and strode forward, obviously intent on checking for injuries.

"Are you all right, ma'am?" he inquired, peering into her car. "Need some help?"

"No thank you, officer. My husband is sending someone to..."

"I'm here, Cassandra."

Cassie twisted her head to see the man she was most angry with, Jefferson Haddon the third, standing behind the policeman, looking as pulled together as always in his gray pinstripe, perfectly pressed shirt and coordinated tie. His black hair lay perfectly groomed against his head. And his hands were clean, Cassie thought miserably.

"It's all right, Officer," she heard him say brightly. "I've called a tow truck. My wife will be coming with me."

Cassie unlocked the door and eased herself out of the car, her muscles aching in the process. There wasn't any point in arguing, she decided laconically. It simply didn't matter anymore.

She followed him woodenly as he led her to his car and climbed inside the plush, cool interior without a word.

"Stay put," he murmured. "I'll be right back." And he was; carrying her sketches of Bored Boris and the box with her wonderful, useless manuscript. Carefully he placed them on the back seat.

"It doesn't matter," she uttered listlessly. "You could have left them there. I don't need them." Tears welled as she thought of what she had lost. And why.

"Yes," he told her firmly, slamming the door as he climbed in beside her. "You do. In about one hour, to be precise."

Cassie frowned at him. "It's too late," she insisted bitterly. "I missed my appointment. And she's tied up in conference the rest of the day."

"Except for one little opening in exactly—" he twisted his wrist to look at his watch "—one hour and three minutes. Look at me."

Cassie turned toward him, wondering at the look of

tender care on his face as he unscrewed a thermos and tipped hot water onto a snowy white towel. Gently he dabbed at the blotches of grease and oil and smeared makeup covering her face, wiping them carefully away with gentle strokes.

"And make no mistake," he continued, eyes flashing. "You will be there." His compassionate ministrations moved to her raw, battered hands and as he cleaned each finger he pressed a kiss to it.

"I would never hurt you, Cassie," he murmured. "Do you honestly believe I would ruin something that I know is so important to you? Do you really think I would do that to my own wife?"

"I d-d-don't know," she stammered, amazed at the strong but kind, considerate touch of his hands when he soothingly pulled a brush, oh so gently, through her tousled hair.

"Well, know this, then," he stated. "I wouldn't. It was simply a stupid oversight on my part. It should never have happened, but I accept all blame." He tipped her chin up.

"The important thing is that you can still make that appointment. If you want to. Do you?"

"Yes!" Cassie voice materialized from nowhere as she stared at him, new hope dawning. "But how, when...what will I wear?" she cried, staring at her ruined clothes.

"I, er, took the liberty of picking out something for you. I hope it's all right." She studied the red spots of color on his cheeks. "You can change at the first gas station," he continued briskly, heading into the traffic with ease. "Meanwhile—" he motioned toward the floor "—there's a thermos of coffee there if you want some."

Gratefully, Cassie poured a mug of the steaming dark brew and sipped it as her sore toes wiggled into the plush carpet of his car.

"Thank you," she said at last, at a loss to fathom it all out. "But how did you know where to phone? Or who?"

"It's whom," he corrected her absently.

"Pardon?" She frowned at him as she filed the now stubby fingernails.

"Whom—the object. Never mind. The answer is that I phoned Mrs. Bennet who had a number you left in case there was a problem with the children. I merely went from there." He pulled off on the access road, finally stopping before a dingy-looking gas station. "We don't have a lot of time," he said in an avuncular voice. "If you're going to change…"

Cassie was out of the car in seconds. He handed her a black plastic garment bag with the elegant gold lettering of La Place across the top left corner.

"There are some other things you might need in here," he added, handing her a paper sack. Cassie's eyes grew even larger. Love and Lingerie was imprinted on the plastic in huge red script. "You'd better hurry."

She scurried into the cubicle, mind whirling as she tried to imagine Jefferson Haddon III entering a shop called Love and Lingerie. It was unthinkable. Gingerly she opened the bag. There were stockings in it. The sheerest black stockings she had ever seen with elastic tops to hold them up.

Cassie slid out of her tattered hose and the ruined suit. Her Christmas blouse wasn't a total write-off; it would clean up nicely. Slowly, with anticipation, she slid the zipper down and stared at the contents of the black bag as her fingers lifted the hanger free. Cassie gasped as she spied the tag, bearing the name of a famous designer. An *expensive* famous designer.

An elegant heavy silk jacket with a full lining swished across her skin like velvet. It was cut in a straight, severe style that emphasized her slim figure. One solid gold button was the only bit of color in the deep rich black. That button and a host of hidden hooks and eyes held the jacket closed around her ample bosom. The skirt was designed in a straight slim cut that smoothed over her hips and fell just above her knee. It was a perfect fit, Cassie decided and the stockings made her feel pulled together, ready to face the world. She fluffed her hair, checked her makeup and stepped out of the bathroom with a swirl.

"You look great," Jeff complimented. He offered her a pair of not quite so high black leather heels and a matching handbag. "The saleslady said these would go with it," he murmured, glancing at her pale broken-heeled shoe. "I think they're the right size. I know they're not as high as you usually wear, but I thought…"

"They're perfect," she whispered hoarsely as the tears formed in her eyes. "I don't know how you had time to do all this, but thank you." She smiled tremulously at him, fingering the rich kid leather. "Thank you very much."

He grinned. "You're welcome." His eyes moved over her with a gleam that warmed Cassie's heart and made her blood tingle. He waved one hand toward his car. "Your chariot, madam."

As they sped down the highway, Cassie transferred her belongings to her new purse with wonder. How had this happened? she asked herself. She wore a designer suit, elegant silk stockings and handmade leather shoes all courtesy of the tall handsome man beside her.

"How do you come to know so much about women's clothes?" she asked curiously, delighting in the flush of red under his skin.

"I don't know anything about them," he answered distractedly, steering smoothly in and out of traffic. "I merely described you to the saleswoman, told her you were a very classy lady on a very important professional mission and asked her to give me something suitable."

"And the stockings?" she asked softly.

His face turned even redder, but he turned, just for a moment and looked directly into her eyes.

"I wanted something especially suitable to show off your legs," he admitted. His eyes fell to inspect her limbs. "And they certainly do a fine job." His voice was a caressing whisper and this time it was she who was blushing.

In a matter of minutes after that, they were driving up beside a tall, glass office building.

"This is the right place, isn't it?" he queried, staring at the bit of paper in his hand.

"Yes," Cassie replied, stepping from the car with a song of hope in her heart. She slid her work from the car and felt someone take it from her.

"I'm coming up with you," Jeff murmured in her ear. "Just to make sure you actually get there, this time."

"Oh. But you're double-parked," she observed, searching the depths of his darkly glowing eyes.

He shrugged. "Who cares?," he murmured as they entered the elevator with a host of other business types. "This is important."

In fact, he walked her right through the door and into the office of Ms. Mary Gaspard, senior editor for Malton's Publishing. And in front of Ms. Gaspard, her secretary and anyone else who cared to see, he kissed her full on the lips.

"You don't need good luck," he whispered. "Just go in there and show them who Cassandra Emily Haddon is. That oughta knock their socks off."

As she listened to the introductions Ms. Gaspard made five minutes later, Cassie's mind slipped back to that kiss.

Who was that man? she asked herself dizzily.

Chapter Fourteen

Cassie got in the elevator and walked out onto the main floor. Somehow. She wasn't aware of anything but the fact that she had just been offered a nice, juicy contract for a series of children's books to be presented to a host of booksellers countrywide.

"Lord," she said in amazement, "when you answer, you really answer."

The feeling of stunned confusion stayed with her as she was driven home with Bennet behind the wheel of her car, now polished to a high gloss with new tires on every wheel. It was hard to believe this car and her old putter were the same one. Even harder to believe Jeff's words as she related the good news later.

"I knew you could do it," he said smugly. "Now we're going to celebrate—really celebrate."

Cassie hesitated, caught off guard as she stared at the phone. "Tonight?" she questioned. "But it's a Monday."

Jeff laughed uproariously at that.

"What's wrong with Monday?" His voice changed, lowering as he murmured into the phone. "I'd really like to Cassie. But the thing is, I have to fly to London tonight. There's a client interested in taking a very lucrative deal with Bytes Inc. I've been working toward this for months now and it looks like it might finally be in the bag." He paused, speaking hesitantly after a few moments. "Are you upset?"

Cassie smiled. "Of course not," she said matter-of-factly. "After what you pulled off today, and the wonderful things you gave me, how could I be mad?"

"What about if we do something Saturday night?" he asked in coaxing undertones. "I should be back Friday and that will give us something to look forward to."

They agreed that it was a date and Cassie hung up, finally, with a grin. Life was getting pretty darn wonderful, she decided happily.

That evening David stopped by her room.

"Cassie you know that uh, tree house thing Jeff's building out back?"

Cassie nodded, wondering at the curious look on the boy's face. "Yes," she said uncertainly. "What about it?"

"It's a mess," he told her bluntly. "If a kid tries to play in that he's going to get really hurt. I went to look tonight and got caught on some of those nails he's so fond of." He showed her the six-inch tear in his sleeve and the red angry welt underneath. "I think we should tear it down."

Jeff's words came back to Cassie just then.

"He tore it down. Said it devalued the property."

"No, David, I don't think we can do that," she murmured. "He's very proud of his work."

"But Cassie…" David's voice died away at the odd look on her face. "You've got a plan, haven't you?"

"Sort of." She beamed up at him. David grinned as she patted his shoulder gently. "Don't worry, I'll look after it. Thanks for telling me."

The plan flew into her mind fully formed. She would have the thing rebuilt. Oh, not some grand edifice. If she could, she was going to have it redone exactly as he'd left it, only stronger. And when Jefferson Haddon the third returned from London he would celebrate with her there.

It was time, her whirling mind told her. A man who took

such tender care of her, bought his wife a suit like that, and made sure she got to her appointment on time had to care a little bit. And, of course, there *was* that kiss.

As she considered Jeff's mixed reactions to her over the past few months, Cassie felt sure he was coming to love her. She prayed it was so. She wanted his love more than anything and since God had brought them together, she was pretty sure Jeff would come to see that light soon, too.

But who would rebuild the tree house as she wanted? She contacted several firms. None of them were interested.

"Ma'am, if our name was associated with that... thing—" one burly contractor growled, jerking his thumb at the sorely built conflagration of boards "—our customers would cancel their house contracts, for sure."

Another claimed it would take too much time to remove everything and then reconnect it solidly.

"Much easier to rip the whole thing down and start from scratch," the man with the wizened old face told her sadly. "That mess wouldn't stand a winter breeze."

Cassie was considering that advice when the Haddons senior arrived for a visit. Mrs. Haddon looked tired, but much better than she had in the hospital. As they sat sipping their tea, Bennet came in.

"Excuse me miss, but I wanted to warn you to stay away from the creek." Cassie knew exactly what he was referring to when he inclined his head sideways. "Whole wall has caved in."

"I was afraid of that. Thank you, Bennet."

Jeffie, as she had come to think of Mr. Haddon, Senior, frowned.

"What wall?" he demanded, searching the interior house walls for imminent structural damage. "I thought Judith had kept the place up."

Cassie took a deep breath and launched into the story, pausing only to take a breath now and then.

"So you see, the tree house is important to him. I just wanted to get it sort of—" she shrugged wearily "—I don't know. Shored up, I guess."

Jeffie hustled to his feet.

"And that's exactly what we're going to do, Missy."

Cassie stared at him, frowning at the elated look on his face.

"What I meant was that I'll have to hire some knowledgeable person..." she began. And never finished.

"I am the best architect this side of the Pacific," he told her, chest puffed out proudly. "And I've got the company to prove it. I can design and rebuild anything you want. Just point me to the place."

Cassie's mouth formed a round, startled 0. "Haddon and Son," she murmured at last. "I'd forgotten all about that." She wondered how to explain this latest rejection of his help.

"I'm sorry, Jeffie, but I don't think that would be a good idea. You see, this was Jeff's baby...his scheme to make a place for the younger kids to come and be out of everybody's hair." She lowered her voice, keeping her gaze on his tanned face. "Apparently it's something of a dream with him. From the time he was a small child."

Jeff senior's face fell as he remembered. He nodded finally.

"Yes," he said regretfully. "I remember that thing." Suddenly he grinned. "Sounds like his ability hasn't improved much." He chuckled. His eyes widened with excitement. "I could do it," he offered raggedly. "I could redo it and he'd never have to know."

"I don't think..."

"Don't think about it, Cassie. Just think about him out there with the kids, having a whale of a time. Oh, please," he begged. "Let me do this one thing for my son. Something I should have done a long time ago."

His face had such a wistful look about it as he told her how rudely he'd had Jeff's dream removed all those years ago. Cassie felt herself giving in long before she said the words.

"All right, all right." She held up her hands at last. "I give up. If you can rebuild the thing so it will be safe and yet make it look like his work, I'll agree. But," she added softly, glancing from him to his wife. "Jeff can never know. I don't think he would appreciate my meddling."

"It'll be wonderful," Jeffie, Sr. crowed, waving his hands madly. "It'll be our little secret." He bent over a piece of paper, drawing madly as he muttered to himself.

Later Cassie left him still muttering, in disbelief this time, as he stared at the mess.

"Hard to believe he comes from a long line of architectural designers," she heard him huff as he tugged away one board after the other, pausing only to write something in his little book.

He worked all day Tuesday and Wednesday, too. On Thursday she was invited to take a look at coffee time.

"It's fantastic," she told him, stomping and pushing for all she was worth. Nothing, not a single board moved. The general work site was just as Jeff had left it last weekend; as if nothing had been touched.

"I can't believe you did this," she told Jeffie, wide-eyed with amazement as she sat inside staring out. "It's perfect." She handed him some coffee in a foam cup.

"It's a long way from perfect." He grinned. "But you can't tell where his work ends and mine begins, I'll give you that." He sank down beside her, laying his hammer aside as he sipped thankfully at the cup. "This is really good coffee." He shook his head, grinning. "Jefferson never serves a decent cup. Always kind of watered down."

Cassie grinned right back at him as she thought about what she would paint on the outside. Considering her sudden success and his part in it, she decided that a dinosaur was indeed appropriate. On Friday she started the project, praying that the forecasted rains would hold off until long after she and Jeff had shared an evening to remember in the tree house.

She had it all planned out and thankfully, the household numbers were back to her, David and Marie by Saturday afternoon when Jeff finally arrived. This was one date she had no intention of sharing.

"I'm sorry," he told her ruefully, kissing her mouth quickly as he came in the door. "I got held up at the last minute and couldn't get free to phone. But it was worth it!" He grinned from ear to ear as he held up his briefcase. "I've got a contract signed, sealed and delivered that will keep Bytes Inc. in the black for a long time."

"Good." Cassie smiled. "Then we can celebrate that, too. Come on, get changed. We're going to have a picnic in the tree house. Just the two of us."

His eyebrows raised at that but only for a second before he frowned.

"Cassie, about that tree house," he began, pulling his tie free. "I'm not sure we should..."

"Oh, come on, Jeff," she encouraged. "Even big business tycoons like you have to slow down once in a while. Besides—" she smiled brightly "—I want you to see what I've painted on it." And not see what your father has done, she added silently.

He was ready at last; wearing a brand-new pair of designer jeans, she noticed ruefully and a silk and linen blend shirt. Oh, well! Not even that was going to spoil tonight, she decided. This was the night she would tell Jefferson Haddon how much she loved him; how much she wanted him in her life.

The light was beginning to fade when they reached the tree house. Here and there through the canopy of newly leafed oak trees overhead, a bit of daylight poked through. It was exactly the right setting for a dinosaur.

"This is fantastic," he declared, touching the wall gingerly. When it stayed in place, his whole face lit up. "It must have been the nails," he murmured to himself. His finger ran down the dips and peaks of the dinosaur's back until he was tracing the puff of smoke that led to the entrance.

"I'm not sure these steps..." His voice died away as she bounded up inside.

"Come on in," she coaxed, pleased with his surprised expression, and watched eagerly as he took in all of her work. It had been a labor of love and Cassie had spared no effort.

Here and there wild animals could be seen. Her favorite was the perky little squirrel whose head rose above the crack between boards, making it appear that he had just popped out of the tree she'd sketched in. Huge vivid green leaves and vines covered the inside walls, a tree branch visible here and there. She heaved a sigh of relief at his words.

"This is wonderful, Cassie. A perfect retreat for kids."

"Sit down," she urged, motioning to the disreputable old cushions she had retrieved from the house. She sank onto one herself. Cassie had nailed a piece of board onto a section of tree trunk he'd left behind and that was their table. Carefully she lit the assortment of candles she had arranged earlier and pointed to the covered trays.

"Your dinner, sir," she murmured softly and lifted the salver on six, plump juicy wieners nestled into buns. "I tried to keep the meal appropriate to the setting," she told him, winking.

The usual condiments stood nearby as did two cans of pop and a bowl of chips. With a flick of her wrist she had poured the ginger ale into two stemmed glasses and held one out.

"To success," she cheered, tinkling her glass against his. "Yours and mine."

"To success," he agreed and sipped the "champagne" thoughtfully. They munched away contentedly and as they ate, Jeff told her about his trip. Cassie, in turn, told him about her week.

"And I'm hard at work to meet that deadline," she concluded. She stared up at him happily. "Isn't *deadline* a wonderful word?" She grinned.

Jeff eased the table away and placed a companionable arm around her shoulders as they sat leaning against the wall, sipping their drinks.

"It's a wonderful world," he concurred thoughtfully. His eyes cast around for one more look as the flickering candles created scary shadows on the wall. "And so is this." She felt his arm tighten around her meaningfully.

"Wouldn't it be wonderful to watch our own children playing here, telling scary stories and having high tea?" She felt his lips move smoothly across her neck. "They might even want to sleep out here. There's lots of room."

"Yes, lots," Cassie agreed, wrapping her arms around his neck and kissing him back with fervor. He kissed her hungrily, like a man who was starving and couldn't get enough of the delectable taste of her lips. His fingers massaged the tender flesh on her upper arms, smoothing over it with gentleness.

"I want you, Cassandra," he growled low in his throat, his lips playing with hers. "I want to make love to you…to create a child with you and watch it growing inside your body. I want to share with you all the things a man and a woman can share." His lips closed over her coaxingly. "Cassie?" His voice was a soft murmur.

"I want you, too, Jeff," she whispered in the stillness of their hideaway. "I want to stay with you forever."

"Thank heaven," he whispered fervently. "All I could think about this past week was how fantastic you looked in that outfit on Monday." He groaned into her mouth. "And those legs!"

Cassie shifted a bit, wanting his arms all the way around her now. And Jeff moved, too. Not much, just a little to stretch his long legs out.

"Ow," he yelped suddenly, sitting up to rub his leg.

"What's the matter?" Cassie asked while her body hummed "not now, not now!"

"There's something sharp here in the corner. I'll just move it. You might hurt…" His voice died away as he stared down at the silver-headed hammer in his hands. "How did this get here?" he demanded.

Cassie stared at it. "I don't know." She pointed to the JWH inscribed on the wooden handle. "It must be yours. It's got your initials." She slid a little nearer, brushing one hand over his chest. "Forget about it. Think of something else," she whispered in her best Mae West voice.

Jeff pushed her away roughly and stood to his feet, towering over her in the dim light.

"I can't forget it," he said harshly. "It's my father's. Rory and I gave it to him years ago." He stared down at her and when he spoke his voice was full of bitter recrimination.

"What was my father doing here, Cassie?"

Cassie swallowed the lump of fear in her throat and tried to ignore the panic that was rising. She stood slowly, grateful for his helping hand, unforgiving though it was.

"He wanted to help with the surprise," she told him softly.

"Help? How? By rebuilding this place?" His fist smashed against the wall in fury. "By redoing what his *useless* son couldn't? By building a tree house that would stay in one place?" He glared at her. "That's what he said, you know. I was useless because I couldn't draw a straight line let alone draft the plans for an apartment complex."

"Oh, Jeff, you're not useless." Cassie slid her arm through his. "You merely have different specialities. You're a master at what you do."

He knocked her hand away roughly.

"Don't ever patronize me, Cassandra. I warned you that I wanted nothing to do with my father. I've told you time and again and yet still you use him against me."

Cassie was aghast. Never had she dreamed he would be so hurt by her actions.

"I only wanted to make it a special place for you and me." She sighed sadly. "I wanted a place where we could be alone for once." She took her courage in both hands and stared up at him with her heart in her eyes.

"I wanted a chance to tell you that I love you," she whispered. "And since I wanted it to be private and David and Marie are up at the house, the only other place I could think to be alone was here." She threaded her hands together in confusion. "I do love you, Jeff. More and more each day. I love the way you're always there for me, cheering me on."

"Then couldn't you have thought to do the same for me, if you love me as you claim," His eyes were cold hard rocks that bit at her with indignation. "Don't you think you might have offered me the slightest courtesy in your so-called love and not have deliberately ignored my feelings about him?"

"Jeff," she pleaded, tears welling in her eyes. "He's your father. He loves you, as I do. He knows he made a mistake but he wants to get past that and try to make amends. That's the way families work." She dashed the tears from her eyes and continued.

"Families are at the root of our society because that's what holds people together, bonds them. Families love each other, no matter what. They don't bail out on one another and they don't quit."

He laughed harshly.

"Heaven spare me all this love claptrap," he snarled, gripping her arms. "I don't want it and I don't need it. What I do want is someone who will understand that I don't need anyone messing up my life with old history. Dead history." He whirled away to the steps but before he could descend them, Cassie stopped him.

"Yes, you do, Jeff. You need us all and if you keep turning your back on everyone who reaches out to you, it's going to be too late for both you and your mother." She covered her mouth as soon as the words escaped but it was too late. He had already heard.

His hands gripped her arms, propelling her backward until she was pressed up against the wall.

"What do you mean, too late for my mother?" he enunciated in a cold, hard voice. When she didn't answer his face dropped nearer hers. "How do you know anything about my mother?" he shouted angrily. Cassie made the decision in a split second.

"I've been visiting her since Christmas. Your mother is sick, Jeff. She's having chemotherapy treatments. The doctors are hopeful but her attitude isn't conducive to healing. She may not have too much longer.''

Jeff's face hardened as she watched, into a bitter, angry inscrutable mask. He let her go and stepped away.

"I trusted you, Cassie," he whispered hoarsely. "I thought you were on my side—that we were a team. And now you go behind my back and become one of them. How could you?" he uttered through clenched teeth. "How could you go and let them come here, into my home? How could you betray me like that?"

With her heart aching inside Cassie stepped nearer and cupped his face in her hands, forcing him to meet her gaze.

"I could do it," she whispered softly, praying that he would hear the words. "I could do it because I love you more than anything and I want you to be whole. I want you to forgive and forget and move into the future with me. Help me build something we can share together, Jeff. Something beautiful, not something full of hate.''

His dark eyes searched hers, blazing into their depths with a scrutiny that rocked her to her soul. They were full of pain and hurt and anger. And something else. Something that tugged at her heartstrings and ached to hold his head to her breast as she reassured him over and over. When at long last, he pulled away, his eyes were dull, lifeless.

"You can keep your so-called love, Cassandra," he said with a measured tone. "It can't fix things this time. I could have used it thirty years ago but it's too late now. I don't need it or you. I don't need anybody." With a lunge he slammed down the steps, dropping the hammer to the floor.

"Yes, you do, Jeff," she murmured sadly, long after he had departed. "You need all of us. More than ever. You just don't know it yet."

And there in the tree house, she sank to her knees and cried out a prayer for him. For both of them.

Chapter Fifteen

Cassie stared morosely at the official document in front of her. Finally, at long last, the words penetrated her almost inactive state of consciousness.

"Oh, no," she whispered in disbelief. "Not now."

"What, not now?" Jeff frowned across the table at her, gulping down a quick cup of coffee as he did every morning now in order to avoid talking to her. When she didn't answer, his long fingers snatched the papers out of her hands. "The court hearing for David and Marie's adoptions."

"Are you still okay with that?" she questioned in a tight voice. Tears burned her eyes as he stared down at her with contempt.

"Unlike some people, Cassandra, I do keep my promises. You made it part of our agreement that I adopt them and I will honor that agreement." His eyes were chips of black onyx as he stared down at her. "Just remember what you promised," he warned finally. "Because I am holding you to it. I still want my own son."

Tears welled in her eyes as he left, closing the front door softly behind him. The pain in his eyes hurt her far more than anything he could say. And it was that pain that made her reconsider the future. A cold dark future without love. A future of fulfilling her rash agreement to give him a child.

Jeff complained all the way into Toronto, even though there was no one to hear him. And he was still fuming when his brother called just before noon.

"What did you do to Cassie?" Rory demanded belligerently. "I just tried to invite her for Dad's birthday dinner tonight and she started blubbering all over the place."

"Maybe she just doesn't like birthdays." Jeff grimaced, hating himself for the sniping response, but feeling fully justified.

"That's baloney and you know it. Cass loves people and she and Dad have been spending a lot of time talking recently...." His voice died away.

"I already know about it." Jeff smiled bitterly. "He would try to enlist her in his campaign," he muttered angrily.

"What campaign?" Rory demanded.

"The one that gets me to join in on this big happy family malarkey," Jeff said in a tight voice. "To pretend that the past never happened."

There was a long silence, then Rory came back on the line, his voice brisk.

"I have to go, Jefferson. I've got a big client on the other line. Seems the electrician goofed. I'll see you at one. At Taylors."

"Wait a minute, Rory," Jeff protested. But his little brother had hung up. "Taylors," he muttered angrily. "Like I need a six-course lunch today." But Jeff went anyway. Just to hear what Rory had to say. His brother was pretty blunt.

"Look, Jefferson, you're wasting your life with this stupid feud. And you're hurting a lot of people besides."

"I'm not trying to hurt anyone. And it's not a feud. I just choose not to get involved in this unrealistic pipe dream you and Cassie have that my father and I could ever be soul mates."

Rory studied him seriously.

"He doesn't believe that, either, Jefferson. He just wants a chance to apologize for the past. And to try to make amends."

Jeff couldn't believe what he had just heard.

"I don't expect Cassie to understand," he said in a tightly controlled voice, glaring at his brother. "She wasn't there. But you were. You know how he treated us—the ranting, the drinking, the misery. How can you sit there and pretend life was rosy when it was the furthest thing from that? How can he make amends for that hellish childhood?"

Jeff stared at Rory, unable to forgive his brother's betrayal. He had been there, for Pete's sake. He'd suffered the same things. How could he just let it all go without a word?

"Jeff." Rory was using the shortened version of his name. It sounded right, Jeff decided, because it made him seem a different person than that sad, needy little boy. "I know you're hurting. And I know that you think that Dad's neglect of us was unforgivable. But that's exactly what you have to do."

Jeff snorted. "Yeah, right. Like I can forgive him for publicly disowning me the day he said he didn't know who I was. And just wipe the slate clean for the time he left me behind because I wasn't in the car at the appointed hour." He glared bitterly at the silver place settings. "Was it so easy for you to forget about the toys Aunt Judith sent? He took them away, Rory. He took them and right in front of our noses, he gave them to his friends. Laughing as he said we didn't deserve them. No," he exploded. "I can't forget that. Don't ask me to."

"All right," Rory murmured at last, his face drawn and sad. "Hang on to it, then. Nurture it inside of you where it can fester and grow and eat away at the rest of your life. It will ruin your relationship with Cassie, though," he warned sadly. "Bitterness and hate have a way of penetrating through to everything we do. It's already ruining your chances to make amends with Mom before she dies."

Jeff glared at him. "I suppose that's my fault, too," he snapped.

Rory rose to his feet with disgust, tossing his linen napkin on the table.

"No, stupid. It's your opportunity."

"To do what?" Jeff demanded.

"To move ahead. To let the past go. Everybody makes mistakes, Jeff. Mom. Dad. Even you. We acknowledge them and then we try to do better. It's called life. Don't waste any more of it."

As he left the restaurant Jeff thought how alone he was. Even his own brother had turned on him. It was even more important now that he have his son.

He'd show them.

He'd show them all that he could be a far better father than the example he'd had.

Cassie sat in the solemn stillness of the courtroom holding her breath. It didn't seem right, somehow. She and Jeff were sitting here side by side, pretending that they were this happy couple, only too anxious to adopt these two children, when Cassie knew that Jeff had only agreed because of their marriage contract.

Just this morning she had given him an escape route once more.

"If you don't want David and Marie as your legal children," she had said quietly, "I won't hold you to that promise. I don't want you to adopt them because of some agreement. I want you to adopt them because you want to be their father."

Jeff had merely raised one mocking eyebrow. "It's a little late to change your mind, Cassandra," he had replied before leaving the room.

"Order in the court."

Cassie jerked to attention, noticing that their judge was

a tall, stately woman with silver-gray hair. She smiled at everyone as she began to relate the purpose for the hearing.

"I know Mrs. Haddon's record with children very well," Judge Pender told them easily. "And I realize that Oak Bluff has been a sanctuary to a number of needy children. I commend those efforts." She nodded her head at Cassie, who felt even more like a fraud.

"What I want to hear this morning is the opinions of the minors in this case, Marie and David. I want to know why they want to make their home permanently with Mr. and Mrs. Haddon. Marie, will you come over here and tell me?"

Marie stood up slowly and walked over to the chair beside the judge. Her fingers twisted the edge of her sweater nervously as she sat down.

"Well," she began softly, her voice betraying an anxious tremble. "I want to stay and be part of their family because I'm a real person there." She glanced up at Judge Pender, who merely nodded her silver head. "You see, Cassie doesn't care about things, like if I mess up her dinner party. And Jeff ate those horrible pork chops anyway because he didn't want to hurt my feelings." The story was slightly convoluted in the telling, but the judge nodded understandingly.

Marie stared at her feet for a moment before continuing.

"It's like you can just be whoever you are there. You don't have to be perfect or pretend you're happy when you're not or agree with everything they say."

"You mean there are no rules?" the judge asked quietly, writing something in her book. Cassie held her breath as Marie continued, praying the young girl would explain clearly.

Marie grinned. "Oh, there are rules," she said laughing. "And if you break them, you are responsible. I should know." She giggled. "I tried them out enough times at first. But even if you do something wrong, Cassie doesn't think you are bad. You just made a mistake and she hopes you'll do better next time."

"Do you and the Haddons ever disagree over things?" Judge Pender questioned next.

Marie's brow furrowed. "Well, Cassie doesn't think I should get engaged to my boyfriend right away. She wants me to finish school and go to university and stuff so I'll see more of the world."

"And what do you think?"

"I think I'm going to marry him anyway eventually. But I guess it's a good idea to be sure." A big smile lit her young face.

"You keep talking about Mrs. Haddon. Is Mr. Haddon not around very much?"

"Oh, Jeff's there whenever we need him. He has this big company to run, of course. And that takes a lot of time."

Cassie felt Jeff shift uneasily beside her.

"So he's mostly pretty busy?" The judge was frowning now, noting another series of scribbles on her pad.

"Yeah, he's really busy. But when I was sick, I called him from school one day and he came right away and took me home. I think he was in a meeting or something, but when I asked him, he said it didn't matter. That I was more important and business could wait."

Cassie frowned. How was it that she hadn't heard anything about this? she wondered.

"Nate, told me—" Marie broke off and grinned at the judge. "Nate's my boyfriend. Well, he told me that Jeff had a talk with him one time and sort of laid down the law. Nate was kinda ticked but I thought it was really nice of Jeff to worry about my boyfriend."

"I see." Judge Pender looked up from her notepad to study the man in question. Cassie felt as if her heart had stopped suddenly. There was a huge pressure building in her chest that demanded release. It hurt to hear all these things about Jeff and know that he had only done them out of a sense of duty. How she wished it could have been different.

"David, I would like you to come here, too, please."

David sauntered up, flopping down in his chair easily. "What do you think about being adopted?" the judge asked.

"It's okay," David muttered finally.

"You don't want to be adopted by the Haddons?" The judge's tone was perplexed. "Why not?"

"It's not that I don't want to be," David said blithely. "But what difference would it make? Jeff's already my dad. At least—" he grinned at Jeff "—that's what I call him now."

"I take it that you and Jeff get along pretty well?" The judge had a funny look on her face that Cassie couldn't discern.

"Well, most of the time." David grimaced. "He can be pretty stubborn but he listens to what I have to say."

"And Mrs. Haddon?"

David beamed. "Oh, she's great. Where I was before, the lady made me call her Mom. I hated that because she wasn't my mom. My mom died." His voice had faded away to a soft murmur. When he looked up, Cassie could see the hint of tears in his eyes.

"Cassie isn't like that," he said stoutly. "It's like it doesn't matter as long as you're comfortable. You know," he leaned forward to face the judge. "I think a person could do just about anything and they'd still love you."

"It's a good place to live then?"

"The best," David agreed. "They really care about each other and about us. Like my dad," he said the words proudly. "He built this tree house for when the little kids come. Or something. Anyway—" David grinned saucily, shaking his head "—it was a real mess. I mean, he tried but the guy's lousy with a hammer. Sorry, Dad, but you are."

Cassie heard Jeff murmur, "That's okay. It was pretty bad."

"Yeah, well anyway, Cassie wanted that tree house to stay there but pieces of it kept hurting people. One day Bennet got hit by a board that fell on him. He made me promise not to tell anybody. Gosh, I hope I don't get him in trouble.''

Just another little thing she'd missed. Cassie grimaced ruefully.

"Cassie phoned all over trying to get somebody to re-build it but stronger, so when the little kids came again they could go there and not get hurt. But she wanted it to look like Jeff had made it, see, and nobody wanted to do that. Know what I mean?''

He looked at the judge to see if she had followed. When she nodded, he continued.

"Finally she got Jeff's dad to help her and he took it all apart and put it back just like she wanted. I even helped a bit. That's what I mean. It was just because she loved him that she did it. She didn't want him to find out, she just wanted him to use it with the little kids. Jeff really loves little kids; almost as much as he loves Cassie,'' David told Judge Pender softly.

"They really do love each other a lot,'' Marie added. "You can see it in their eyes when they look at each other. Jeff tries to pretend he's not watching her when Cassie's drawing and she stares at him all the time. And they are always touching each other. And they're like there for the other one when things get bad. I've seen Jeff get this look on his face sometimes that makes me feel kind of, I don't know, special. I think that's the kind of look I want Nate to have when he looks at me.''

The room was silent as they all watched the solemn-faced woman write down a few more phrases.

"And do Jeff and Cassie love you two?'' she asked.

Cassie flinched, wondering how the kids would answer. Everything was so important; each word they said would determine their future. Let them say the right things, she prayed softly, closing her eyes. They flew open when Jeff's hand wrapped comfortingly around hers and she felt the strength he was lending her.

"Yes,'' they answered in unison, with no hesitation.

"How do you know? Do they buy you lots of stuff or get you neat things or what?"

"Well, we did get some really nice things for Christmas," Marie offered. "But that's not what tells you if someone loves you and cares about you."

The judge smiled. "What does then, Marie?" she asked quietly.

"It's more the way they act around you," she replied hesitantly. "Like Cassie showing me how to use makeup even though I ruined her lipstick and eye shadow. And Jeff showing me how to use his new computer game that he designed for some big company. That was cool!" She grinned happily. "And he didn't have a fit when one of the kids knocked him out with a snowball, either. He just got up and went on with things."

"And like my driving lessons." David glanced at Cassie with a grin. "I got to drive his car a little bit each day after I got my learner's. Some of the guys can't do that, you know. They have to take lessons from the driver ed people."

"Don't you want lessons?" the judge asked curiously.

"Oh, yeah! But by then I won't be so uptight. I'll know a little bit to start with and the other kids won't make fun of me. I was pretty bad at first," he admitted, frowning.

Cassie wiped away the tears at the look of relief on the young boy's face. She hadn't known about that, either. What was the matter with her?

"And when all the other kids came to our house, Cassie let me have my own room. That felt really...I don't know. Kinda special. Like I was important enough to rate my own private place."

"Thank you very much, David and Marie," the judge said. "You've helped make this decision much easier. You can sit down."

When they had returned to their seats, Judge Pender snapped her notes together and laid them flat on the desk. She stared out at them for a moment before speaking.

"In my work I have seen many families in all sorts of

conditions," she told them thoughtfully. "And always, it is the families that have a care and regard for one another that survive the tough times. I see that here." She smiled.

"David and Marie want to be part of the Haddons' family because they can see and feel the love and regard that is present between Mr. and Mrs. Haddon. It's a love that includes rather than excludes. Mr. Haddon has shown a nurturance and care for these children that I hadn't expected given his unfamiliarity with children. Mrs. Haddon has continued the excellent care she has always shown to children under her roof. I commend them both for their careful handling in such a situation and find no reason why David and Marie should not be legally adopted by them after a period of not more than sixty days, making them and the Haddons a family."

The judge gathered her documents together before glancing down at the group of people gathered before her. Cassie felt like a fraud as she listened to the words.

"A strong, loving marriage is always the best basis for children to be nurtured in. Often, in our society, our children have less than optimum conditions during the most formative years of their lives. They emerge as bitter, hardened adults who cannot allow themselves to forget the past and care deeply for another human being, or to accept the love offered to them. You have opened your hearts and your home to David and Marie and others, without reservation. May God bless you for your efforts. We are better for it."

It was a moving tribute that was totally undeserved. As she left Jeff outside the courthouse and drove the children home, Cassie felt the sting of tears prick her eyelids. It would have been so wonderful if it had been true; if only Jeff loved her even half as much as she loved him.

Cassie wanted nothing so much as to lock herself in her room and give way to the misery that held her in its grip. She ignored the happy whispers coming from the back seat as she contemplated the future. Everything seemed so futile now. All her dreams of a happy family at Oak Bluff were just that—unrealistic dreams, illusions. It was time to face reality. She had agreed to a loveless marriage with a man she loved more deeply than her own life. She would soon be the mother of these two teenagers who had based their future plans on her hopes and dreams.

How would she endure it?

"Cassie?" It was Marie looking apologetic, except for the tiny sparkle at the corners of her eyes. "I forgot that my geometry set broke yesterday and I have to have another for class tomorrow. Could you possibly drop us off and then pick one up?"

"Why don't we all go," Cassie suggested. "We could have a drink or something to celebrate."

"Uh, no, thanks. I've got a chemistry test tomorrow and I have to memorize formulas." Marie's face flushed a bright red. "You know how much I hate chemistry. I've just got to study."

Actually, Cassie had always thought Marie found her subjects rather easy, but then she'd been missing a lot lately. This was just another thing to add to the list.

"Yeah," David said quickly. "Uh, me, too. I mean I have to work on my English paper. Again."

Cassie frowned. "Didn't you finish that last week?" she asked curiously.

"Um, no. That is, this is another one." He stumbled out the door without looking at her and then turned back. "Oh, by the way," he added. "Dad said he'll be a little late. And not to make anything for supper. He's ordered pizza, or something, I think. To celebrate."

"Fine." A celebration. Great, just great. In slow motion, Cassie put the car into gear. "See you later then," she muttered.

"Yeah. Later." David and Marie scurried into the house without a backward glance.

As she drove down the road watching the sun slowly

sink behind the ridge of trees in the west, Cassie swallowed her tears.

There's no time to cry, she told herself sternly. You've gotten exactly what you wanted. Haven't you?

Chapter Sixteen

The entire house was lit up like a Christmas tree when Cassie finally arrived home after scouring the stores for a geometry set. This late in the season, no one seemed to carry much in the way of school supplies in the local drugstore.

Searching for some enthusiasm, she walked up the path to the front door, starting backward when it was flung open.

"Cassandra! Where have you been? Where are the kids?"

Jeff stared at her with a strange look on his face as Cassie moved past him to toss her jacket on a nearby chair. She pushed the heavy fall of hair back off her face and turned to look at him, emotions held in check. For the moment.

"They were here when I left," she told him, walking through the dining room and jerking to a halt. "What is this?"

There was a trio of three uniformed waiters standing behind an elegantly set table of Judith's best crystal, silver and china.

Jeff studied her with a thoughtful frown.

"I thought you'd ordered it. David said you had something special planned tonight and not to be late."

"He told me you were bringing pizza," she told him, smiling bitterly at the irony of the situation.

"What's so funny?" he asked pointedly.

"It's obviously an attempt to give us some privacy," she answered. "They're not here, are they?"

"No, but..."

"Dinner is served, sir. Whenever you are ready."

They both turned to gape at the tall white-gloved man who stood behind them. Jeff searched Cassie's face with a questioning glance and she shrugged.

"Why not?" she murmured. "It saves me making dinner."

The big, brilliant chandelier was switched off. Instead, a huge silver candelabra with many candles gave off a golden glow in the room, faintly accenting the rose centerpiece.

"Marie," they said together.

Jeff grinned at her. "She alone could cause a rise in candle stocks!"

Soft stringed music played in the background sending out the smooth mellow tones of a romantic ballad. Cassie studied her food with bitterness. There was no love for her here. Not for her. It was just a pipe dream she'd had.

The food was elegantly served and should have been delicious. Cornish game hens in a mandarin cherry sauce with wild rice and tiny peas; it was a dish she'd enjoyed before. But tonight everything tasted like sawdust including her favorite key lime dessert.

When the last dish was finally removed and the coffee poured, Cassie breathed a sigh of relief. The tension was killing her. Jeff hadn't said two words in the last five minutes and she couldn't think of anything else to break the long silence between them.

"Is there anything we can get for you, sir? Madam?" Their waiter stood, smiling benignly at them as if he couldn't feel the stress tangible in the rose-scented room.

"No, that's everything. Thank you very much." Jeff handed the man a tip which was refused.

"Oh, no, sir. Everything's been taken care of."

Jeff frowned. "It has? How?"

"Everything was arranged by telephone and credit card. We appreciate it, sir. You've been very generous."

Jeff groaned. "*My* credit card, I'll bet," he muttered. "I gave it to David when he went on that trip. Just in case there was an emergency." He frowned. "I never got it back."

"Sorry," Cassie apologized bitterly. "Just another little side effect of raising children. My fault. Sorry."

Jeff frowned at her, hands thrust deep in his pockets as he watched the caterers move out through the front door.

"I didn't mean that," he said, inclining his head. "I was just..."

"I'm going to drink my coffee in the family room," she mumbled, cutting him off.

He followed along behind like a meek little puppy, Cassie thought grimly. As if he were afraid she didn't know where to go or something. The sofa closed around her tired body like an eiderdown and she laid her head back on the seat with relief.

"It was a tense day, wasn't it?" Jeff began, coming behind her to massage the tight cords on her neck. "But, in a way, I'm glad it's over. Finally settled." She felt his lips against her throat and jerked away.

"Cassie..." He paused, thoughtfully studying her face as he walked around the sofa and sank down beside her. "That judge gave me some things to think about today. I wanted to tell you..."

"Yeah," she snapped. "Me, too." The sadness of their situation overwhelmed her like a tidal wave swamping her with the futility of pretending any longer. She had everything: the home she'd always wanted, a husband whom she loved more than anyone could imagine and two wonderful children.

She had far less than she had ever dreamed, Cassie realized. Because without Jeff's love, the house, the kids...they were just dreams. Idle dreams.

"I can't do this anymore," she whispered, the tears

coursing down her cheeks. "I love you more than anything, Jeff, but I can't adopt those children. I can't pretend to be your wife when you won't let me in…not really into your life."

She let all the pain and hurt flow out like a river bursting its banks. Nothing could stop it.

"I'm not your wife, Jeff. You want some glamorous society woman like that Melisande who can put on fancy dinners and dine at elegant restaurants and shoot the breeze with the best of them. And that's not me," she wailed.

"Cassie, if you'd just let me explain…."

She ignored him. "I'm not the wonder woman the kids think I am, either. I'm not strong. I need somebody to lean on—someone to talk over the hard parts with and help me deal with the kids who need so much help. I don't even know half of what's going on with Marie and David." She sobbed the words out. "They've gone to you when I should have been there."

Cassie stared at him through her tears and acknowledged her defeat.

"It isn't right," she admitted at last. "We can't bring another child into all these problems. I can't ever be the mother of that son you want so desperately, Jeff. I can't, I won't do that to a child." The words were harsh and full of pain.

When she jumped up to race out of the room, Jeff caught her arm. He pulled her tightly against him, burying his face in her hair.

"Cassie," he groaned, holding her close. "You already are the mother of my son. The judge said so today. And if David and Marie are the only children we ever have, we will be the luckiest parents in this world."

She glared up at him tearfully, pushing away as she did so.

"No, we won't. Because those kids need love—all that they can get. They need parents who are committed to their family, close and extended. I want my children to grow up in a circle of love. I want them to hear the old family tales and feel the bonds of love that knit us all together." She stared down at her hands miserably. "But you can't forget the pain in your past."

Cassie didn't dare look at him. She knew the loathing that she'd find on his face as soon as she mentioned his father.

"I thought God led me here," she whispered. "I thought I was following his will when Judith left the house to both of us. I thought that eventually you'd understand how much family means to me." She paused and then said it. "Eventually, I thought, you'd come to love me, too."

She did look at him then. A piercing scrutiny that told her more than any words could how wrong she had been.

"God didn't lead me here," she whispered sadly. "I just wanted it so badly, I thought He did, too. But wishing and hoping can't make it so."

She turned to leave the room as fresh tears cascaded down her cheeks.

"Sit down, Cassandra." Jeff's voice was soft but firm as he tugged on her arm. "I have something I want to say."

"You don't have to," she began, but he ignored her.

"I came here six months ago, after my aunt died, full of anger that she would dare to manipulate me. And then I got to know you. That was an eye-opener!" He grinned at her.

Cassie sank back onto the sofa, unnerved by the look on his face.

"You didn't take those kids into your heart and love them because you were supposed to. Or because someone said you had to. Or even because you would benefit from them. You took kids in and cared for them, loved them, and then sent them back home because it was the right thing for you to do. And you stuck to that, no matter what obstacles I put in your way.

"I admired that, Cassie. And I've seen the difference it makes, that love of yours. I've watched the children come and go and they never left here the same. Each one of them took away the knowledge that he held a special place in your heart. And gradually I came to realize that what you were so freely doling out to everyone else, was exactly what I had always wanted. To belong, to matter."

Jeff slipped to his knees and grasped her hands with his, staring straight into her eyes with a light of wonder in his face.

"I was so jealous of your childhood. You had all the things I wanted and never had. And here you were, transplanted to Judith's and you made your own little world again. The people at the church, the kids that came and went, the agency people. They were like one big happy family to you and I thought, 'At last! This will be my own special little corner of the world.' And I began to enjoy the kids. Then you started harping on my dad."

He stopped and swallowed, obviously organizing his thoughts.

"And every time his name would come up, so would the word *love*." He grimaced. "I began to hate the sound of that word. And yet, somehow, I knew it was exactly what I wanted—what I had to have."

Jeff smiled sadly, fingering the beautiful rings he had given her.

"I was head over heels in love with you at Christmas and more than anything I wanted to make our marriage a living and breathing partnership. But I just couldn't swallow the hate that I felt for my parents. You, sitting there, laughing and joking with them made it worse. I felt like you had taken their side."

"Oh, Jeff," Cassie murmured, tightening her fingers. "They can never make up for the past, although they will spend the rest of their lives trying to get you to see that."

"I went to see them today, Cassie. After the court hearing." He flushed a dull red as he stared at their entwined hands. "Something the judge said got to me and I realized that the only reason I didn't have a family wasn't because God had given me a rotten one. It was because I had pushed them away."

He kissed her lightly. "I'm not doing that anymore, Cassie. I'm not pushing my parents or you away ever again. It will take awhile for my family to work out our differences, but we've made a start this afternoon.''

His eyes, huge and melting, met hers and searched their emerald depths for an answer.

''What I need to know now is whether you'll help me? I love you more than anything in the world. I don't care about Judith's money or the estate or anything but you. You're the most important thing in my life.''

''But, Jeff, I'm not at all the type of wife you need. I can't bake, I'm no good at society things. I certainly won't be an asset to your business. And I can't guarantee that I'll have that son you want.''

He kissed her then, full on the lips, with all the fervor she could ever have asked for. And when she was breathless and only wanting more, he cupped her face in his hands.

''Cassandra Emily Newton Haddon, you are the only person I will ever need and you're exactly the woman I need to teach me about love. I'm only beginning to understand the meaning of that word, but I know that you are a master at loving. You've proven it over and over. It doesn't matter about children. Not anymore. There are more than enough kids in the world to care for. Besides—'' he grinned happily ''—I'm already a parent to the two most wonderful kids in the world. David and Marie are the perfect additions to our family. If God sends us more, fine. But if not, can't we be happy with what we have?''

Cassie gazed at him with love shining out from her happy face. God had promised and He had more than fulfilled her dreams. Her heart sang His praise.

''Cassie, why don't you say something?'' Jeff was peering at her worriedly. ''Didn't you mean what you said about loving me? Were you just saying it?'' He swallowed and straightened his shoulders. ''It doesn't matter, you know. We can still build something beautiful if you'll just say you care for me at least a little, that you'll stay with me.''

Cassie placed a finger over his lips to silence him. As he kneeled there in front of her, she thanked God for his mighty mysterious works.

I will use this gift of love wisely, she promised. *And with Your help we will make it grow and spread out to encompass others who need it so badly.*

"Jefferson William Haddon the third," she began softly. "I love you more than life itself. I think I have since the day you tried to put out my campfire." She smiled. "And yes, I'll live with you. I'll love you and work with you to raise our children, with God's help."

She kissed him gently; a kiss full of promise and love. And Jeff kissed her back.

"I love you," he murmured. "And I will never tire of saying that to you."

He picked her up in his arms and carried her up the steps.

"And tomorrow," he promised softly, "after we visit Judith and tell her how much we appreciate her hand in everything, you and I are going away for a real honeymoon."

"We are?" Cassie breathed, as he closed the bedroom door and set her down to face him. "Where?"

"I really think it would be best if we went back to Banff," Jeff whispered in her ear, his hand curving down her back as he pulled her closer. "After all, we've already seen the scenery and I want to spend my time looking at my wife."

Cassie moved back just slightly as his lips drew near.

"What about Marie and David?" she asked.

"They're not coming." He chuckled intimately. His lips feathered the delicate skin at her neck. "We'll have lots of time together as a family, Cassie. But for a while, I want you all to myself, Mrs. Haddon."

"Wonderful idea, Mr. Haddon," she agreed.

And then neither of them said anything for a very long time.

Chapter Seventeen

The stately old brick house resounded with the sound of families laughing together. Outside, on the vast leaf-covered lawns, David looked at Marie and grinned at the giggling children throwing the brilliant red oak leaves at one another.

"Doesn't seem that long ago, does it?" he asked. "Two years goes past pretty fast in this place."

"Just wait." She chuckled. "It will go even faster now that you're a senior."

Half an hour later everyone gathered in the conservatory for the christening of Robert—Bobby for short—Jefferson Haddon and Emily—Emmy—Judith Haddon who slept like angels in their parents' tender arms.

"Father, we thank You for Your great blessings to Cassie and Jeff. We ask that You keep Your hand on them. Guide them gently as they raise these babies and Marie and David and remind them often of the love that binds all families together—a picture of the love that You, Father God, have for us."

As the reverend pronounced the benediction, a gentle wind suddenly jingled the chimes, sending their light airy tinkling reverberating through the open window and into the house that was now a home.

Cassie glanced at her husband and smiled happily at the love she saw glowing in his eyes.

"She knows," she told him softly. "Judith knows."

* * * * *

Dear Reader,

Thank you for reading my first book in the Love Inspired series. I'm a strong believer in the benefit of a good laugh and I love a happy ending, so I particularly enjoy writing Christian romances full of hope for the future. If my readers come away from my books feeling as if they've escaped their own confusion for a little while; if they've laughed and cried along with my imaginary friends, I have done what I set out to do.

I grew up in a small prairie town where everyone knew everyone else. My parents had their own business and I was constantly in the company of their friends, neighbors and customers for miles around, which provided wonderful fodder for my imagination and world of pretend. I remember being Laura Ingalls hiding from the enemy in a "cave" of carraganas. I stalked an elderly town hermit in the best Nancy Drewish fashion, and I was the Cinderella of more imaginary romances than you can imagine. But I was also Joan of Arc, a missionary to the Congo and Dr. Livingstone's special assistant. Much of what I now write stems from my memories of those happy, carefree days.

As a child I was always puzzled by the dour expressions of some Christians. I still am. The joy that comes from God is large enough to encompass all of our daily problems and carry us through even the worst of times. Sometimes it's difficult to see even the next step, let alone visualize a whole lifetime, but isn't it wonderful to know that there is someone who sees it all and will guide us perfectly if only we trust in Him?

I wish you joy and much love for each new day.

Lois
Richer

Merry Christmas from
Love Inspired!

**'Tis the season for hearth,
home and holiday joy!**

And Love Inspired is proud
to share with you the gift of romance in
three special, memorable stories.

You won't want to miss any of these heartwarming
tales of faith and family:

CHRISTMAS ROSE
by Lacey Springer

A MATTER OF TRUST
by Cheryl Wolverton

THE WEDDING QUILT
by Lenora Worth